He'd become famous. He'd fulfilled his dream.

But he'd also left her, after years of shared joys and tears, when it was most convenient for him. And she'd spent the past twenty-three months trying to come to terms with the loss of him—her high school sweetheart, the guy she'd waited for throughout army basic training and deployment, the man she'd traveled all over the United States with as they'd performed their music and chased their dreams.

Sawyer had been her soul mate. She was once closer to him than any other person on earth.

Until fame came calling.

"Rory? Aren't you going to say anything? Welcome me home?"

Without giving it a second thought, Rory turned and grabbed a half-full glass of ice water.

"Welcome home," she offered and then tipped the water over his head.

Dear Reader,

Think about your best memory. Focus in on that. Try to remember every little detail of that moment, how it touched you, embedded itself in your soul.

Now imagine having that memory taken from you. Not just that one, but every one that came after and each one that came before. You don't just lose your memories but the emotions and people that went with them. You lose your loved ones, then you lose yourself.

Alzheimer's leaves you without memories, recognition, understanding, even the most basic forms of knowledge, like tying your shoe or using a phone. Early-onset Alzheimer's is a rare form of the disease that can develop as young as one's thirties, effectively stealing not only past memories...but future ones.

My goal when I set out to write *A Song for Rory* was to find hope within such tragic situations. But that job had already been accomplished for me in the countless personal stories I've read about this disease. Patients and caregivers for Alzheimer's (especially early-onset) have my utmost respect and admiration. You are all fighters, battling to keep what you should never have to lose.

That's why for every purchase of *A Song for Rory*, I'm dedicating a portion of sales to Alzheimer's charities.

In *A Song for Rory*, I hope you find this truth: that even when memories are taken, love is not.

If you have a personal story on how Alzheimer's has touched your life, I'd love to hear from you. You can contact me through my website at www.cerellasechrist.com or by mail at PO Box 614, Red Lion, PA 17356.

Cerella Sechrist

HEARTWARMING

A Song for Rory

———

Cerella Sechrist

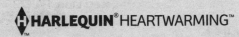

Recycling programs
for this product may
not exist in your area.

ISBN-13: 978-0-373-36829-7

A Song for Rory

Printed in U.S.A.

www.Harlequin.com

Cerella Sechrist lives in York, Pennsylvania, with two precocious pugs, Darcy and Charlotte, named after Jane Austen characters. Inspired by her childhood love of stories, she was ten years old when she decided she wanted to become an author. These days, Cerella divides her time between working in the office of her family's construction business and as a barista to support her reading habit and coffee addiction. She's been known to post too many pug photos on both Instagram and Pinterest. You can see for yourself by finding her online at www.cerellasechrist.com.

Books by Cerella Sechrist

Harlequin Heartwarming

Gentle Persuasion
The Paris Connection
Harper's Wish

To my brother, Caleb Sechrist. Because you're awesome. But you already knew that.

I don't care what I said all those years ago when I found out Mom was having a boy. It turns out having a little brother is one of the best things that ever happened to me. Thanks for making so many of my days brighter.

Acknowledgments

To my sister, Carissa Sechrist, for allowing me to "borrow" many of her original lyrics for *A Song for Rory.* You're the true genius behind Rory's and Sawyer's talent. And extra-special thanks for writing "Rory's Song" just for this story. Your payment (i.e., pound of coffee) is in the mail.

To my editor, Laura Barth, for helping shape the Findlay Roads series thus far, and to Karen Reid for doing a wonderful job picking up where Laura left off. I'm blessed to work with not just one but two amazing editors. This story is better because of it.

A special shout-out to all my fellow baristas and customers at the Randolph Park Starbucks in York, Pennsylvania. Especially Bruce K. Davis, who kept me on track every week by asking me if I was meeting my book deadline. That next triple-shot cappuccino is on me, Bruce.

Finally, to every family member, caregiver and Alzheimer's patient who has had the courage to share their personal struggle with this disease—you have taught me about persistence, pride, love, patience, and the power behind each and every memory. Thank you.

CHAPTER ONE

"AND THE WINNER of this year's Artist of the Year is…"

Sawyer Landry tensed in his seat as the reigning country music diva, Daisy Elliot, slowly untied the red satin ribbon from the envelope. He knew the cameras would be watching him, so he tried to appear relaxed and prayed the stiffness in his shoulders wasn't obvious. The auditorium sat hushed in anticipation of Daisy revealing American Heartland Radio's most prestigious award.

If he managed to win, he could just hear his manager's reaction. *Well, butter my butt and call me a biscuit, sugar! I knew you had it in you!* Perle Jackson peppered all her conversations with such colorful dialogue. It was part of a carefully cultivated persona that she put on to disarm others. Sawyer had quickly learned not to trust her redneck shtick. Perle was as ruthless as a Mafia crime boss when the occasion called for it, which made sense if you believed the rumors that she'd actually grown up in Brooklyn, and her Southern accent was as fake as her fingernails. It made Sawyer glad she was working for him and not against him.

Daisy fumbled with the envelope, her bracelet catching on the satin ribbon. She laughed breathlessly, the sound a whiffle of air against the mic.

Sawyer realized he was balling his hands into fists, so he slowly eased them open. There was a collective shifting of the audience as they grew impatient with Daisy's delay. At long last, she tugged the gold-edged ivory card from the envelope.

"There we go," she announced, her voice carrying an air of relief. "As I was saying, the winner of this year's Artist of the Year is…" She drew a breath. "Sawyer Landry!"

The tension broke as the audience swept to their feet in a standing ovation. Sawyer was a beat behind as the announcement hit him. He'd done it. Artist of the Year.

"Come on up here, darlin'," Daisy exhorted.

He received several congratulatory thumps on the back as he navigated his way up the red-carpeted runway to the stage. From his peripheral vision, he noticed a montage of his concert performances and various awards ceremonies displayed on the massive auditorium screens.

The applause rose several octaves as he

tossed a wave toward the audience. He felt himself warm to the reaction. It was heady enough to hear a crowd of two thousand fans screaming his name, but having such a strong reaction from his peers, even his idols, in the industry cheering him—that was a rush at an entirely new level. He nearly tripped over his cowboy boots—a gift from Nashville's premier designer—as he moved toward the podium.

The audience was still on its feet, hooting and hollering, as he accepted the bronze statue from Daisy.

"Congratulations, Sawyer," she murmured for his ears alone as she leaned in to press her cheek to his.

He hefted the weight of the award in his hand. It was an elongated sculpture with a crystal sunburst radiating from the top. He glanced down to read the description: "An artist of the highest caliber, displaying showmanship and talent, Artist of the Year," followed by the date and year.

Sawyer swallowed hard as he read the words, making an effort to keep his emotions in check. He'd done it. After years of living out of a van, playing dive bars and community events, never knowing where his next paycheck would come from, he'd finally reached the top. He raised his head and looked out over the auditorium. The stage lights were too bright for him to make out individual faces, but the applause still rippled on.

He finally let out a breath and grinned. The sight of his smile set the crowd off once again, and the clapping intensified a few more notches. He raised a hand to quiet them, but it was still several long seconds before the room was silent.

"I don't even know where to begin, there's so many people I need to thank." He drew a breath. "My band, my manager, Perle, and all the talented folks at Americana Records." He quickly ticked through his mental list of industry partners, executives and collaborators.

"My family, especially my parents, for buying me my first guitar. I told you I'd pay you back for it one day, and now I guess I can." He was rewarded with a rumble of laughter from the audience.

"I'm especially grateful to my fans. Every single one of you who bought an album or downloaded a single or attended a show— you are what has made this possible." He laid a hand across his heart. "And I thank you for that."

He stopped then, his gaze fixed on the sunburst at the top of his award. He experienced a tug in his chest, as he so often did when he was onstage, staring out at a crowd or accepting an award. In all those times, there was still one individual he had yet to thank.

She was the one person who had made all the difference in his life and his journey to this stage. But he hesitated to name her. After all, it was unlikely she harbored any fond memories of him after the way he'd ditched her.

But wasn't this the moment? The occasion when he was meant to pay homage to those who had shaped and defined him, the ones who had believed when others had withdrawn their support? If that was the case, there was only one person whose belief in him had been unfailing, no matter the hard times. It was his own pride—the recognition that he was the selfish one who had given up on her and not the other way around—that had kept him from voicing her name.

Well, there was no time like the present.

"There's one more person I need to thank. And she may be the most important person of all."

A hush swept over the auditorium. With the stage lights blinding him, he could have almost believed he was alone in the room. He drew a breath and closed his eyes, struggling to find the words.

"Rory, if you're watching—" he opened his eyes, trying not to wince at the bright glare "—I'm sorry."

Saying those two words eased a bit of the ache in his chest. He hadn't realized what a relief it would be to speak them aloud. It bolstered him to continue.

"You deserved so much more than what you got. And truth be told, you hold more talent in your pinkie finger than I have in my entire body."

If the audience still remained in the auditorium, they had fallen utterly silent—he could imagine he was speaking directly to Rory. Only the faint electrical hum of monitors and amplifiers could be heard.

"If anyone deserves an award for best artist, it's you. Because you're the best artist I've ever known or collaborated with. Your faith in me helped me to believe in myself. I dedicate this award to you."

Daisy cleared her throat, and a soft guitar riff from the speakers signaled it was time for him to wrap it up. He also heard a faint reverberation from the crowd, a wave of whispers traveling through the room.

"So, thank you…for everything."

He tipped the award in acknowledgment and then moved toward Daisy, who was waiting to direct him off the stage. There would be a crowd of reporters wanting to interview him. Applause followed him into the wings, and he heard the ceremony's host segue the proceedings into the next performance.

Sawyer paused at the hallway that led to the press area and looked down at the award he held in his hands. Though he felt relieved at having finally recognized Rory after all this time, a weight of grief still hung over him. Most days, he was too busy to acknowledge it, but in moments like this, the truth hit him full force.

No matter how many albums he sold, concerts he played, or awards he won, he wondered if he would ever shake the regret of letting her go.

RORY CALLAHAN TRIED not to fidget as the scones were passed.

It wasn't that she was bored or having an awful time, she was just uncomfortable. High-tea luncheons weren't really her type of scene, especially when she'd been forced to dress in a frilly pink sundress and strappy heels thanks to Paige Worth's stringent dress code for the bridal shower. She tried to slip off the tight heels, but her best friend, Erin, nudged her gently in the side.

"Stop moving so much," she whispered in an aside. "Paige is shooting daggers."

Rory frowned and stopped working one open-toed shoe's heel against the other. She slid a glance in Paige's direction and caught her fellow bridesmaid glaring in disapproval.

"Well, it's ridiculous," she hissed back at Erin, her Irish accent more pronounced with her exasperation. "Why do we have to dress up in these fancy frocks anyway? Harper doesn't care. In fact, I'm sure she'd have been just as happy having the shower at the Moontide, like I suggested." She looked in her soon-to-be sister-in-law's direction. Harper was smiling graciously. If she was unhappy with the choice of venue, she didn't show it.

Beside her, Erin's shoulders slumped. "That's what I would have preferred, too," she acknowledged, "but Paige insisted. And as the matron of honor…"

"I know, I know." Harper's sisters were sharing the role of matron and maid of honor, and that meant that whatever Paige wanted trumped anything Rory or Erin suggested. Tessa, as the maid of honor, occasionally spoke up to veto her older sister's ideas, but on the whole, Paige was the one running the prewedding events.

"The Moontide would have been a lovely

choice," Rory continued, trying to keep her voice low so as not to be overheard by the other shower attendees, "and I'm sure Aunt Lenora could have used the business."

Aunt Lenora was Erin's great-aunt by marriage, and the proprietress of the bed-and-breakfast in Findlay Roads, the Moontide Inn. Erin and her young son, Kitt, lived there while her husband, and Lenora's great-nephew, Gavin, was deployed overseas in the army.

Erin didn't reply, and Rory guessed she'd decided to say nothing if she couldn't say anything nice. Rory bit her tongue and tried to do the same. Harper was about to become her sister-in-law, and it was no good to start things off by complaining about Harper's oldest sister.

"All right, everyone!" Paige, positioning herself in the center of the room, clapped her hands to draw the group's attention to her. "Now it's time for another bridal-shower game!"

Rory stifled a groan. After pin the ring on the groom, when she'd nearly choked on a macaroon at the blown-up photo of Connor used for the pinning, along with bridal bingo and shower charades, she'd had her fill of wedding-game antics. But Paige wasn't done yet.

"I've saved the best for last." Harper's older sister was glowing with excitement. Rory had never been one of those girls who became giddy over weddings, even less so in the past couple of years since her breakup with her longtime boyfriend. But over the last two hours, she'd concluded that Paige's enthusiasm more than made up for her lack of it, where matrimonial mayhem was concerned.

"Tessa is passing around your cards right now."

As one of Harper's bridesmaids, Rory already knew what was coming. Both she and Erin had been given the shower itinerary during one of Paige's bridesmaid meetings, which occurred on a weekly basis now that the wedding was only three weeks away. So it was no surprise when Tessa handed her and Erin one of the scavenger-hunt cards, but still, Rory deflated a little.

Tessa paused to squeeze Rory's shoulder in encouragement. Rory straightened. Tessa was keenly observant and definitely the sweeter of Harper's two sisters. But still, Rory didn't want to seem sour, especially as a member of the wedding party. She'd just have to make the best of Paige's bridal-shower scavenger hunt. Tessa moved on to the next table.

"As you can see," Paige continued with her instructions, "you have a list of items for our bridal scavenger hunt. Some items are easier than others."

Rory scanned the list she'd be sharing with Erin.

A piece of candy.

No problem there. Erin always carried some in her purse, to appease Kitt when he got antsy.

Paper clip.

That shouldn't be too hard. They could just ask at the hotel's front desk.

A penny.

Easy.

She didn't get a chance to finish perusing the items as Paige began speaking once again.

"Now remember, ladies, you only have twenty minutes to find everything on the list. The first pair back here with all of their items wins this deluxe mani-pedi gift certificate!"

Rory took a look at her fingernails. She kept them trimmed short, not only because of her server's job, but also to make it easier to play guitar. She supposed she could use a manicure, especially for the wedding.

"All right, let's get ready..."

Rory and Erin pushed back their chairs and joined the other guests, who were preparing to sprint for the doors. Erin neatly tore the sheet in half and handed the bottom portion to Rory.

"This will go faster if we split up."

"Good idea," Rory agreed.

"Set…" Paige prompted.

Rory glanced at her list as Paige shouted, "Go!"

There was the clicking and scuffing of shoes along the tile as the other shower attendees made a dash from their private reception room to commence the hunt.

"Meet you back here once I have all my items," Erin offered, and then Rory was on her own.

RORY REGRETTED ERIN splitting their list by the time she reached the second item. Paige had obviously increased the difficulty with each sequential object. While she doubted Erin had had much trouble locating the penny, paper clip, or candy, Rory had gotten creative in tracking down a fork, newspaper, postage stamp and piece of hotel stationery.

But the final item on her list was the oddest. *An umbrella.*

Rory stared at it for a full thirty seconds, wondering how in the world Paige had come up with these items. She stood in the hotel lobby, a gift bag—compliments of the resort gift shop—filled with her scavenger items hanging from her fingers. Where to find an umbrella?

She looked around, wondering if Paige meant for her to steal it from the coatrack. No way was she taking it that far. It was just a stupid game, after all. This is what came from letting Paige take charge. Rory sighed and tapped her foot then winced as the straps of her sandal pinched the side of her ankle. She was tempted to just take off her shoes and walk around barefoot, but Paige would probably be scandalized at the sight.

She moved toward the other side of the lobby and leaned against a column, which was hidden behind the large fronds of a potted palm, and rubbed at the offending sandal strap. She supposed she could always ask at the front desk for help. She knew some hotels kept umbrellas on hand for the convenience of their guests. But then her attention fastened on the placard sign standing nearby, advertising happy hour in the hotel lounge.

She grinned. Ah. Paige didn't specify what *type* of umbrella. Surely one of those little cocktail ones would suffice.

Rory straightened and headed in the direction the sign indicated.

She couldn't wait to see the look on Paige's face when she and Erin showed up with all their items.

RORY ENTERED THE hotel lounge, which was pretty quiet this time of day. She imagined it was a much livelier place during the evening hours. But right now, there were only a few businessmen seated at the bar, and a young couple in a corner. Rory's eyes drifted to the stage that dominated the room. There was no live entertainment taking place at the moment, but the sight was still a familiar one to Rory. Over the years, she'd played in over a hundred bars and lounges just like this one as she and Sawyer traveled around the country, performing their special blend of country and Irish folk music as they tried to make a go of a musical career.

She'd given up that life after Sawyer left her, though, and while she may have missed the man, she didn't miss the smoke and gloom of the bar scene. In some ways, it had been a relief to walk away from it all…even if she did still resent Sawyer for the way he'd abandoned her.

"Excuse me." She approached the bartender. "I need an umbrella."

He eyed her with a look he must have reserved for customers who'd had too much to drink. She frowned at his reaction. "You know, one of those little ones you put in fancy cocktails?" She held up her torn sheet of the scavenger list. "I'm on a scavenger hunt."

The man's eyes cleared. "Ah, part of the bridal-shower party, are you? I've seen a few of you going back and forth."

Rory nodded in confirmation. "So, do you have any tiny umbrellas?"

"I think we have some in the back. Give me a minute to see if I can scrounge one up for you." He gave her a wink, but she pretended not to see it as she shifted her attention away from the bar.

She hoped the other shower guests weren't way ahead of her. She didn't normally have a very competitive streak, but she didn't want to end up dead last in this game. She had a feeling Paige would somehow hold it against her. She wouldn't be surprised if the other woman had a game planned to name the worst bridesmaid in the wedding party. Not that Rory was shirking her bridesmaid duties. It was just that Paige always seemed to expect so much more.

While Rory waited for the bartender to return, she reached for the bowl of peanuts on the bar. She picked through them, not really all that hungry even though the shower luncheon had consisted of mostly dainty finger foods. She'd probably be starving by the time she punched in for her shift at Callahan's that night. Maybe she'd try to get there a little early and grab a bite.

She pushed the peanuts aside, then tapped her fingers restlessly on the smooth plane of the bar. With nothing else to occupy her, she turned her attention to the hi-def televisions mounted behind the counter. An entertainment channel was running—she recognized several of the starlets that flashed across the screen. There was no sound coming from the TV, but the captioning was announcing which of the featured celebs were going to be on the next season of some hit reality show. She leaned against the counter and watched the monitor without any real interest. She was just starting to space out, wondering what was taking the bartender so long and whether Erin had found all the scavenger items on her half of the list, when the entertainment host shifted to the next story on his agenda.

She stiffened as the familiar face of her ex-boyfriend flashed across the screen.

"Sawyer," she breathed.

The headline ticker across the bottom of the screen announced him as the winner of the coveted Artist of the Year honor at the American Heartland Radio awards show. She experienced a pang of grief and a thrill of pride, both at the same time.

He'd done it. Not only had he found success as a country music star, but now he also had the most prestigious award in the industry to back it up.

The image shifted to him on a stage, holding his prize and speaking to the audience. Her heart fluttered as she noted that success had only enhanced his handsomeness. The light brown hair that he'd always kept on the longer side had been trimmed and styled, and the dusting of scruff along his jaw added a layer of cowboy cute that was surely a hit with female fans. She swallowed, peanut crumbs sticking in her throat.

"You a fan?"

She jerked, realizing the bartender had returned. He was holding out a miniature yellow drink umbrella, and it appeared as if he'd been standing there waiting for her to take it for some time.

"No, I'm not," she replied, her voice clipped.

"If you say so." He looked at the television, and Rory tried not to follow his gaze. She didn't need to see Sawyer again, didn't need to feel the stab of betrayal and heartbreak once more.

After nearly two years, she'd thought it wouldn't hurt so much. Wasn't that what everyone had told her? It takes time. Wounds heal.

You'll find love again…and all that. But Rory wondered how much more time she'd need? How much longer would her tender heart ache at the mention of his name or the sight of his face on a magazine, website or on TV? When could she finally stop avoiding country radio, afraid to hear his latest hit and wonder if he ever thought of her, if he ever missed her like she missed him?

"Don't you need to get back to your party?"

Rory snapped to attention a second time as the bartender spoke to her. She tried not to bristle. What business was it of his if she wanted to hide out in here, away from the fuss and frills of this wedding business? Every time she turned around these days, she was confronted with reminders of love and happily-ever-after. She was thrilled for her brother and Harper—of course she was. But their impending nuptials were a reminder, every single day, that she was alone. Maybe that wouldn't have been so bad if she and Sawyer hadn't been together for so long, if they hadn't had so many dreams and plans of a life together.

She shook her head. No use going there. She forced herself to look back at the television. Sawyer still dominated the screen, but it appeared to be a post-awards interview. Her eyes flicked to Sawyer's face as he was being interviewed on a red carpet. She didn't know what the reporter was asking, didn't allow herself to read the captions. But she watched Sawyer's face, the happy glow, and let the hurt and anger take hold of her once more.

All of Sawyer's dreams had come true. And after almost two years of silence, she doubted that she even entered his thoughts anymore.

CHAPTER TWO

SAWYER STOOD OUTSIDE the restaurant and tugged his baseball cap farther down on his forehead. So far, he'd escaped recognition on the streets of his hometown, but he hadn't spoken to anyone directly, either. He'd only arrived in Findlay Roads an hour ago. He'd flown into BWI Airport and rented a car for the hour-long drive to town. The trip had been impulsive, but he'd taken the text he received from his brother the night of the AHR awards as a sign.

He pulled out his phone and thumbed into the text app to read Chase's message once more.

Way to go on the awards, bro! It's a good thing you can sing since I'm the one who inherited the brains in the family.

Even after reading the text multiple times, Sawyer still smiled at his kid brother's teasing. He supposed he deserved some ribbing. After all, as the older sibling, he'd tortured Chase unmercifully while they were growing up. It was hard to believe his baby brother was finishing up college next year…

Seriously, tho, long time, no see. When are you coming home for a visit? Haven't seen you since Thanksgiving. Mom and Dad won't ask you, but I think it's important you come home for a while. Final exams wrap up on Friday, and then I'm going to be free all summer. Hope 2 C U soon?

Sawyer frowned, as he had the first time he'd read the text. There was something in Chase's suggestion that hinted of uncertainty, even perhaps vulnerability. But then again, how much could a person really read into a text message?

Still, Chase was right. It had been way too long since Sawyer had last seen his family, and he couldn't even remember when he'd last visited his hometown. Certainly not since he'd moved to Nashville, and his career had taken off. Then it had hit him.

Rory.

It was the perfect chance to see her again, since his schedule was free for the next few weeks. Sure, Perle would probably prefer that he spend that time doing interviews and the like to leverage his recent AHR win, but he'd wrapped up his concert tour the weekend before last. Soon he'd have to hit the studio to begin laying down tracks for his next album, but he only had a few songs ready to record. Songwriting hadn't come so easily in the last couple of years. He'd taken for granted how much Rory had influenced his desire to compose songs—without her in his life the music didn't flow like it once had. Maybe talking to her would spark some fresh ideas. He'd always been eager to get the words and music down so he could play them for her and get her feedback. Besides, he reasoned, he deserved a minivacation after the breakneck pace he'd set over the last two years.

And just like that, he'd made the decision to come home. He'd booked the flight immediately and replied to his brother that he'd see him soon. But even though he was looking forward to time with his family, he was most excited about reconnecting with Rory.

And that was how he found himself in front of Callahan's restaurant, trying to muster up the courage to head inside. He'd put this off for too long, and even though he didn't want to wait another minute, he wasn't sure what to say other than "I'm sorry."

He owed her an apology. But even more than that, he wanted her back. It had become crystal clear to him in the hours after the awards show, when all his dreams were coming true, that something was missing. That some*thing* was really a some*one*.

He wanted Rory. *Needed* her. No amount of awards could replace her. She'd been his greatest source of inspiration for as long as he could remember. She had been his constant, through years of doubt and failure. He'd been foolish to think he wouldn't need her once he hit the big time.

It hadn't taken too much investigative work to learn she was working that afternoon. He knew, from previous phone conversations with his mother, that Rory had gone to work for her brother after she and Sawyer had split. He also knew she'd moved back to town and into the apartment above the restaurant. According to his mother, Connor's restaurant had finally taken off. It was mentioned as a four-star dining experience in numerous travel and culinary magazines, and it had gained huge recognition when Connor was the runner-up and then the grand prize winner in the annual Best of the Bay competitions two years in a row.

Sawyer had to admit that the exterior of the place didn't look anything like he remembered back when Rory's dad had owned it. The Rusty Anchor sign had been replaced with a sharp, pub-style design, and the name had been changed to the family one of Callahan's. The place had a cozy but classy feel to it, from the redbrick facade to the black-trimmed window frames. His gaze skipped upward, toward the second floor. He wondered if Rory was up there now or if she was already down below in the restaurant. Either way, his stomach somersaulted at the thought of her being nearby. He was close. So close.

He was a ball of mixed emotions, excitement and nerves competing for first place. What would she think of him showing up here? Would she recognize it as an effort on his part to make things right? Or would she merely see it as an intrusion?

He guessed there was only one way to find out. With another tug on his baseball cap, he drew a deep breath and headed inside the restaurant.

WHEN RORY CLOCKED in for her shift at Callahan's that afternoon, she prayed there would be no discussions about Sawyer's Artist of the Year award. Given that he was a hometown boy and she and he had been known so long as a couple, it was often impossible to dodge his name in conversation, especially from those who didn't understand that Rory was no longer a part of his life. She had become adept at pat responses: "No, I don't know what he's up to these days. He's so busy recording and touring, you know." Most people missed the sarcastic edge to her words, but occasionally, someone would cock their head and make their apologies before blessedly changing the subject.

She grabbed her apron from the back room and said hello to Rafael. He mumbled an incoherent greeting in response, his attention fixed solely on the washing machine he was attempting to fix. Rafael had been with the restaurant well before it had become a highly rated, popular establishment. As one of the few original employees, Rory was fond of him, in large part because of his longtime loyalty to her brother. Now that Callahan's had become a success, Rafael had been promoted from busboy and occasional line cook to maintaining the restaurant and property.

Tying her apron in place, Rory left Rafael to his work and headed back through the kitchen to check what section she'd be working that evening.

Twenty minutes later, she had settled into her server's routine. She'd topped up the beverages at all six of her tables, provided a fresh bread basket to table eighteen and put in the appetizer order for table sixteen. She approached the computer to tabulate the bill for her four-top at table twelve and noticed the hostess seating a lone diner at table fifteen on the outer edge of her section. It was a slightly isolated table by the window, and one that was sometimes requested by customers dining alone.

Vanessa, the hostess, caught Rory's eye and hurried over. "I just seated a cute guy at table fifteen."

"I saw," Rory replied as she stuck table twelve's bill into the receipt folder. "I'll get to him in a minute. I have to finish up with twelve."

"Okay, but I wanted to give you a heads-up— he asked to sit in your section."

That got Rory's attention. She raised her head and zeroed in on the newcomer. He was slouched over the menu, a baseball cap pulled low over his forehead. His posture was relaxed, but she noticed him drumming his fingers impatiently on the tabletop.

Her stomach clenched. She'd seen that gesture a thousand times over the years, in the back rooms of bars before they'd gone onstage, in the airport before he'd shipped out for army basic training, and the day he'd sat her down in a restaurant not nearly so nice as this one to

tell her about the record deal from Nashville…
right before he broke up with her.

She knew every emotion that accompanied
that gesture—excitement coupled with adrenaline and just enough nervousness to keep him
cool under pressure. Her entire body tingled,
and she wondered if she should try to pass off
his table to someone else.

She immediately dismissed the thought.
He'd asked for her section. He knew she was
here.

Drawing a deep breath, she headed for his
table, dropping off table twelve's check and
promising to return for the payment shortly.
Ten steps later, she was at his side.

He was facing away from her, looking out
the window and over the water. She debated
how to begin, whether to admit she recognized
him through his thin disguise or behave as the
server she was and ask if he'd like to start with
something to drink.

In the end, he saved her from having to decide. He shifted in his seat, pulling his eyes
away from the gray-blue of the Chesapeake's
water, lifting his gaze to meet hers.

"I forgot."

"Forgot what?" she asked.

"How beautiful it is here."

The way he said it made her realize he wasn't

referring to the view, and she fought back the heat flooding her cheeks. He looked the same, maybe better than when she'd last seen him in person. Or perhaps it was her complicated emotions making him seem that way. Sawyer had always been confident, but he seemed to hold himself with even more surety now. But then, setting country music records was likely to do that to a person.

Stabs of both jealousy and grief sliced through her. He'd become famous. He'd fulfilled his dream. And beneath the layers of frustration, a part of her was exceedingly proud of him. But he'd also left her, after years of shared joys and tears, when it was most convenient for him. And she'd spent the last twenty-three months trying to come to terms with the loss of him—her high-school sweetheart, the guy she'd waited for throughout army basic training and deployment, the man she'd traveled all over the United States with as they'd performed their music and chased their dreams.

Sawyer had been her soul mate. At one time she'd been closer to him than any other person on earth, her brother included. She hadn't had many close relationships in her life, and Sawyer knew that. But she'd had him.

Until fame came calling.

"Rory? Aren't you going to say anything? Welcome me home?"

He'd called her beautiful, as if that could make up for the heartache he'd caused her.

Without giving it a second thought, Rory turned and grabbed a half-full glass of ice water on a table waiting to be bused.

"Welcome home," she offered and then tipped the water over the top of his head, dousing him.

And with that, she turned on her heel and stalked away, deciding Sawyer Landry could starve before she'd serve him.

SAWYER BLINKED THE water out of his eyes and groped for a napkin to wipe his face. He dabbed at his wet chin and pulled his baseball cap lower over his forehead, hoping he wouldn't be recognized with the attention Rory had just drawn to him.

"I suppose I deserved that," he admitted aloud and used the sleeve of his T-shirt to mop some water from his jaw.

Seconds later, the hostess appeared with a handful of napkins, uttering profuse apologies for Rory's behavior.

He shrugged. "I should have seen that coming. Rory never was one to take things lying down."

The girl blinked, obviously puzzled. Then her eyes narrowed as she studied him, her brow furrowing in concentration. Sawyer looked away, hoping she wouldn't recognize him.

"You know Rory?"

He pushed back his chair. "Yeah, I'm her—" He stopped. "An old friend," he said after a beat and stood.

"Sir, please. I don't know what came over her, but I'm sure the manager will treat you to a meal on the house—"

"Not bloody likely."

Sawyer turned as Connor, Rory's older brother, approached the table. The other man's expression was tight with anger. Sawyer held up his hands in surrender.

"Hey there, Connor. Good to see you."

"What are you doing here?"

"The place looks great. Your dad would have loved it."

Connor made an angry noise in the back of his throat and took another step toward the table. Sawyer shifted his eyes to the hostess, in hope of reminding Connor they had an audience. But she wasn't the only one watching them. From his peripheral vision, Sawyer noticed that most of the customers in the immediate vicinity had paused to witness the confrontation.

"I just wanted to see Rory," Sawyer admitted. "I thought I'd surprise her. In retrospect, maybe showing up here wasn't exactly the smartest way to go about it."

Connor's jaw clenched in reply.

"Listen, I know it's more than I deserve, but I'd really like the chance to talk to her."

"I'm not sure she wants to talk to you," Connor growled.

"Fair enough. But would you mind asking her for me?"

"She's working right now."

Sawyer nodded. "Okay." He sat back down in his chair. "In that case, I'll just wait right here."

Connor crossed his arms. "You're not welcome here. I'm going to have to ask you to leave."

Sawyer released a breath, trying to keep his cool. He and Connor had always gotten along in years past. Sawyer had a tremendous amount of respect for the other man, especially his devotion to his family and his dream of becoming a successful restaurateur. He'd always known Connor possessed the same Irish bullheadedness as Rory; he'd just rarely come up against its full force like this.

Still, the man was protecting his sister. And for that, Sawyer couldn't blame him.

"What if I order something? I'd love to see what you—"

"No." Connor's voice was flat, brooking no argument.

Sawyer opened his mouth to respond but never got the chance.

"Oh, my gosh! You're Sawyer Landry!"

Recognition suddenly bloomed on the hostess's face. Sawyer grimaced. Connor blinked.

"You're him! You're Sawyer Landry!"

Her excitement spread through the restaurant dining room, first hushed and then louder, like the click of falling dominoes gaining speed.

Sawyer knew it wouldn't be long before he was assailed by autograph-seekers and picture-takers. Normally, he didn't mind—it went with the territory, after all. But he'd come here to see Rory, and he didn't imagine a rush of groupies in the restaurant dining area would endear him to Connor.

"Please, Connor, just tell her I want to talk."

Connor's arms remained crossed, his nostrils flared.

One of the servers timidly approached and thrust her order pad in Sawyer's direction. "Would you mind giving me your autograph?"

"Dani, go see to your tables."

"But—"

"Now."

Sawyer heard the snap of photos and looked past Connor to see several restaurant patrons brandishing their phones and clicking away in his direction. He smiled at them and gave a little wave.

Dani began to slink away with an air of disappointment surrounding her.

"How about I drop by later and bring you a signed copy of one of my CDs?" Sawyer offered to her retreating back.

Dani turned, her face lighting happily. She nodded and then caught Connor's eye before scurrying away again. Vanessa took her cue from her coworker and followed.

Before the two men could continue their argument, a customer approached and held out her napkin, along with a pen.

"Excuse me? Mr. Landry? My daughter is a big fan, and she'd just love it if I could get her your autograph." She held out her napkin and a pen, and he took the items in hand.

"Sure, what's her name?"

The woman beamed. "Allison. Allie, that is. Or whichever you prefer."

He scribbled a quick note, wishing Allie all the best, and then signed his name with a flourish.

He sensed Connor's mounting irritation.

"Oh, thank you, thank you so much." The woman paused. "And…would you mind taking a picture with me? Just so I can prove to her it was really you?"

"No problem." Sawyer stepped to the side so the woman could move in beside him.

She turned to Connor and handed him her cell phone.

"Would you mind terribly?"

Connor did mind, Sawyer could see it, but he wasn't about to deny a customer. He wordlessly took the phone, framed the shot and clicked as Sawyer grinned broadly for the camera.

"Oh, that's just wonderful. Thank you!" The woman was speaking to him, barely sparing Connor a glance as she reclaimed her cell phone. "Thank you so much! Allie will be so excited."

Sawyer looked at Connor, eyebrows raised as though daring him to allow this to continue. A few chairs scraped, and Sawyer had the sense a receiving line was about to form. Connor must have realized it, too, because he grabbed Sawyer by the arm and hauled him away from the table.

"In the back. Now."

Sawyer shot one last look over his shoulder and saw several crestfallen faces as he was dragged away. Once the dining room disappeared from view, Connor warned him, "I'll take you to her, but if she doesn't want to talk to you, you leave through the back. You got it?"

"Got it."

Connor hesitated, his green eyes cold. "You don't deserve her forgiveness, you know."

Sawyer grew serious. "I know. But I'm hoping she'll grant it anyway."

Connor gestured for him to follow and didn't comment further one way or another.

RORY PACED IN Connor's office, her black Converse sneakers squeaking on the hardwood floor each time she pivoted on her heel. Normally, she found this room soothing. After the fire that had damaged a large part of the building, Harper had seen to it that the back office was remodeled into a charming work space for Connor. Though it wasn't overly large, the slate-blue walls and sea-glass collage artwork were calming. Harper shared the space with Connor, too, and while his half of the room was usually a jumble of papers and notes, Harper's tiny glass-topped desk remained neat and tidy, often with fresh flowers in the pottery vase displayed on the corner surface. Rory had caught Connor adding flowers to that vase on more than one occasion. It warmed her to think her brother could be such a romantic where Harper was concerned.

Today, however, she spared little thought for her brother's love life. She was too overwhelmed with her own.

Sawyer was here. Back in Findlay Roads. In the restaurant. Sawyer was here…for her? After the last couple of years trying to separate herself from the idea of ever seeing him again, he was suddenly back. And he'd sought her out.

She was still trying to wrap her head around this revelation when a soft knock sounded on Connor's office door.

A second later, it eased open, and Connor stuck in his head.

Behind him, she caught a glance of Sawyer. She stepped back and shook her head.

"No. Connor, *no*. I said I don't want to talk to him."

Connor grimaced. "I know, but I can't have him in the restaurant."

"Then kick him out!"

"He won't go without talking to you first." She scowled.

"Rory, please." Sawyer's voice sounded from the crack in the doorway. He edged it open and stood next to Connor. "Just five minutes. Five minutes, and then I won't bother you anymore. Please."

She raised her chin. "I can't. I'm on the clock."

"Not anymore," Connor said. "You're taking a break."

"I just got here," she protested, but Connor's gaze pleaded with her.

"Vanessa can fill in for you for a bit."

Rory opened her mouth to protest and then closed it. If Connor was asking her to do this then she should. He wouldn't make such a request of her lightly.

"Fine," she snapped. "Five minutes."

Connor appeared relieved and then sheepish. "Um, would you both mind discussing things…elsewhere?"

Rory raised an eyebrow.

"I think it would be better if Sawyer left the premises," he explained.

"Oh." Rory wasn't sure what that was about, but decided that if she was going to talk to Sawyer, it didn't matter whether it was here or somewhere else.

"Why don't we take a stroll on the promenade?" Sawyer suggested.

Rory folded her arms across her chest.

"Fine. But your five minutes starts the next time you open your mouth."

Sawyer nodded but wisely didn't utter a sound.

THE PROMENADE WAS blessedly vacant this time of day as people spent the late afternoon hours shopping or sailing on the bay. A few couples were scattered along the boardwalk and one man was fishing over one of the railings, but they were spread out so that Rory and Sawyer were mostly alone.

Sawyer had taken her at her word about when the timer on his five minutes would begin. He said nothing as they'd walked from Callahan's to the promenade and still remained silent as they began strolling the stretch of boardwalk. After a good three minutes of silence, Rory grew too uncomfortable to allow it to continue. She stopped and turned to face him, crossing her arms over her torso. She made a point of tapping her wrist.

"Okay. You can start talking now."

But he didn't, not right away. At first, she thought he was antagonizing her, but then she realized he seemed to be searching for the words. His struggle gave her a moment to study him more closely. His light brown hair was trimmed short around his ears and behind his neck. She couldn't see any more, since he still wore the baseball cap he'd been sporting in the restaurant. He didn't wear any sunglasses, despite the afternoon sunshine. A part of her wished he had. It was difficult to stare into the familiar warmth of his blue eyes. He had a faint dusting of scruff along his jaw, and she wasn't sure if it was an intended effect or whether he'd just not bothered shaving that morning. Maybe he'd been in too much of a hurry...to see her?

She tensed. She couldn't let herself think such things.

It was hard not to, though, when he kept stealing glances at her, his mouth twitching slightly every time she met his gaze. It was also strange to be standing so near to him, after so much time apart.

He was somehow different...and yet still Sawyer. The way he carried himself was new to her. He moved with an easy confidence, maybe even a touch of arrogance, as if he'd finally found his place in the world, and no one could take him from it.

She hated that. She admired it. She envied it.

"I'm going to start timing you whether you speak or not," she announced, as much to jump-start the conversation as to take her mind off her emotions.

"You said you wouldn't start timing until I started talking."

She smirked at his slip. He made a face.

"Okay, round one to Rory."

She didn't reply, simply tapped a finger on

her hip, pretending to tick off the seconds—though she was really just waiting to hear what he'd say next.

"Please stop that."

She ignored him. He groaned.

"Fine. Listen. I'm sorry. I was a jerk. I was selfish and inconsiderate, and maybe a little bit dazzled by the idea of my name in lights."

"A little bit?"

He looked at her, managing to catch her eyes with his so that she couldn't look away.

"I don't know how else to say it except that I shouldn't have treated you the way I did—you didn't deserve that. I've missed you."

Her heart began to pick up speed.

"You're unhappy?"

He hesitated. "No," he admitted. "I can't say that I'm unhappy. I…love what I'm doing. I love performing, and I've gotten to travel the world. It's—" he drew a deep breath "—it's everything I ever dreamed."

Her heart continued racing, but this time in anger.

"You came all this way to tell me that? 'I'm sorry, Rory,'" she said, mimicking him, "'but really, my life's great now. Just thought you should know.'"

She grunted in disgust and turned away from him, stomping down the boardwalk. She passed an elderly couple seated on a bench and only barely registered their frowns of disapproval. She wrapped her arms tightly around her midsection, holding herself together or holding back her fury, she wasn't sure which. Seconds later, she heard the soft thump of Sawyer's footsteps behind her, trying to catch up.

"You didn't let me finish."

"You've said enough."

"But I haven't told you the most important part."

She almost stumbled in hesitation, but righted herself and took two more steps before he spoke again.

"You didn't let me say that it hasn't been worth it."

She stopped abruptly, and he ran into her from behind so that she staggered forward. The next thing she knew, his hands were around her waist, keeping her from falling. For a moment, just the span of a heartbeat or two, she let him hold onto her and savored the memory of his embrace. But by the count of three, she came to her senses and pushed him away.

"Don't touch me." She whirled on him. "Don't you touch me."

"Sorry, sorry." He backed up, hands in the air. He looked pained.

"I didn't come back to rub things in. I know

I'm not the best guy, but do you really think I'm that cruel?"

She shifted from one foot to the other, uncomfortable with the question. As much as she'd tried to vilify Sawyer in her mind over the last couple of years, she didn't know if she could call him cruel. Selfish, yes. Insensitive, sure. But cruel? No, he'd never been that. The man who had cradled her in his arms the night she'd lost her father was not mean. But even so, he'd broken her heart, and while he might not have done it out of cruelty, his selfishness had wounded her just the same. Just because he was ready to make amends didn't mean she was ready to let him.

"Why now?" she asked him.

Sawyer hesitated, his eyes flickering with some emotion she didn't recognize. Guilt? Embarrassment? Whatever it was, she pushed the question to find out.

"After two years of complete and utter silence, why did you come back now?"

"Because I missed you."

She wanted to believe him, but something didn't ring true. He wanted something from her, something that went beyond simply missing her and wanting her back in his life.

"A lot may have changed between us in two

years, Sawyer, but I can still tell when you're holding something back."

He tugged at the baseball cap, a sign of his discomfort. "I'm telling you the truth. I miss you, Rory. More than you can imagine. I think about you all the time. There are nights when I toss and turn because my dreams are full of you and how I let you go. Some days, I forget to eat because my stomach is in knots, wondering what you're doing, worrying that you'll move on and find somebody else. I try to write music, but the words won't come to me because I don't have you there to tell me which lyrics are good. Sometimes, I can't even—"

"Wait, back up."

Sawyer stopped speaking as she held up a hand, but his mouth remained open as he registered her words.

"You're having a hard time composing music?"

His jaw snapped closed, and he looked almost guilty.

"That's it, isn't it?" She began pacing, her steps trying to keep rhythm with her racing heart. "You're *blocked*. That's what all this is about. You're feeling the pressure to top your first album, and you don't have anything to write about."

"Rory, that's not it."

She couldn't even look at him. Because if she did, she might be foolish enough to believe his protests.

"It makes sense you'd come back now. You're probably due for some studio time, am I right?"

When he remained silent, she had her answer. She found the courage to stop moving and turn her attention on him.

"You thought you could come back here and have some sort of…what, summer fling with me? To kick-start your creativity?"

He appeared offended by the suggestion but a little embarrassed, too. Which only proved her point.

Sawyer hadn't come back to Findlay Roads because he loved her, because he missed her. He'd come back because he needed a muse. This realization drained the last of her anger and left her feeling sad and tired.

"I really need to get back to work."

"Rory."

He stepped toward her, but she automatically took a step back. The hurt in his expression was like a knife to the chest, but she steeled herself against it.

"I'm not here because I need to write new songs. I'm here for *you*."

"But it's not that simple, is it?" she countered, her voice flat.

He conceded with a nod, and for some reason, it felt a little too much like surrender on his part. Was he really giving up so easily? She shook her head, confused. Shouldn't she want him to give up? To go back to Nashville and leave her in peace?

"I really do need to get back to the restaurant." Connor was probably worried about her, plus she didn't like asking her coworkers to pick up her slack.

Sawyer sighed. "Okay. Then is there another time we could talk? There's some stuff I'd really like to get off my chest."

She bristled. Not only did he need a muse, but he also wanted her to be his confessor? Nearly two years without a word, and now he was asking her to find time for him to unburden his guilt? Well, maybe she'd show him what it felt like to be humiliated and abandoned.

"Fine then. How about tomorrow?" she offered, keeping her tone cool. "You can stop by the restaurant in the afternoon, before the dinner rush. That's when I normally get my break."

Sawyer brightened considerably, and she felt

a twinge of guilt. She'd just outright lied to him. She wasn't scheduled to work tomorrow.

"You don't think Connor will mind?"

"Leave Connor to me."

Sawyer smiled. "Tomorrow. I'll look forward to it."

His hopeful expression cut into her heart, and she nearly opened her mouth to tell him the truth. But then she remembered how she'd felt, when he'd broken things off with her at the diner beside the Motel 8 in Little Rock, Arkansas. All because he'd been offered a recording contract, on the condition that he was a solo act with no Rory in tow.

She still remembered the words he'd spoken when he sat her down to end their relationship...

"I'm sorry, Rory, but it's the opportunity of a lifetime. I can't just pass it up for..." He'd trailed off, looking sheepish.

"For me," she'd said, finishing the sentence for him. "For us."

He'd sighed, the sound a huff of impatience. "They think I have a real shot, Rory—that I could be the next country music superstar. Only...it would be better if I was unattached, both musically and personally."

"So I'm excess baggage, is that it?"

He'd made a gesture of dismissal. "You

know it's not like that. But sometimes, a person has to make sacrifices to go after what they want. And you and I have been together for so long. It's probably about time we go our separate ways. You understand, right?"

She shuddered at the memory. Oh, she'd understood him all too well. It had been easy for him to toss her aside when something better came along. She had been his sacrifice, but she'd felt more like an old shoe, thrown out when no longer useful.

Because just like that, he'd severed thirteen years of love, friendship and collaboration. He'd drawn a line between who he was and who he wanted to be. He had never even checked in to see if she'd found her way safely back home to Findlay Roads.

Recalling that low point in her life, she managed to shake off her guilt at leading him on.

"Tomorrow," she repeated, forcing her tongue around the lie. "I'll see you then."

CHAPTER THREE

SAWYER SHOWED UP at Callahan's the next afternoon with a bouquet of flowers—purple freesias, Rory's favorite—and a stack of autographed CDs for the restaurant staff. He felt a tingle of anticipation as he stepped toward the restaurant door, catching a brief reflection of himself in the windows. He'd chosen a casual, white button-down shirt, rolled up to his elbows, and he was wearing a faded pair of jeans. He'd ditched the baseball hat from yesterday, but he did wear a pair of sunglasses, both to combat the late-afternoon light and to hopefully stem any recognition as he walked into Connor's establishment.

Fortunately for him, business was apparently slow this time of day, and he only glimpsed a few tables with patrons. He saw several servers moving around, though, probably preparing for the dinner rush. He approached the hostess stand and found the same young woman from the day before. She was speaking with another woman, petite and curvaceous with blond hair. She held a stack of menus in her hand, and he couldn't help noticing the ring she wore. A claddagh ring, on her left hand. The two women turned as he stepped up to the podium.

Even with the sunglasses, the younger one from yesterday recognized him.

"Oh! It's you!"

He smiled for her as he removed his shades. "It's me," he agreed.

The second woman cocked her head, as though trying to place him. He'd seen that look before, on the streets and at airports or at coffee shops, and even the grocery store. It was the look people got when they thought he was familiar but couldn't quite believe he was someone famous.

"I'm Vanessa." The younger woman held out a hand.

He shifted the CDs and flowers into one arm to respond to her handshake. "Nice to officially meet you, Vanessa. I'm—"

"Sawyer Landry. Of course you are." She let her hand linger in his until he withdrew.

He slid a glance in the other woman's direction and caught her frowning at him.

"Vanessa, can you take these into the back?" She shifted the stack of menus neatly into Vanessa's arms.

"Oh, but Harper…can't I stay here?" She looked from the blonde to him, and back again, obviously conveying some sort of coded message.

The one named Harper shook her head. "No, I think I'd better handle this."

Sawyer steeled himself. Harper may have looked sweet and pleasant, but he had the feeling she was a formidable gatekeeper. He wondered if Rory had actually put her in place to keep him away. But why invite him back to the restaurant if she didn't want to see him? Maybe just to get him off her back temporarily. The thought filled him with dismay. He'd been looking forward to this for the last twenty-four hours.

As Vanessa walked away with the menus in hand, Harper turned to face him.

"We haven't met," she began. "I'm Harper Worth, Connor's fiancée."

Sawyer's eyebrows lifted. "Connor's fiancée? Sorry, I didn't realize he was engaged."

She smiled, and he had the sense she couldn't help it. She seemed excited about her role as Connor's bride-to-be.

"I'm Sawyer Landry," he belatedly offered.

"I know. Even if I didn't recognize you from your music, I've seen photos from when you grew up around here."

"Oh." He wasn't sure how to respond to that. Just how much did Harper know about him? How much had Rory shared?

He held up the CDs. "I brought these for some of the staff. One of the servers—I think her name was Dani—asked for an autograph yesterday. I promised I'd bring some albums by. Can you make sure she gets one of them?"

"Of course." Harper took the CDs from his hand, her gaze darting to the flowers though she didn't comment on them. "That's very nice of you. You have several fans here, so I'm sure they'll appreciate it."

He dipped his head in acknowledgment, and then the two of them fell into an awkward silence.

"Um, did Rory tell you I was coming?"

Harper cocked her head. "No. Was she supposed to?"

He didn't know how to answer that. There wasn't a reason for her to inform Harper he'd be stopping by. After all, she'd said they could talk on her break since it wouldn't interrupt her work. But then, this woman was going to be her sister-in-law. Wasn't that the kind of thing sisters shared with each other? He'd only ever had a brother, so he'd never had a chance to observe a lot of sisterly interactions. And he supposed it was different between sisters and sisters-in-law anyway. He cleared his throat.

"Rory and I made plans. She said to stop by around this time—that she'd probably be getting a break before the dinner rush. Is she available?" He shifted the freesias from one hand to the other, feeling increasingly awkward under Harper's steady scrutiny. He could only imagine how Connor had railed about him to her. He doubted Rory's brother had given the best impression. He again wondered what, if anything, Rory had said to her.

Harper hesitated, and he had the sense bad news was coming.

"I'm sorry, but Rory isn't working today."

He frowned in confusion. "Was there a last-minute schedule change or something?"

She shook her head. "No, there have been no changes to the schedule, at least none involving Rory, this week."

Had she forgotten he was dropping by? Or had she simply gotten her schedule confused? Maybe she didn't have his number anymore, to let him know plans had changed.

"In fact, she never works on Fridays," Harper went on. "She has a standing gig at the Lighthouse Café on Friday nights, so she's always off those days."

Sawyer's face heated. Rory wasn't the forgetful sort. If she'd told him to come by today, on a day she never worked, she'd done it on purpose. She'd stood him up.

"Oh." He cleared his throat. "Well, I must have gotten the day wrong then."

Harper looked at him with pity, seeing through his lame excuse, and that only served to stoke his frustration. Okay, so maybe he'd deserved this little trick on Rory's part. It wasn't as if he wasn't due some payback. But he was still embarrassed and disappointed. He'd thought there'd been a crack in the wall she'd erected between them, but he realized now that her defenses were still solidly in place. Well, round two to Rory. That didn't mean he was giving up. If she wanted to play hard-to-get, he'd just have to step up his game.

"Wait. Did you say she's playing at the Lighthouse tonight?"

Harper hesitated, and he wondered if she hadn't meant to give up that bit of information. But then, he thought he saw a sparkle in her eyes, just before she lowered her face from view.

"Did I? Oh, well, everyone around here knows that Rory plays there on Friday nights. She goes on at the same time every week. Eight o'clock sharp. Anyone in town could have told you that."

Harper wasn't looking at him. She was studiously swiping at the hostess podium, as if brushing away dust, but it was obviously already clean. He had the feeling Harper Worth was on his side for some reason. He grinned even though she hadn't looked at him.

"That's handy information, Miss Worth."

She glanced up. "Please, call me Harper."

"Harper," he said, "it was a pleasure to meet you. Connor is clearly a lucky man."

She smiled broadly at the compliment.

"I'm sure we'll be seeing you again soon," she offered.

The words gave him hope. Whatever Rory had or hadn't shared with her future sister-in-law, he seemed to have Harper's stamp of approval—at least to attempt winning Rory back.

He considered the freesias in his hand. Rory had never been much of the chocolate-and-flowers type. Showing up with them might only make it look as though he didn't know her anymore.

But he did. He still knew her.

He held the flowers toward Harper.

"Why don't you take these? My way of saying thanks for all your help."

Harper looked as though she might protest,

but he pushed them into her arms before she could say anything.

"Well, thank you." She eyed him. "And if you don't mind me saying so...good luck."

He nodded.

Where Rory was concerned, he'd take all the luck he could get.

RORY SAT AT the coffee-shop counter, a half-finished glass of iced tea in front of her, and waited anxiously to take the stage. The Lighthouse Café was always busy on Friday nights, but this evening it was particularly packed. Every table, from one end of the room to the other, was filled with patrons. The sofas and love seats along the walls overflowed with customers of all ages, from teens to people in their thirties and forties, and even a couple she swore had to be approaching their eighties.

The crowd didn't really bother her. Performing to ten was the same as performing to two hundred. Once she was onstage, she always experienced a rush of self-confidence. But something about tonight had her tied up in knots, and it had nothing to do with the audience.

She couldn't stop thinking about Sawyer. She wondered if he'd stopped by the restaurant, like she'd told him to. The thought made her squirm with guilt. As much as Sawyer deserved a little payback, she didn't really feel right about what she'd done. She wasn't the vengeful type, and she'd never stood a guy up before. Then again, the only guy she'd ever really dated was Sawyer, unless she counted Bobby Hughes in fifth grade and that one guy she'd gone to dinner with last year. But a stolen kiss on the playground and a boring evening out didn't come close to what she'd had with Sawyer. Still, she'd never been so coy before as to lead someone on.

Even if he was six feet tall with eyes that could turn her into a puddle with one look. She shook her head and took a swig of iced tea. *Nope, don't go there, Rory.* Sawyer may have come back to town talking big about apologies, but it didn't mean they'd pick up where they'd left off. How could they? They were different people now. Especially him.

"Rory, you all set?"

She shook off her reverie as Dave Ridgley addressed her from behind the counter. He was the owner of the café and hosted most of the Friday night performances. He'd been the one to approach Rory about playing at the Lighthouse. He'd seen her perform at the annual 4th of July celebration in town last year and asked if she'd be interested in a weekly gig at his newly established coffee shop in town.

At first, she'd been hesitant. She hadn't been doing much with her music since she and Sawyer split. But the invitation niggled at her until she agreed to a trial run, of sorts. Within the first month, not only did she have a solid following of friends and acquaintances coming to see her perform, but she also became hooked on the opportunity to play her music on a weekly basis. And over the last year, she'd gained quite a few fans who made the effort to come out every Friday and hear her sing. It was encouraging, and a boost to her ego, to realize she had enough talent on her own, without Sawyer, that people wanted to hear her music.

"Ready when you are, Dave," she said and stood to follow him.

They stepped onto the stage together, and Rory grabbed her guitar from its stand as Dave tapped the mic. A few conversations continued, but most of the crowd turned their attention to the platform.

"Looks like we've got a full house tonight," Dave began. "I'm guessing it's not because you came to hear *me* sing."

There were a few chuckles, and one guy near the front let out a heartfelt "boo."

"All right, Jeremy, you've obviously had too much caffeine already. I'm cutting you off. No more espresso shots."

More laughter rippled around the room, and Rory had to grin. It was soothing to be in such a familiar atmosphere. She'd spent most of her life playing one show after another in a line of bars, lounges, community events and weddings. There were a few places she and Sawyer would frequent, but it wasn't like this. Playing in her hometown, week after week, gave her a sense of comfort and belonging.

"Well, if you're not here for me, then maybe you all came out for this lovely lady." Dave gestured in her direction, and the café erupted in cheers and applause. Rory was hard pressed not to blush at the enthusiastic response.

"I think that's a yes," Dave concluded. "Then let's get this show on the road. Rory, you're up."

More cheering ensued as Rory stepped to the microphone, adjusting her guitar strap around her waist.

"Now that's what I call a proper welcome," she said into the mic. Jeremy let out a wolf whistle. "You really have had too much caffeine, haven't you, Jeremy?"

He laughed, and the others in his vicinity joined him. Rory strummed her guitar, listening to make sure it was in tune. She made a minor adjustment and checked again.

Perfect.

"You've all been patient with me these last few months while I worked on some new songs. Well, tonight, your patience will be rewarded. I have something new for you."

She waited while they clapped with excitement.

"I take it you're ready to hear it?"

More cheers.

"Okay then." She drew a breath and strummed a few notes before launching into the song.

I can't help what I feel,
But I know that wounds heal.
And time is all it takes,
But right now it's heartbreak...

Though she'd told herself she wasn't going to think of Sawyer as she sang, her mind couldn't help drifting to him. He was the inspiration for the lyrics, after all.

I've fallen in love with you,
And now I'm bleeding and bruised.
'Cause I let down my guard,
And I fell pretty hard...

The audience was rapt. She sensed it as well as saw it when her gaze swept the room. A few couples were wrapped in each other's arms, and several others swayed to the music. A pair of teenagers even got up and started dancing. She was glad to see it was being received so well. It wasn't exactly a happy song, but it had come from her heart—from the deepest part of her injured pride and wounded spirit.

She launched into the bridge and caught a few people brushing tears from their eyes. She kept going, into the final round of the chorus.

What else can I do?
I've fallen in love with you.

She strummed the final notes on her guitar and stepped back from the microphone as her audience launched to their feet, clapping and whistling in a standing ovation. She smiled and gave a tiny bow, pleased with the reaction and doubly grateful that she'd made it through the song without breaking down. She'd had more than one crying session when she wrote it, thinking about Sawyer and how much she missed him.

But then, as if the music had conjured him, her eyes drifted to the back of the room, and there he stood.

Sawyer was here.

CHAPTER FOUR

How LONG HAD he been standing there? And how much had he heard? Enough, she guessed, because he was clapping along with the rest of them, as though he'd witnessed a fair share of her performance. He was too far away for her to read his expression. Had he realized the song was about him? She hoped not. It was one thing to bare her soul before an audience, but it was another to reveal her insecurities to the man who'd caused them.

What was he doing here anyway? How had he found out where she'd be tonight? Unless someone at the restaurant told him. Her weekly gig at the Lighthouse was well known. She supposed any one of her coworkers could have mentioned it to him. But then, the idea of him actually having gone to Callahan's looking for her gave her a tiny thrill. He'd been true to his word and tried to see her.

And she, of course, had left him hanging. Stood him up. The stunt still didn't rest well with her, but a part of her was pleased that he'd gone to the trouble of finding out where she would be. Though she didn't plan on forgiving him just because he'd made a little effort. She was still miffed that he'd appeared like he had yesterday, showing up where she worked and expecting her to drop everything for him.

She'd like to see how much he enjoyed being put on the spot like that.

She stepped up to the mic again, an idea taking hold. "Thank you," she said as the applause began to die down, and people resumed their seats. "I'm glad you liked it."

"It was worth the wait," Jeremy called from his table, and she gave a nod of thanks in his direction.

"I have another surprise for you this evening."

She sensed a ripple of interest run through the crowd. "Some of you know that I lived on the road for years, performing with my…" She paused for a second as she tried to find an appropriate word other than *boyfriend.* "A mate of mine," she amended. She didn't look in Sawyer's direction, but from the corner of her eye, she thought she noticed him straighten.

"Now, for those of you who are new to the area, I should tell you that my friend went on to bigger and better things. He's known now for his debut album, *Chasing the Wild*, and he recently won American Heartland Radio's Artist of the Year award."

A few whispers ran through the room. Rory couldn't hear exactly what they were saying, but she recognized Sawyer's name being mentioned.

"It's been a while since he's been back home, but tonight, we have the privilege of his presence, as well as a performance."

She finally looked at Sawyer, her gaze cutting straight to the back of the room and meeting his eyes.

"I'd appreciate it if you'd all welcome Sawyer Landry to the stage."

As the room erupted into shouts and applause, she smirked in his direction.

Now he'd see what it was like to be put on the spot.

SAWYER HAD TO give her credit. He hadn't expected Rory to point him out like she had, much less try to push him into a performance. He'd hoped to speak to her privately, after her set was over. No chance of that happening now. Though he'd done pretty well not being recognized until Rory pointed him out. Most of the coffee-shop patrons were focused on the stage when he'd slipped inside, just in time to hear Rory begin her song.

The song that still had awareness humming in his veins. The mournful melody and soulful lyrics had put him to shame with their truth. He marveled at his own selfishness back then. But he could only dwell on his mistakes so long. He had to focus his efforts on making it up to her.

And if she wanted him to take center stage in this café, then that's what he would do. As more and more customers turned in his direction, he kept his sights set on the stage and Rory. He tipped his head toward her, acknowledging the challenge, and began making his way from the back of the room up to the front. Several hands clapped him on his back. There were likely former friends here that he'd greet later, but for now, he had a show to put on.

As he took the two short steps onto the platform, Rory began to remove her guitar. She placed it on its stand and moved as if she planned to leave. His hand grabbed her wrist before she could escape. He felt her pulse jumping erratically beneath the skin. Was it the thrill of performing that had her blood pumping? Or did he have something to do with that reaction?

"Don't go too far," he warned her.

She shrugged. "Okay."

"Promise me."

She looked over his shoulder and out at the audience. He didn't want her trying to sneak out while he was distracted. She'd never been one to break a promise, which is why he tried to force one from her.

"Give me your word that you're staying."

She shifted uncomfortably, and he wondered if her plan had been to bolt as soon as she got the chance.

"I'm staying," she agreed.

He waited, eyeing her, uncaring about the impatient murmurs sounding behind him. She sighed and tugged her wrist free from his grasp.

"I *promise*," she agreed.

Satisfied, he reached for the guitar she'd set aside and adjusted the strap to better fit his broad shoulders. Rory hopped off the stage and took a place at the bar, people moving to accommodate her. He kept a steady eye on her until she nodded, and he decided she'd keep her word.

Only then did he turn to the audience.

"How y'all doing tonight?" It was the standard way he opened his performances, giving his audience the chance to express their enthusiasm. Tonight was no exception. The crowded coffeehouse exploded with applause, whistles and hollering.

"How about Miss Rory Callahan? She's something, isn't she?"

More shouts and some foot stomping. He glanced Rory's way, and she was focused solely on him, ignoring the reactions from the crowd. He strummed a few notes to get a feel for the instrument.

"I hope you don't mind me taking the spotlight away from Rory, since she's the one you came to see."

The audience responded with reassurances as Sawyer finished tuning the guitar to his satisfaction. In some ways, it was strange to be performing for such a small group again. He'd grown used to stadium crowds, massive sound systems and rows of bright lights shining down on him. Up here, on such a tiny platform with only a few house lights, he felt himself relax. As much as he loved the thrill and adrenaline of a powerhouse performance, there was something familiar and comforting about such an intimate venue.

"Well, if you don't mind me playing a song or two, how about we pick things up a little?"

With that, he strummed the first few chords of one of his recent hits, a slightly rockabilly tune about a teenage boy trying to impress a hard-to-win girl. He looked at Rory a few times as he sang and caught her frowning at the lyrics. He wondered if she'd ever heard it before, if she knew he'd written it with her in mind. When they were younger, she'd been a vulnerable, guarded girl, but that had been part of what drew him to her initially. He could see she was wounded, still trying to find her place. But she was tough and unapologetic about being different from the typical teenage girls he knew. She'd caught his heart without him realizing it, and, as the lyrics said, "Drew him in with a smile."

The audience enjoyed the song, clapping along and singing the chorus in unison with him. When he wrapped it up with a riff on the guitar strings, the crowd broke into rowdy applause.

He raised a hand to settle them. "Glad you enjoyed that," he offered. "It seems like you guys know some of my music."

There was a ripple of laughter that went around the room.

"Any requests?"

For the next half hour, Sawyer played several songs from his album and even a tune he hadn't performed in years, thanks to a request from an old high-school friend in the audience. He kept an eye on Rory as he sang and even managed to catch a smile on her face at one point, which she quickly wiped away when she saw him watching her.

He'd learned to read an audience quite well in his years of performing, especially a small group like this. So when he sensed they were ready, he thumbed a couple softer chords.

"I appreciate you guys giving me the chance to play a few songs here this evening, but I know you didn't come to hear me. You came for Rory. Some of you know that Rory and I were a joint act for years. Now, I've played with a lot of talented people since. But I've got to tell you that none of them quite measure up to her."

There were murmurs of approval moving through the room.

"I don't know if it's those Irish roots of hers or something she inherited from her parents, but you've got to give it to her—the girl's got spirit, and she knows music."

The murmurs grew louder, and a couple people even clapped. He slid a glance Rory's way. She was looking down at the bar, and though he couldn't see her face, he suspected she was blushing.

"So, to finish up tonight, I'd like to ask her to come up here and join me."

Rory's head snapped up, and his suspicions

were confirmed. Her cheeks were tinted pink, and her eyes were wide with surprise.

"And we'll perform a duet for you."

There were more whistles and shouts of approval, but Sawyer didn't pay them any mind. He didn't need this crowd's permission. He only needed Rory's. He looked at her, trying to convey his thoughts with his eyes.

Please. Come and sing with me once more.

He wasn't sure she'd do it. Rory was stubborn, and she wouldn't stand for being bullied or manipulated. Neither of which he was trying to do, but he wasn't sure she'd see it that way. So he was a little surprised, but mostly relieved, when she pushed away from the counter and stood to her feet.

She made her way back to the stage and came to stand beside him. And having her there, it was almost as if the last two years had ceased to exist, and they'd never been separated at all.

RORY'S HEART WAS thundering in her chest so loudly that she feared the microphone would pick it up. She should have known Sawyer would find a way to turn the situation around on her. But what worried her most was what a thrill it gave her. It had been nearly two years since they'd shared a stage. But standing here next to him, all that time melted away, and for a brief moment, she could have almost convinced herself that nothing had changed.

Sawyer kept the guitar, and though she waited to hear the opening chords, she knew which song he'd choose. As she'd expected, he launched into a duet they'd performed many times—a heartbreaking song about love and loss and the determination to keep going through it all.

He took the first verse, and she waited to join him until the chorus. When she did, their voices blended in such achingly sweet harmony that she had to blink back tears.

Why had Sawyer come back now, after all this time? She'd waited for him at first, thinking he'd realize what he'd done, that he couldn't live his life without her. But as seasons changed and summer turned into fall and then winter, and she heard his first single on the radio, she had to accept that they were finished. She had spent nearly as much of her life with Sawyer as without him, so it had taken her a long time to adjust to his complete and utter defection. Most days, it still felt a little odd not to see him. They had been such a constant part of each other's lives that something still felt missing in her day when he wasn't there, like forgetting to brush her teeth or how to tie her shoes.

Not that she equated her relationship with Sawyer to those things, but he had always been such a steady part of her life. When he'd taken that away, she'd been adrift for a long time. And now here he was, back in the center of her world. She didn't quite know how to deal with that.

As she sang her part of the song, she felt his eyes on her. She kept her focus on the audience, not wanting to see the look on his face, but at the same time, craving his attention. This was not good. She didn't want to wish for anything from Sawyer, not even so much as a glance. But having him beside her filled up a vacant pocket of her spirit that she'd tried to forget was empty. Now with the two of them on the stage together, everything that had been misaligned for the last two years shifted into place.

She gave herself over to the song, closing her eyes and soaking in the lyrics and the soft strum of the guitar as their voices blended together on the bridge.

When you get lonely,
I'll be everywhere you are...

When Sawyer strummed the last note, she kept her eyes closed for only a second longer before the coffeehouse crowd rattled the walls with thunderous applause. She opened her eyes and instead of looking at the audience, her gaze went straight to Sawyer. He was watching her, happiness lining his features. Her heart tugged at the sight of him, those warm blue eyes, the trademark scruff along his jawline and that light brown hair that occasionally fell over his forehead and into his eyes. She had missed him. Too much. She couldn't let him back in again, after how thoroughly he'd shattered her world with his leaving.

She'd promised him she'd stick around, but their time on the stage was up. She had to get out of there before her heart overrode her head.

"Thanks for a great night, everyone!"

With that farewell, she moved past Sawyer and off the stage. He was still holding her guitar, but she decided she'd pick it up sometime over the weekend. Dave would see it was taken care of.

She nearly tripped down the two steps leading off the stage and began making her way to the door. Several people tried to stop her, but she cut off each of their comments with a thank-you and kept forging her way toward escape.

When she reached the exit, she spared a glance behind her. She saw Sawyer, surrounded by fans but his eyes centered solely on her. His expression had shifted from joy to hurt. He was obviously wounded by her quick departure. For a moment, she wondered if she should wait for him. But no, she couldn't risk it.

She exited the café and headed for her pickup, at the far end of the parking lot. The sight of the truck's peeling blue paint caused her to sigh with relief. It was like a refuge, offering shelter from everything going on outside its cozy little cab. Technically, the pickup was Connor's. He'd started using it after their father's death. But Rory had a lot of memories wrapped up in the vehicle. Patrick Callahan had purchased it shortly after he'd immigrated to the States with his two young children, following their mother's death. To this day, the smell of sunbaked vinyl upholstery and engine oil always made her think of Sunday drives, wedged in the middle of the cab between her dad and brother. She hadn't minded that Connor inherited the pickup because she knew he'd take good care of it, as their father had. But now that the restaurant was doing so well, and Connor was marrying Harper, he'd bought a more family-friendly SUV and given her use of their dad's old truck.

She nearly ran the last few steps, then pulled open the door with a creak and climbed inside. She never locked it. It wasn't worth stealing, and she kept nothing of value inside. But when she reached for the keys she usually kept hooked on the belt loop of her jeans, she frowned.

Oh, no. She'd left her keys beneath the counter of the bar inside. She pushed her head against the headrest and groaned. She couldn't go back for them. No way.

Which meant that if she wanted to avoid Sawyer, she'd better start walking.

SAWYER MIGHT HAVE missed her if he hadn't decided to swing by her apartment and make sure she'd made it home okay. It was a thinly veiled excuse to see her, but he didn't much care at this point. She'd dodged him twice, and while he probably deserved it, he'd been hurt that she'd broken her promise to stick around at the coffee shop. He was preparing what to say to her as he drove, speaking the words aloud to the silence of his rental car.

"Rory, I know I don't deserve it, but I would appreciate it if you could respect the relationship we had enough to hear me out."

He cringed, considering how she'd respond to that little speech. It wasn't as if he'd exhibited a lot of respect for their relationship when he'd dumped her. He drew a breath and tried again.

"It would mean a lot to me if you'd just listen to what I have to say."

No better. He didn't think she was much interested in what would mean a lot to him.

He cleared his throat and considered how to rephrase his request, then stopped as he noted a lone figure, striding briskly down the sidewalk ahead. He'd know those stiff shoulders anywhere. He accelerated a few feet ahead and slid the car into an empty space on the street. He killed the engine and exited the driver's side just as Rory came abreast of the truck. She took one look at him and her jaw went slack.

"You followed me?"

"Hardly. You didn't give me much of a chance to follow you anywhere after you bailed back at the Lighthouse." He tried to keep his tone even, but a note of accusation still leaked through. "You promised you'd stay."

She shifted from one foot to the other, and he recognized guilt in her expression. "I did stay," she protested. "I stayed for your entire performance. Although if I'd known you planned to ambush me into taking the stage with you—"

"Which was not so different from what you did to me," he pointed out. He had her there, and he could tell she knew it, too, by the way she wouldn't meet his eyes. Her shoulders remained set, however.

"Rory, can we please talk?"

"You mean can *you* talk? I don't imagine I'll have much to say. And even if I did, it's not as if you asked my opinion the last time we *talked*."

He grimaced. Okay, so she was still hurt. Not that he could blame her, but maybe it had been a touch of arrogance on his part to assume she'd welcome him back, if not exactly warmly, then at least not with this degree of vehemence.

He glanced down the street. "Look, your apartment is only a few blocks from here. Let me drive you home. I'll talk on the way. If you don't like anything I have to say by the time we reach your place..." He drew a breath, afraid to gamble away his chance but knowing he couldn't exactly keep showing up where he wasn't wanted. "Then I'll leave you alone. For good. Deal?"

She didn't answer him right away but scuffed her heels on the pavement as she considered. After a long minute, during which he was pretty sure he'd held his breath for the entire sixty seconds, she nodded.

"Fine. Just until we reach the apartment."

He should have felt relief, but he only experienced a wave of apprehension. He had less than five minutes to convince her.

He would have to talk fast.

CHAPTER FIVE

"FIRST OF ALL, I apologize for the way I treated you."

Rory had to admit, it was a good place for him to start. She kept her arms crossed over her midsection and looked out the window as he drove. It felt as if the vehicle was moving well under the speed limit, but she decided not to push him about it. She'd agreed to hear him out, so she might as well let him talk. She was determined that nothing he said would change her mind anyway.

"The way I left you was wrong. I wish I had never have broken things off the way I did. We should have at least talked. You deserved the chance to be heard. And I regret that I didn't give you that. You can't know how much."

She felt some of the tension leave her shoulders. He paused as though waiting for a response from her.

"Keep talking." It was the most encouragement she was prepared to give. Besides, it felt good to hear him admit he was wrong. She never thought he would.

"It was a dream come true for me—which doesn't excuse what I did," he added as she stiffened again. "I was so distracted by the opportunity that I didn't consider what I was giving up in exchange."

She frowned. "What was it you were giving up?" She asked the question so softly that she thought he might not hear her. But he did.

"You. And everything you are to me. More than just my girlfriend, but my soul mate. The person who's always been there, the one I wanted to protect and cherish for the rest of my life."

The words caused her heart to catch in her throat as tears threatened. She'd dreamed of hearing him say these things. But it had been too long. "It's been almost two years, Sawyer. Why didn't you come back before this? You never called. Not so much as a text or email to see how I was doing."

"I know. At first, I thought a clean break was better, that it would only make things worse if I got in touch. And I admit, there was so much going on that it was easy not to think about it. But you have to know that even in the midst of this whole new life I was experiencing, you were still in the background of my every thought. Before I could stop it, I'd often find myself wondering, 'What would Rory think of that?' Or 'I can't wait to tell Rory about this.' That should have been my first clue that I'd made a horrible mistake in giving you up."

"I'm sure the recording deal and fan base made up for it." She didn't mean to sound so bitter. When had she let her emotions become so ugly?

"Those things distracted me from what I was feeling, but they didn't make up for it. And like I said, there were so many new experiences for me that when I did begin to miss you, I could force it to the back of my mind."

She wanted to make some sarcastic remark like "out of sight, out of mind" or "glad to know I'm so easily forgotten." But she knew that wasn't what he meant, and it wasn't fair to mock him when she sensed he was being sincere.

"I've been lonely without you," he went on.

She couldn't help herself this time. She scoffed.

"I'm serious." He turned his head in her direction. "There's always someone around, it's true. I have fans and my band, makeup artists and stylists, executives and management teams, collaborators and fellow musicians. I'm surrounded by people almost twenty-four-seven."

He blew out a breath. "But none of them really *know* me. Not like you do."

"Not like I did," she replied. "I don't know you anymore, Sawyer."

"But you do. I haven't changed so much. I'm still Sawyer Landry, deep on the inside."

"Except now you've got millions of fans the world over, and your face is instantly recognizable wherever you go. And don't forget the house in Nashville and your ranch in Texas. And that starlet you were dating for a while... what was her name?"

He held up a hand to stem the tide of facts, which she knew sounded more like accusations than observations. "Okay, okay. So *life* is different for me. My situation is different. But I'm still Sawyer Landry, son of Ford and Olivia Landry. Brother to Chase, best friend to Gavin...and if I had my way, boyfriend to Rory Callahan."

He fell silent after that last part. She had the feeling he hadn't meant to speak that possibility aloud. Probably because he didn't want to scare her off. But she wasn't scared. In fact, him speaking those words gave her a tiny thrill of hope—hope that part of her wanted to smother. But even if she did, she knew it would just resurface.

"How do I know you're not back just because you need some fresh inspiration for your next album?"

He seemed to take her concern seriously and didn't answer immediately. "Music has always been at the heart of who we are, Rory, and I admit, I miss that inspiration. And I've always relied on your opinion because I trust you. But that's just it—it's about you, not the music. Because even if all that went away, and I never wrote another lyric or played another song, you'd still be the one thing that inspires me, in anything and everything I do."

This little speech left her breathless and entirely without words. Fortunately, Sawyer continued.

"I know it will take some time," he said, his voice hushed, "but I was hoping maybe you could learn to trust me again. And that we, the two of us, we could, you know…" He faltered and came to a stop.

She saw the turn toward the restaurant, and her apartment, up ahead. His time was almost up.

"Can you… Is that something you can do?"

She swallowed, looking out the window so she didn't have to face him. "I'm still not sure what it is you're asking from me," she hedged.

He didn't hesitate in his reply. "I'm asking you to forgive me, for a start. Beyond that…

maybe we could just try to talk, like we used to. I want to know what life's been like for you the last couple of years—what you've been up to, if you've written any new songs and if you like working for your brother. And maybe it's possible we could, I don't know, start again?"

She chewed on her lower lip as she contemplated these words.

"Will you at least think about it?" he asked as they neared the restaurant.

Rory considered but stayed silent as he pulled into a parking space in the back alley, near the steps that led to her second-floor apartment. He cut the engine, and she suspected he planned to walk her to the front door. He'd always been a gentleman about that sort of thing. Or maybe he was trying to buy himself more time.

She tugged on the door handle and let herself out of the car. Sawyer hurried to exit the vehicle and meet her on the opposite side.

"Rory?"

She turned to look at him and felt her heart catch. Maybe he *was* still her Sawyer underneath, the one person she knew as well as, maybe even better than, herself.

"I'll think about it…"

His face lit up, a smile breaking through.

"On one condition."

His smile faltered. "What's that?"

"I'll tell you later. Just show up here tomorrow morning. Eight a.m. sharp, you got it?"

"You promise you'll be here?" he countered.

She offered him a little smile of her own. "I'll be here. Just make sure you are. And bring your guitar."

He frowned. "Why—"

"No questions. Just come. And I'll give you my answer after."

"After what?"

She didn't reply but rather turned her back and headed up the stairs to her apartment.

She couldn't resist throwing the words down to him once she reached the landing.

"Thanks for the ride…cowboy."

SAWYER ASSUMED THAT when he showed up at Rory's place the next day, he'd find out what she had planned. He was wrong. She had her truck back, presumably she'd gotten it before he showed up, or else someone from the coffee shop had dropped it off for her.

Rory stowed their guitars in the small space behind the front seat before climbing into the driver's side. When he hesitated, she waved a hand impatiently.

"Come on, we don't want to be late."

"Late for what?" he asked as he opened the passenger-side door.

She didn't answer but rather started the engine, and he decided he'd better get inside the cab before she changed her mind and took off without him.

He tried asking again after they'd passed the town limits and once more when they merged onto I-95 south, but Rory only smirked. He'd just have to trust her. He decided to give up asking and simply enjoy the chance to be with her, just the two of them. Trapped in a vehicle like this, at least she couldn't dodge his questions.

"So, tell me what you've been up to since you moved back to town?"

She was hesitant with her responses at first, sharing only minimal details about working in Connor's restaurant, which had become wildly popular over the last two years, and what some of their acquaintances were up to these days. She opened up a bit more the longer they drove, and filled him in on how Connor had met Harper, the restaurant critic who'd nearly destroyed his career only to find herself working for him some time later. She caught him up on the antics of Molly, her young niece, and how Gavin, Erin and their son, Kitt, were doing since he saw them last. He noticed that she directed a lot of the conversation away from herself, instead bringing him up to date on the town and community. He recognized this as a defense mechanism, but he wasn't satisfied. He wanted to know more—about her.

"But what about *you*?" he persisted after she'd told him about Harper's sister, Paige, and how she had appointed herself wedding planner. "What are you up to these days?"

She fidgeted, the cracked vinyl seats squeaking as she did.

"I told you. I work for Connor, and I live in the apartment above the restaurant."

"But I knew that already. What else do you do? I take it you play at the Lighthouse every Friday night."

"Most Friday nights," she agreed. "Once in a while, I'll skip it for a girls' night in with Harper, Erin, Tessa and Molly."

"No Paige?"

She shook her head. "Paige lives in DC. She drives into town fairly often to help with the wedding stuff, but she has her life in the city, with her husband and daughter."

"Ah. You're still writing songs?"

"Some."

He paused. "I liked that song you performed last night. 'Falling for You'?"

"Oh, right. Um, thanks." She kept her eyes

on the road, studiously avoiding his gaze. He'd hoped that maybe referring to a song that he assumed was about him might get her to open up a bit, but if anything, it made her even more quiet.

"It was a good song," he said.

She didn't respond, and he searched for another way to keep her talking.

"Are you still performing at the Independence Day festival every year?"

She nodded. "Yeah, I've kept that up. It was...tough, that first year. Right after..."

"Oh, right." He'd broken up with her just weeks before the festival was to take place, leaving her to handle it on her own. While he was deliberating on whether he should apologize for that or let it pass, Rory reached over and turned on the radio.

"So, still no hints as to where we're going?" He decided to let it go and change subjects.

She turned the music up louder.

"You'll see when we get there," she announced over the steady rhythm of classic rock and roll.

He settled back in his seat, recognizing that Rory was done talking for now. He might as well enjoy the music. It was obvious he wasn't going to learn anything more for the time being.

OF ALL THE places Sawyer might have guessed Rory would take him, the inner city of Baltimore hadn't even been on the list. But when they pulled into a parking lot, flanked by a basketball court on the left and a shabby brick building on the right with a sign labeling it the Harbor House Youth Center, he assumed they'd reached their destination.

"Rory?" he asked uneasily, wondering exactly what they were doing in one of the most crime-ridden neighborhoods in the area.

"Don't worry," she assured him. "I'll protect you from the gangbangers."

Her nonchalance put him at ease, and he laughed. "Way to emasculate a man."

She climbed out of the cab and grabbed her guitar from the backseat before slamming the door. Sawyer followed her lead. Five minutes later, they were in a classroom of sorts, with floor-to-ceiling windows and industrial lighting overhead. Despite the shabby appearance of the building's exterior, the inside was warm and welcoming with strings of multicolored lights dangling from the ceiling, and polished wooden floors. The walls were covered in graffiti artwork with uplifting messages like Stay Strong, Survive and Hope. There were folding chairs and a few tables in the room, and Sawyer noticed a collection of instruments dominating one corner.

A group of around fifteen dark-skinned youth ranging in ages from maybe eight to fourteen or fifteen were scattered throughout the room. Only one other adult seemed to be monitoring them.

"Yo, Miss Rory!" called one of the older teens as they moved farther into the room. "What's up, girl?"

"Hey, Jamal," Rory replied with a wave. "Have you been practicing that song I gave you?"

"You know it," Jamal replied, eagerly confident.

"You didn't say you were bringing some guy with you," another of the kids pointed out.

Rory glanced at Sawyer. "This is Sawyer," she offered and then introduced each of the kids in the room, though he knew it would take him a bit to remember all the names.

"Sawyer. He your boyfriend or something?" one of the girls asked. Sawyer thought Rory had introduced her as Kenesha.

Rory laughed, and the sound of it drew his head around. He hadn't heard Rory laugh once since he'd come back, much less at a question like the one Kenesha had just asked.

"Something like that," Rory replied. "He's

famous, you know. A country music singer. Just won a big award."

The kids eyed him skeptically.

"He don't look famous," Jamal said.

"Hey," Sawyer protested. "Give a guy a chance, would you?"

Rory shook her head. "I'm serious. He and I used to perform together, but then he got a big recording contract. Lives in Nashville now."

They eyed him warily, not sure what to make of this.

"What's he doing here?" Jamal asked.

Rory shrugged. "I thought you might like the chance to meet him. Show him what you can do."

Jamal grunted, not giving in so easily. From the corner of his eye, Sawyer saw the only other adult in the room approach.

"Well, this is a surprise." He shifted his attention to the dark-skinned, fortysomething man who had stepped up to them.

"Hi, Leland. Sorry, it was sort of a last-minute thing to bring him along. Sawyer, this is Leland. Leland, Sawyer."

Leland held out a hand, and Sawyer took it. "No problem, Rory. In fact, it's a pleasure to meet you, Sawyer. I have your album, and I love your music."

"Thanks."

With these words, Leland confirmed what Rory had told the kids. They began talking and moving closer.

"You're really famous? For real?"

"You know Beyoncé?"

"How much money you make?"

Leland held up a hand. "Whoa, slow down there. Is that any way to welcome Sawyer to the group?"

There was some grumbling, but the kids backed off.

"Tell you what, why don't we show Sawyer what we've been working on the last few weeks?"

This suggestion restored the mood, and the kids broke off to prepare. As soon as it was just the two of them, Sawyer turned to Rory.

"So, this is the 'one condition' you mentioned?"

She nodded. "I wanted you to come here and meet these kids. Talk to them. Show them... I don't know, that they matter. That they're worth the time of someone...like you."

"Like me?"

She turned away. He looked back over the room.

"How often do you come here?"

"I try to come at least twice a month," she replied. "It's part of the Baltimore inner-city

Kids and Culture campaign. They have some after-school programs, and then these weekend events. The kids come, and we sing and learn about different styles of music. And just hang out. Sometimes, that's all they really want— just to chill and have someone listen to them. It gives them somewhere to be other than the streets and a creative outlet to pour their energy into."

Sawyer was staring at her now.

"How long have you been doing this?"

She finally looked at him. Her eyes were bright in a way he'd never seen them, her cheeks flushed. She looked away again.

"A little over a year. I don't always get to come as often as I'd like. Sometimes, work interferes. And lately, bridesmaid duties have kept me from showing up regularly."

"Rory, that's…" He shook his head, amazed. "That's great." He was humbled. Rory had taken her music and used it for a cause greater than herself. How much had he given back, especially after how blessed he'd been the last two years?

Maybe he shouldn't have, but he couldn't stop himself from reaching out and grabbing her hand. She stiffened at his touch, but then, after another few seconds, she relaxed. He squeezed her fingers, leaned in and whispered,

"I think this is a lot cooler than any Artist of the Year award."

She didn't say anything, but when he looked at her face, she was smiling.

TWO HOURS LATER, Rory was in awe of how easily Sawyer had won over the kids in the group. They'd performed their current song for him—a mash-up of folk rock and rap, which Sawyer enthusiastically applauded once they were finished. She'd forgotten how he could manage to do that, make someone feel so special. He'd done it for her often enough, but it warmed her heart to see how he behaved around these kids. Within the first hour, he'd had them gathered around as he strummed out one of his singles on the guitar for them to learn. Once they had that down, he invited them to freestyle some rap lyrics into his verses. The kids took turns coming up with various rhymes until they'd laid the groundwork for an entirely new version of Sawyer's song.

They took a break halfway through, after Jamal challenged Sawyer to a rap-off. Sawyer was better at it than Rory would have suspected, but he still couldn't compete with Jamal's quick and inventive rhymes, especially when one of them referenced Rory as Sawyer's "lady." There were a lot of "oohs" after that one, but Rory brushed them off and kept braiding one of the younger girls' hair as she'd been doing when the rap-off began.

But even though she didn't allow herself to be drawn into the interaction between Sawyer and the kids, she couldn't resist watching him. Once he'd realized what they were doing there, he'd relaxed and began exhibiting a camaraderie with the kids. Over the course of a couple hours, she watched them embrace him, the girls making attempts to flirt and the boys cutting on him until they saw he was a good sport, then asking him to join them in some of their freestyle hip-hop. At one point, a hip-hop dance battle began, and though Sawyer tried to bow out of it, the kids insisted he join in.

So he did. He had them all rolling with laughter over his poorly timed dance steps. Even Rory couldn't contain her giggles as he tried to keep up with Jamal and some of the other kids' quick and graceful movements. He shrugged off their ribbing and asked them to teach him some moves. They were merciless in trying to get him to beatbox, and he did his best to keep up.

Rory wondered what Sawyer's fans would think if they could see him now, but then she thought they might enjoy this as much as she was. Seeing Sawyer without inhibitions, sacrificing any sense of dignity in order to buoy these kids' spirits... It moved her. It reminded her of the Sawyer she'd once known, who was kind and selfless and giving. Maybe he was right. Maybe he hadn't changed as much as his circumstances had. Perhaps breaking up with her really had been a mistake he'd come to regret. Could she continue to hold that against him? To make him pay for that one mistake, especially when he was so desperately asking for her forgiveness?

She was so deep in this thought that she didn't realize she'd stopped braiding Zara's hair until the little girl nudged her. "Are you finished, Miss Rory?"

"Oh. Sorry, love, no." She began moving her fingers in and out once more, keeping her attention focused on the braid.

When she looked up again, she found Sawyer watching her. Their eyes locked, and he held her stare, his expression serious.

She'd promised him that if he came today, she'd consider his request—to forgive and forget, to move on and be friends and...maybe more. He'd certainly lived up to his end of the bargain.

Sawyer didn't turn away until one of the

kids jumped onto his back, forcing him to shift his focus.

Rory knew he'd be expecting her answer soon.

CHAPTER SIX

THEY STOPPED FOR burgers and fries at a diner on the way home. Sawyer insisted it was his treat. Rory had softened in the hours they'd spent at the youth center, and Sawyer had the sense that she was seriously considering his request for a second chance.

He pulled out his baseball cap again and tugged it low over his forehead as they placed their orders. Their waitress eyed him suspiciously but didn't comment on his disguise. When she walked away, Rory clucked her tongue. "It's strange, the way you have to hide now."

"I'm not hiding," he amended, "but sometimes, being recognized can be overwhelming."

She arched an eyebrow.

"Not just for me," he went on, "but for whoever's with me. I wouldn't want you to feel awkward."

"Hmm."

He decided to change the subject.

"Rory, thanks for today. That was a lot of fun."

She tugged a napkin free of the tabletop dispenser and began folding it into squares. "You were really good with the kids."

"They're a good group."

The waitress reappeared with the drinks, a Sprite for Sawyer and iced tea for Rory. He didn't speak until they were alone again.

"So, what's the story there? How'd you get involved?"

Rory took her time tapping one end of the straw on the table until it poked through the other end. She pulled the wrapper free and slid the straw into her glass.

"I wasted a lot of time my first year back, just...moping. After a while, I decided I needed to find something bigger than myself to invest my time in. And not long after that, I read an article about the Kids and Culture thing. The program is a way to keep kids off the streets. It gives them an outlet, a place to go, a way to express themselves in a safe and controlled environment."

"It seems like a good program."

"It is." She became more animated as she spoke. "Sawyer, you should see some of the situations these kids come from. Almost all of them are from single-parent homes, and several, like Jamal, are being raised by a grandparent while their mom or dad is in prison."

She straightened, gesturing as she continued. "And Zara? The little girl whose hair I was braiding? She and her mom are living out of a van in the alley behind the building. Leland and I have tried to help out to get her off the streets, but she's a proud woman."

"That's terrible," Sawyer sympathized.

"It is," Rory agreed. "Zara is such a sweetheart. She's shyer than a lot of the other kids, but you should hear her sing. She starts quiet, like a sparrow, and then her voice grows as she goes along."

"I'm sorry I didn't get to hear it. Maybe next time."

Rory straightened, her eyes widening. "Next time?"

He realized how this sounded. "Well, I mean…if it's a standing invitation, that is."

Rory blinked and then looked down at the tabletop. He remained quiet, letting her work out whatever she needed to say. Before she found the words, the waitress reappeared with their food and set the plates in front of them, sashaying away after Sawyer confirmed they didn't need anything else.

He didn't touch his food, though, but watched Rory instead.

"I just don't know how to wrap my head around the fact that you're back," she finally said. "And especially when you say you want for us, to be, you know."

"To be together."

She let out a breath and met his eyes. "I don't know if I'm ready for that, Sawyer. I—I want to be, but I'm not sure that I am."

He weighed his words carefully. "I'm willing to wait for you, Rory. I'll wait as long as you need me to."

She licked her lips. "I appreciate that, but—"

"No." He rested his hand on the table. "No, you're not hearing me. I will wait, however long I need to wait. I owe you that much. And I'll do whatever it takes. If I need to commute to Nashville and spend more time in Findlay Roads, then that's what I'll do. If you're here then there's nowhere else I'd rather be."

He stretched out his hand across the table, willing her to take it. "You're it, Rory. You're the one thing that's been missing from my life the last two years. And, I don't know, maybe I needed that time to recognize just what an integral part of my life you are."

"Or maybe you just need someone to bounce ideas off of, to jump-start your music writing again."

He didn't flinch at her words but rather kept

his gaze steady on hers. "I miss that part of our relationship, I'll admit it. But that's not all I miss. Not what I miss the most."

He kept his outstretched hand on the table, palm up.

"Give me another chance. You might think it's a risk, but I know the truth."

"Which is?"

"That I love you. That you mean more to me than anything else, and that I'm not going anywhere. I promise you that."

She hesitated for a long time, but he waited, as patiently as he'd promised, until she finally rested her hand in his.

"I want to believe you," she softly stated.

"Then believe me. I messed up, Rory. Please don't doubt me, doubt *us*. Don't keep us from being happy."

She licked her lips, her expression thoughtful. "It's a lot to take in all at once, yeah?" Her Irish accent was more pronounced in her uncertainty. "And I think I do trust you, Sawyer, but I just have to be sure. Of me, as much as of you. I don't believe it would be wise to re-enter a relationship with resentment. I need to make sure I won't hold the past against you, in the future. Or this—" she used her other hand to gesture to him and then her and back again "—will never work."

He was both surprised and pleased by her wisdom on that score.

"Okay," he agreed. "We're in total agreement then. I want you to be sure, too. And I promise I will do whatever it takes to earn your trust again, to prove to you I'm in this for the long haul."

She offered him a faint smile, and it buoyed his hope.

"Give me a bit more time to think on it," she said.

"You can have all the time you want."

She nodded and toyed with a French fry, even as Sawyer continued to hold onto her fingers. "If you'd like, maybe you could come with me to this dinner I have tonight." She made it sound like an off-the-cuff offer, but he suspected it was more.

"Sure, what kind of dinner?"

She shrugged. "It's just a get-together that Connor and Harper are having, sort of a thank-you to everyone involved in the wedding."

"Oh." He wasn't sure how he felt about facing Connor again, given her brother's reaction to him at their last meeting.

Rory tugged her fingers free of his and awkwardly reached for a napkin as she avoided his eyes. "It's okay if you'd rather not come. I understand."

He insistently reached for her hand once again. "Hey." He waited until she met his eyes. "I'd love to. Just tell me where and when."

The way her eyes lit up at his words soothed something deep within him. Being with Rory was right. It had always been right. He'd just had a brief period where he'd forgotten that.

"Be at my place by five."

"It's a date."

She looked startled at this statement, but she didn't protest. Instead, a small smile played around her lips as she reached for another French fry with her free hand.

It was a long time before he let go of her other one.

SAWYER TURNED THE radio up loud on the way to his parents' after he'd dropped off Rory at her place. He slapped his hand on the steering wheel as he drove and when the DJ announced the next song, he couldn't help letting out a small whoop of happiness. The first strains of his breakout hit reverberated through the speakers, and he found himself singing along to his own voice, marveling at his good fortune. How could he be so lucky? All his dreams had come true, and best of all, Rory was about to give him a second chance. He felt like he was on top of the world, that everything was going his way.

> Take me or leave me
> On this long stretch of road.
> Love me forever,
> Or leave me here cold...

He remembered the first time he'd ever heard this song on the radio. He'd been driving to an interview to promote the upcoming release of his first album. None of it had seemed quite real yet at that point. He'd seen the album, held it in his hands. He'd heard the song played in the studio. But it wasn't until he was in his car alone, navigating the Nashville highway, and hearing those opening notes filter from the speakers that he realized how far he'd come in such a short time. He'd been both overjoyed and humbled, and the only thing spoiling it was the sudden and unexpected desire to have Rory sitting in the passenger seat beside him.

Now, he was being given the opportunity to see that wish come true. He couldn't imagine being any happier than he was right now.

As the last notes of the song faded away, he turned his dad's pickup into the driveway and flicked off the radio. He felt another wash of happiness as he recognized his brother's Honda Civic parked in front of the garage.

Chase was just exiting the vehicle as Sawyer pulled in. He quickly put the truck in Park and hopped out of the cab. He'd driven their dad's pickup this morning while his dad used the sedan he and Chase had both learned to drive on. Though he'd offered to keep his rental while he was home, his dad insisted he use the truck, saying the sedan never got driven enough anymore anyway.

"What's college done to you?" he teased his brother as he came around the front of the truck. "You've turned all preppy on me."

Chase ran a hand through his neatly cut hair and then tugged self-consciously on the button-down shirt he wore. Sawyer almost felt badly for teasing him, but what else were big brothers for if not to tease their siblings unmercifully?

"Is that a *vest* you're wearing?"

Chase rolled his eyes. "I'm a business major. I have to look the part."

Sawyer gave him a once-over and arched an eyebrow. "You catch many girls in that getup?"

Now his brother looked mortified. "That's none of your business."

Sawyer smirked. "Or, maybe there's just one girl in particular, huh?"

Chase frowned, and Sawyer finally relented.

"Come here, bro." He drew his brother into a hug and then dutifully mussed the kid's hair. Chase pushed him away, but he was grinning as he did it.

"What are you, twelve? I'm not in grade school anymore, you know."

Sawyer shoved him playfully. "You'll always be a kid to me, Chase."

His brother huffed. "Now you sound like Dad." Suddenly, he grew sober. "Have you talked to them yet?"

Sawyer frowned. "Who? Mom and Dad? Sure, I got into town the day before yesterday. We caught up over dinner my first night here."

Chase didn't say anything, just eyed his brother meaningfully, as though he was searching for some answer.

"Did they tell you what's going on?"

Sawyer frowned again uncertainly, trying to think what might have been said that would cause Chase to look so grave. He belatedly realized that most of his conversations with his parents had revolved around him and his career.

"No," he slowly admitted. "What's wrong?"

Chase shook his head. "I don't know. But they're keeping a secret. I can tell."

"What makes you think so?"

Chase glanced toward the house and then back at him. "Little things. When I call, they both somehow manage to change the conversation as soon as I start asking about things at home. And I got this weird call from Dad a while back. He needed directions."

Chase had always been the more perceptive son, but Sawyer was still skeptical. His brother was far more serious than he was and more inclined to magnify things that weren't really such a big deal.

"Okay, so maybe that's a little odd, but Dad never was good about finding his way around, so calling for directions is—"

Chase shook his head as he cut off Sawyer. "Home. He called me for directions on how to get home from work."

Sawyer blinked. Okay, so that was strange.

"Did you know he cut back his hours? He's only working part-time."

"Part-time? He loves his job. Why would he do that?"

"That's not all," he continued. "When I was home at Christmas, I caught him out back, whistling for Tucker."

"Tucker?"

"Yeah." Chase didn't need to elaborate because Sawyer saw where he was going with this. Why would their dad be looking for the dog that had died eight years ago?

"Have you asked Mom about it?"

"That's just it—I tried. I didn't tell her about the directions thing because Dad begged me not to. But I asked her if she thought everything was okay with him. She brushed it off, told me he'd been stressed lately, and their doctor wasn't concerned."

"She took him to a doctor about it?"

"I guess."

Sawyer ran a hand across his mouth as he considered. "If she took him to the doctor, then she's worried, too. No matter what she says."

"Exactly."

He understood why Chase was uneasy now. Sawyer found it hard to believe his parents were keeping some big secret, but still, something was definitely off.

"That's part of why I texted you and suggested you come back home. I thought, between the two of us, we could find out what's going on."

"That was only part of it?"

Chase shrugged one shoulder but his grin gave him away. "Well, that, and I kind of miss having you around. You haven't been back home at all since you went and became all famous. We fly down to see you in Nashville, but you need to come back here more often. If you don't return to your roots once in a while, this celebrity stuff is going to go to your head, you know."

Sawyer gave him a playful shove. Chase stumbled back but laughed anyway. "Plus, I don't think anyone at college believes you're my brother. Think you could come visit my campus this fall? Maybe sign some autographs, tell a few girls how much you've always admired me?"

Sawyer reached out and knocked a fake punch against his brother's arm. "I have a feeling you're probably doing just fine on the girl front."

Chase didn't answer, but the way his ears grew red told Sawyer more than any words could have. He wrapped an arm around his brother as they turned toward the house.

"Maybe we could set you and your friends up with backstage passes on my next tour."

Chase's face lit up. "Seriously?"

"Sure. Anything for my little bro." He leaned Chase's head down and raked his knuckles across his scalp, disregarding Chase's protests. They were laughing as they headed inside the house, but deep down, Sawyer couldn't shake his faint uneasiness.

IT DIDN'T TAKE long for Sawyer to see why Chase suspected their parents were hiding something. Their mom was ecstatic when they walked through the door, thrilled to have both of her boys under one roof again. She ushered them into the kitchen and set out a pie she'd baked that morning. Their dad came in from his workshop to join them, and Sawyer had the chance to fill them in on his morning with Rory while Chase boasted about how well his finals had gone. However, as soon as Sawyer made the effort to turn the conversation around to how his parents were doing, they found ways to steer it back to him.

"So… Rory was glad to see you?" His mom eyed him pointedly, and he felt his father's and brother's curious glances.

"Not at first," he admitted, reluctant to talk about her until he knew where they stood, "but she's getting there, I think."

His mother beamed with happiness, and that's when he realized something. Since he'd returned home a few days ago, he hadn't once seen her without a shadow of some sort over her features. Even when she smiled, it felt strained. This was the first time her expression was filled with pure joy.

"I miss that girl," she commented, almost to herself.

Sawyer cocked his head. "Don't you ever see her? Talk to her?"

Olivia sliced off another tiny sliver of pie, neatly avoiding his eyes. "She needed time to heal, Sawyer, after she came back here. If she'd wanted to see us, she would have. You know that. I decided not to make your break with her more difficult by seeking her out."

"Oh." He felt a wave of shame at this candid response, saddened that his choice had deprived his mother of a friendship with Rory. The two of them had always gotten on so well. Rory had grown up without a mother, and his own had never had any daughters. He'd never considered before how they each might have filled those roles for the other.

"Well, here's hoping she comes around more often," his dad said. "I always liked her. She's sharp. Keeps you in line."

Sawyer grinned, again feeling that flutter of happiness at the progress he and Rory had made that morning. "She definitely does." He nudged his brother. "Now, if we could just find someone like that for Chase…"

"Hey." His brother held up a hand. "My love life is not a topic for discussion here."

"Why not?" their dad asked. "You're taking Jessica Barnes to homecoming, aren't you?"

Chase had his fork raised halfway to his

mouth but froze when their dad asked this question. His gaze leaped to Sawyer's. Sawyer felt an odd twist in his stomach, the echo of Chase's earlier concern sending a shiver down his spine.

"Dad. Chase hasn't dated Jessica in six years. That was back when he was a sophomore in high school," Sawyer reminded him.

He expected his dad to laugh or make a joke—something about how Chase was so popular with the ladies, it was hard to keep track of his girlfriends. That's the sort of teasing they often did with each other. But his dad looked confused, his eyes shifting to their mom in question.

She reached out and patted their father's hand. "Chase is in college now, Ford. Remember?"

"College?" He looked from his wife, back to his youngest son and then at Sawyer. The struggle in his dad's eyes startled him. He seemed to be…lost. And then, he looked down, hiding his face from view.

"Hard to believe how fast you boys are growing up."

Chase was still frozen, his fork partway to his mouth. After another beat, he set it back down, and Sawyer wondered if his brother had lost his appetite. Because the churning in his stomach wouldn't allow him to finish his pie, either.

"Mom?" He looked to his mother for an answer. "What's going on?"

She glanced at Sawyer then gave a quick swipe of her head.

"Mom?" he demanded. Chase pushed his pie plate aside.

He watched his mother's expression cycle through several emotions—frustration, anger, grief. Her jaw hardened and she pursed her lips. Sawyer didn't know how long they sat there, in this emotional standoff, when he noticed his father's hand reach toward his mother's.

"Tell them."

She blinked, breaking her gaze from Sawyer's and looking to his dad.

"It's time, Olivia. We said we would, when they were both back here, together." He looked at her. "Tell them."

Sawyer felt a weight settle into his stomach, solid and unmovable, and somehow, he knew. He knew, in that moment, whatever his mom was about to tell them would change everything.

CHAPTER SEVEN

SAWYER WISHED HE could turn back time, just for one hour. One hour ago, he'd been the happiest he could ever remember being. He had a successful career, the chance to restore his relationship with the woman he loved and a future bright with possibility. Now, a mere sixty minutes later, he felt as if his world was crumbling around him.

"I still don't understand how this works," he said. "Dad's only fifty-three. I thought Alzheimer's wasn't something you had to worry about until you were much older."

His mom twisted her fingers in her lap and slid a glance toward his father. His dad seemed remarkably at ease considering the diagnosis he'd been given. But then, he'd had a lot more time to get used to the idea, Sawyer thought with a touch of resentment.

And then another sickening thought—what if his dad's nonchalance was because he didn't understand what was happening? What if his mind had already deteriorated to the point that he didn't realize what they were discussing? Sawyer felt a wave of nausea at the idea.

"That's why it's called early onset Alzheimer's," his mom patiently explained a second time. "It strikes people in their fifties or younger. Only about five percent of the Alzheimer's patients are in the early onset group. It's very uncommon."

"That's not much consolation, is it?" Sawyer replied, trying to temper the sharp edge in his tone. "I mean, who cares how uncommon a disease is if you've been diagnosed with it? Is it supposed to make you feel special or something?"

"Sawyer..." Chase spoke his name softly, under his breath, in warning. Sawyer knew it was illogical to feel irritation. It wasn't as if his father had asked for this to happen. But his fear needed a target, and since his parents had been withholding this information for some time, they were the easiest choice.

"How could you have kept this from us all these months? How hard would it have been to pick up the phone or send an email or a text or *something*?" He raked a hand through his hair and realized his fingers were trembling. He dropped his arm and tightened his knuckles into a fist.

"We didn't want to distract you from everything you had going on." His mother's tone was sympathetic but unapologetic. "We wanted you to enjoy this time in your life for as long as you could."

"I think the news that my father is dying is worth the distraction, don't you?"

"You don't die from Alzheimer's," Olivia calmly corrected. "It weakens your body's defense mechanisms so that eventually, you become vulnerable to infections and unable to fight off disease, and then..."

The words hung in the air as his mother looked down at her lap. If her words had been meant to be reassuring, they had the opposite effect. It made Sawyer even more aware that his father's diagnosis was a death sentence.

Chase spoke up, obviously trying to diffuse the tension.

"How serious is it? His symptoms don't seem too bad yet, so how much time do we have?"

Sawyer perked up at this. "That's true. He should have years before he'll need any real care, right? There has to be medicine to delay the progression of the disease. I mean, even if there's no cure yet, it's not like Alzheimer's is a new thing. I'm sure there are drugs and therapy and experimental trials and stuff." A thought came to him. "And if it's about the money, you don't have to worry. I can take care of any costs that health insurance doesn't cover. Money isn't a problem."

His mother was silent, and that alone said more than any words could.

"It's not…that simple," she finally offered.

"How can it not be?" Sawyer countered. "There has to be some clinical trials he can join or something. If you had told us sooner, Chase and I could have helped you look into options. Now that we know, we can find a way to fix this."

For the first time, his mother's steady voice cracked. "Don't you understand? There is no way to *fix* this, Sawyer."

"You don't know that," he countered, his words sharp. "How can you know that when you've been keeping things to yourself all this time? How is that fair to Dad? You should have told us," he accused.

"This is the worst part."

Sawyer had been so focused on his mother that when his dad spoke, it took him a second to shift his attention.

"What? What's the worst part?"

His dad gestured between them. "This. People talking about you like you're not in the room, referring to you in the third person when you're sitting right in front of them. Making decisions as if you're already too incompetent to understand what's happening to you."

A wave of shame washed over Sawyer.

"Dad, that's not what I was trying to do. I'm just…confused. And upset. You guys have had months to come to terms with your diagnosis, and I'm just learning about it now."

"You think we've come to terms? That we've accepted this is happening? Make no mistake, son, I'm not *at peace* about this. I'm angry. And I'm depressed. And I'm frightened. The last thing I am is *okay* with it."

Sawyer leaned back as his father spoke. He'd never heard his dad talk in such a manner, and the words—as well as the emotion behind them—gave rise to sudden grief. His dad was dying. Not only that, but also dying in one of the most inhuman ways possible. He was passing before his time and losing his identity, his dignity and his memories as he did.

"Dad—" His voice caught, and he coughed to muffle the sob forming in his throat.

They all sat silent for a minute, letting the tension settle. Sawyer tried to remember what little he knew of Alzheimer's. With all of his grandparents long gone, it hadn't seemed like something he'd need to think about anytime in the foreseeable future. He still couldn't wrap his mind around the news his father, only in his early fifties, had the disease. He was only twenty-two years older than Sawyer.

"Sawyer." His mother reached across the table. "You have to understand, we kept this from you for your own good."

He shook off her hand. She grimaced, and he felt a stab of guilt but not enough to keep him silent.

"My own good?"

"You had a lot going on, and we didn't want to interfere with that."

His jaw clenched. He was torn. Torn between lashing out at the hurt he was experiencing, or embracing his parents and never letting go. His emotions were convoluted, a jumble of tangled feelings he couldn't unravel. He stood to his feet.

"I can't talk about this right now."

"Sawyer, we're not finished here—"

He heard his mom's voice calling after him as he headed for the door, and then his father said, "Let him go, Olivia. Give him time."

It was the last thing he heard before he slammed the front door behind him.

SAWYER AVOIDED GOING back home after he'd stormed out following his parents' announcement. He spent the afternoon driving around town, circling the shoreline of Chesapeake Bay until it intersected with the Susquehanna River along the city limits and then looping back toward the center of town. He had no particular destination in mind; he just kept driving as he tried to wrap his head around his dad's Alzheimer's diagnosis. His emotions skipped back and forth between anger at his parents for having kept this secret so long and guilt for not coming home more often to give them the opportunity to share it.

He was so mired in his worry and self-recrimination that he lost track of time, belatedly realizing he'd better head toward Callahan's so he wouldn't be late to pick up Rory for the dinner at Connor's. By the time he pulled in to the back alley of the restaurant, he had only seconds to spare. Rory was already waiting for him, sitting on the steps leading up to her apartment.

She was dressed in a pair of navy blue capris and green ballet flats with a pale jade sleeveless blouse that flowed in soft lines down to her hips. The color drew attention to the dark ebony of her hair, which she'd let loose to fall in soft waves around her shoulders. His breath hitched at the sight of her. He wasn't sure how she got more beautiful each time he saw her. Maybe it had something to do with their time apart. His memories of her had softened, grown hazy, and whenever he was in her presence since he'd returned home, it was as if things were being brought into sharper focus.

She stood and began walking toward his vehicle. He quickly exited the truck to come around and open the door for her.

"You look beautiful, Rory."

The compliment seemed to throw her off balance. She hesitated, her eyes darting from the open truck door to his face and then down to the ground. At last, she offered a slow smile and murmured her thanks.

They drove to Connor's house without much conversation except for Rory's directions. Sawyer wasn't uncomfortable, and he didn't sense Rory was, either. It's just that they'd spent so many hours on the road together over the years that driving together was second nature to them. He turned on the radio but left the volume on low, content to let it run as background noise. They kept the windows down, and a nice breeze ran over his skin and kept him cool.

It was only as he pulled up to the curb by Connor's house that he felt the first ripple of nerves. He wondered what Rory had told her brother about inviting Sawyer to come with her today. He doubted Connor was keen on the idea of him joining the party. Despite his uneasiness, he couldn't help wishing he'd been privy to that conversation. Connor and Rory were both bullheaded. He could only imagine what she'd said to convince him that Sawyer was coming to the get-together.

As he exited the vehicle and went to open Rory's door, his doubts assailed him once more, and he swallowed at the thought of what he'd say to Connor if the other man questioned his intentions toward Rory. He thought about taking her hand as they walked up to the house, but he hesitated, uncertain of whether she'd accept the gesture.

They reached the porch, and Rory rang the doorbell. His nerves must have been evident because he suddenly felt her hand slip into his. She squeezed gently, and just like that, he relaxed. Seconds later, the door opened, and Harper greeted them with a welcoming smile.

"Hey, you made it!"

From the surprise in her tone, Sawyer wondered if his attendance had been in doubt. Rory released his hand, and he worried it was because she didn't want to be seen holding it. His fingers cooled at the loss of her touch, and he felt the rise of butterflies once more.

"Sawyer, this is Connor's fiancée, Harper," Rory began. "Harper—"

"Sawyer Landry, I know."

From the corner of his eye, Sawyer saw Rory's

brow wrinkle. She glanced his way, her expression suspicious. "Have you two met?"

Harper laughed, but it sounded slightly forced to his ears. "Rory, come on. He's famous. I mean, who doesn't know Sawyer Landry?"

Sawyer decided to play along. If Harper wasn't going to reveal they'd met before then he thought it might be better if he didn't, either. He stuck out a hand. "Pleased to meet you... Harper, was it?"

Harper's caramel-brown eyes practically twinkled as she placed her hand in his. "Harper Worth, soon to be Callahan," she added with a touch of pride. "It's nice to meet you, too, Sawyer."

Before Rory could question them further, Harper opened the door wide enough for them to step through.

"Come on in, dinner's almost ready."

Sawyer placed his hand at the small of Rory's back, felt her stiffen momentarily, and then relax. He didn't take his hand away until Harper ushered them into the dining room, and he was introduced to the rest of the dinner party.

RORY COULDN'T STOP herself from stealing surreptitious glances in Sawyer's direction. She felt like a teenager again, in the early days of her and Sawyer's relationship, when everything was new and tentative. She would do the same thing then as she was doing now— sneak covert glances at him, as if to reassure herself he was really her boyfriend. Her emotions were much the same as they'd been then, too—she was uncertain he really wanted *her* and not some other girl.

But he'd come back to Findlay Roads. For *her*. And declared his love, offered to make amends for how he'd left her. Though part of her remained wary and wounded, the larger part believed him and wanted to trust him again. For nearly two years, she'd tried to find a way past her grief at their breakup, and now, it seemed there was no need to. Sawyer had come back. And he loved her.

Of course, there was a lot to consider, she thought as she watched him catching up with their friend, Erin. Sawyer lived in Nashville now, and his music career had given him a new way of life. He'd be traveling, on tour for much of the time. But she could join him, couldn't she? Or at least, she could fly out occasionally to wherever he was performing and spend some time with him. She frowned at the thought. She didn't want pieces of Sawyer, though. After how close they'd been before, traveling cross-country for months at a time and spending nearly every waking moment together, could she really be satisfied with the occasional weekend or a couple of weeks at a time? If she committed to this relationship, what did their future look like?

As if he could hear her thoughts, Sawyer turned, in midconversation with Erin, and caught her eye. Even as he was speaking, his mouth lifted in a grin, and he sent a brief wink her way. Her heart sped up, and she couldn't keep the smile from her lips. She'd missed him. She'd almost convinced herself she was doing okay until he'd appeared and upended her world by telling her he wanted her back.

"Uncle Sawyer, look!"

Sawyer's eyes shifted to Molly, Connor's eight-year-old daughter, as she tugged his arm. In Molly's time line, Sawyer had been gone for far longer than he should have been, a fact that she pointed out less than five minutes in the door.

Now, her niece was intent on making up for lost time by demanding Sawyer's attention as often as she could gain it and showing him the various highlights he'd missed while he'd been away, via photographs and mementos.

"And this is the article they put in the newspaper when the restaurant almost burned down," she informed him, thrusting a tattered newsprint clipping into his hand. Sawyer took it and patiently skimmed it. Rory felt her heart warm at the care he took to give Molly his full concentration. He'd make a great dad someday.

She dropped her head at the thought. She'd entertained the idea of her and Sawyer settling down one day and having children, but that seemed like ages ago. She wasn't quite prepared to invest her heart so fully again just yet.

She missed Sawyer's response to Molly as Harper sidled up next to her.

"You look deep in thought," Harper observed.

Rory shrugged one shoulder. "Maybe I'm just hungry."

Harper laughed. "Isn't that usually my line? At least, that's what Connor says."

Rory looked at Harper just in time to catch her friend gazing in Connor's direction. The love on Harper's face caused Rory to experience a surge of affection for her soon-to-be sister-in-law. Harper really did love Connor and Molly, body and soul. Despite her initial doubts, she couldn't have imagined a better wife for Connor or mom for Molly.

"He chose well, you know."

Harper snapped to attention and looked in Rory's direction. "What?"

Rory shook her head. "Nothing." And then,

simply because she wanted to, she wrapped her arms around Harper. "I'm excited you're going to be my sister. That's all."

Harper seemed flustered by the sudden affection, but after a beat, she tightened the embrace. "I'm happy, too. More than you can imagine."

When they pulled away, Rory noticed a faint sheen of tears in Harper's eyes. She fanned herself dramatically.

"Whew. It's getting a little emotional in here, isn't it?"

Rory nudged her. "We can't have that, can we?"

Harper nudged back. "Well, I suspect it has something to do with the handsome cowboy over there."

Rory couldn't help herself. She immediately looked in Sawyer's direction. Tessa had joined the conversation with Sawyer and Erin while Molly had moved on to pester Rafael for a piggyback ride. Rory watched them for a moment—her friends. The man she loved, even if she couldn't admit it to him just yet.

Seconds later, she felt Harper's hand on her arm.

"In all seriousness, Rory…is everything okay? With him being back?"

Rory thought about this question, weighing

the risk of being hurt again with the longing to let Sawyer back into her life. He was still Sawyer. Yet, if she was honest with herself, she sensed something more in him. He was… steadier, somehow. He'd always been strong, someone she could rely on…until that fateful day when fame came calling. But since he'd returned, he seemed more conscious of who he was and how his words and actions affected others. Perhaps that was a result of his fame, of being in the public eye so much. Maybe scrutiny had made him take a harder look at himself. At some point, didn't she have to trust that he was a man of his word, and he wouldn't leave her a second time?

Then again, what was that old saying? Once burned, twice shy? Maybe that was why she was so hesitant. She knew what heartache felt like now and wasn't in a hurry to experience it again.

"Yeah, everything's okay," she finally answered.

Now, if only she could make herself believe that.

SAWYER WAS A little worried when dinner got off to a bit of a rocky start. Molly had practically attached herself to his hip since he'd walked in the door, and when they gathered around the dining table, she insisted he sit next to her with Rory on his other side.

"Here, Sawyer." She pointed to the chair next to hers.

He knew better than to argue. Even at eight years old, Molly was as stubborn as her father and aunt. He took the seat beside her while Rory sat next to him. Connor had spent most of the evening in the kitchen, and Sawyer had easily relaxed in the rest of the company. Harper's sister, Paige, and her husband, Weston, had been unable to attend since they lived an hour-and-a-half away in Washington, DC, but the rest of the wedding party was in full attendance, including Harper's sister, Tessa; Erin, as one of Harper's bridesmaids; Rafael, who was serving as DJ for the reception as well as a groomsman; and Rory, as another of the bridesmaids. Erin's husband, Gavin, was also a groomsman, but with his current army deployment, he wouldn't be home until the week of the wedding. Connor had another friend, from his time in culinary school, who would be flying in for the event but since Jake owned a restaurant in Portland, Maine, he couldn't make it before then. So it was a relatively small group gathered around the table for the thank-you dinner that Connor and Harper were hosting. For his part,

Sawyer was just fine with the intimate number. Though he didn't mind large groups, it could sometimes feel awkward if someone became starstruck—which was more likely with a greater number of people. And he'd had to disentangle himself from more than one fascinated fan over the last year.

As they waited for Connor to bring in the food, Sawyer focused on Molly.

"So what's this I hear about you being in a wedding? You're not getting married, are you?"

She sighed with childlike gusto. "No, silly. It's *Dad* and *Harper* getting married, not me. I'm only eight."

"Eight going on eighteen," Harper muttered, grinning as she spoke.

"That sounds about right," Sawyer teased. "So, does that mean you're dating yet?"

Molly giggled. "Nooo. Dad says I can't date until I'm thirty."

"Your dad's right."

She rolled her eyes with little-girl exasperation. "But Aunt Rory just turned thirty, and you guys were already dating *forever*."

He felt Rory shift beside him, but he did his best not to look in her direction. He didn't want to draw attention to Molly's statement and make things more awkward.

"Molly, I'm not sure any boys will be able to handle you until they're thirty," Rafael remarked. This observation drew a round of laughter, thankfully pulling the attention away from him and Rory.

Before anything else could be said, Connor entered the room balancing several dishes in his arms. They all moved to help him, and Sawyer's mouth began to water. He didn't need to read the reviews of Connor's restaurant to know he was an incredible cook. Though he was wary of how Connor would behave with him being there, he had to admit he was looking forward to the meal. And he hoped Connor wouldn't be too critical of him in everyone else's presence.

"Sawyer," Connor greeted him with a nod after all the dishes were on the table. "Nice to see you again. We're glad you could join us tonight."

Connor's tone was pleasant enough, not at all disapproving as Sawyer feared it would be.

"Um, thanks," Sawyer mumbled, thrown off by the unexpected hospitality.

Harper was beaming with pride, and he suspected she'd had no small part in her fiancée's politeness. He shot a glance in Rory's direction just in time to see her shoulders lose some of their stiffness. So, she'd been as nervous as he had.

Bless Harper Worth. She was clearly a good influence on this family.

For the next few minutes, the conversation revolved around small talk as Connor took his seat, and the food was passed around. Sawyer loaded his plate with crab-stuffed rockfish, asparagus in lemon-brown butter sauce and the roasted new potatoes that Connor had prepared. As soon as everyone was served, Sawyer made a point to compliment Connor on the meal.

"I have to admit, I've missed your cooking," he told him.

Connor made a sound of disbelief. "No need to stroke my ego, Sawyer. I'm sure you've had food that was just as good during the last couple years."

Harper pointedly cleared her throat at the slight edge to Connor's tone. The other man frowned.

"That is, I hear Nashville has quite the culinary scene."

"Oh, sure," Sawyer agreed, trying to be as polite as Connor was obviously striving to be. "But I haven't had much of a chance to try the restaurants there. I've been too busy touring, which means eating at odd times and whatever's available. It's not quite the same as this."

"As this?" Harper prompted, her tone curious.

"Sitting down with friends, at a real meal. Like a family."

This response obviously pleased Harper. She smiled, and gave a slight nod. And he didn't miss the look she shot in Rory's direction, as if to let her know she approved.

"Will you be traveling less now that the tour for your first album has ended?" Tessa asked.

He thought of his father, knowing the remaining time they had together was limited. "I really hope so," he replied without elaborating. "I have to put in some studio time, begin working on my second album."

Harper's eyes lit with interest. "Oh, yeah? So you'll be writing new songs?"

Connor sighed. "What she's trying very hard not to tell you is that she's a big fan of your music."

Harper blinked several times and looked flustered. "Well, of course, I enjoy all kinds of music…"

"You might as well give it up, love. You know every word to every song on his album."

Harper's face turned a soft shade of pink.

"Really?" Rory said. "I didn't know that. How did I not know that?"

"Well…maybe not *every word*," Harper hedged.

"But you never listen to country music," Rory pointed out.

"Not when you're around," Connor mumbled beneath his breath.

"Oh." Rory's eyes grew wide. He wondered if Rory had been avoiding country music, too, so she didn't have to face any painful reminders of him. He cringed at the thought. He'd really broken her heart, hadn't he? It didn't make him proud, nor did it boost his ego. He didn't deserve her. After all the years, after everything they'd done and seen together, she deserved so much more than to be tossed aside.

"Harper and me listen to Sawyer's CD every time we're in the car," Molly stated and then broke into an off-key version of his first single, "Firefly Nights."

"Molly, not at the table," Connor admonished.

Sawyer was humbled, amused and embarrassed all at once. Fortunately, Erin and Harper seemed to recognize the need for a subject change, and they steered the conversation in other directions, toward talk of the wedding and the reception that was to be held at the restaurant, as well as Connor and Harper's plans for their honeymoon in Ireland. Rory spoke with envy about their trip, and he remembered that revisiting her homeland was something she'd always wanted to do. He allowed his mind to wander briefly, wondering if they might consider a trip to Ireland for their own honeymoon...provided he could win back Rory's heart and convince her to become his wife. Or maybe he could schedule several stops there on his next tour, and Rory could join him.

Talk eventually turned to the music for the reception, and he and Rafael found common ground in comparing rockabilly classics to current music trends. Despite the occasional tense exchange between him and Connor, dinner turned out to be a pleasant affair, both in terms of company as well as food.

After a dessert of strawberry pie and ice cream, Molly was sent to bed while the adults retired to the living area for conversation. Sawyer was preparing to sit beside Rory on the couch when Connor tapped him on the arm.

"Mind if I have a word, mate?"

Sawyer didn't see how he could deny him. Fighting uneasiness, he glanced at Rory and found her talking to Erin. Rather than disturb her, he followed Connor toward the back of the house and onto the patio, anxious to hear what was on the other man's mind.

When they stepped outside, Connor gestured for Sawyer to take a seat on the porch's cushioned chairs.

"No thanks. I think I'll stand."

Whatever Connor had to say, he wanted to hear it on his feet. Connor shrugged as if it made no difference to him. But then he hesitated, shifting from one foot to the other, as though reluctant to share his thoughts.

"Rory'd kill me if she knew I'd asked to talk to you," he finally began.

Sawyer released his breath in a soft laugh. "You almost sound like you're afraid of her," he said, unable to resist ribbing the other man.

Connor made a face. "I'm surrounded by females. Between Harper, Molly and Rory, I'm always apologizing for something."

Now, Sawyer laughed outright. "I don't know about Harper, but my experience with Rory is that her bark is worse than her bite."

"Yeah, well, that might be because she's in love with you."

CHAPTER EIGHT

ONCE THE WORDS were out there, the atmosphere grew serious. Sawyer said nothing and neither did Connor. They stood there, the silence growing until Connor sighed.

"Why did you come back here, Sawyer? After the way you left, after all this time…why now? Your life is so far removed from here. Your face is recognized everywhere you go."

Sawyer tried not to wince, remembering how he'd shown up at Connor's restaurant, his presence disrupting business.

"Why couldn't you just leave things well enough alone?"

Sawyer let the question hang there for a minute as he carefully formed his words.

"Because I can't live without her," he finally admitted. He considered how best to explain it to Connor. "What if you had everything a chef could want? What if Callahan's was even more successful than it is now? Let's say you owned several restaurants, you had a contract for cookbooks, your own television show, you'd won multiple competitions."

Connor cocked his head, and Sawyer could tell he had his full attention.

"What if you could have all that…but not Harper?"

Connor blinked, and Sawyer could see by the widening of the other man's eyes that he'd driven his point home.

"That's what it's like," he said. "I was foolish when I broke things off. I'd convinced myself it was time, that it was better for both of us if we parted ways. Worst of all, I told myself that she'd be happier without me."

Connor's jaw hardened, and Sawyer held up a hand.

"Look, I know it was selfish. But it was just one of the things I told myself to justify leaving her. And by the time I realized how wrong I was, it was too late to simply call her up and tell her I'd made a mistake. So I kept going, assuming that missing her was no different than being homesick. I thought it was something that would go away in time. Only, it didn't."

He released a breath and, to his surprise, felt a weight lift off his chest. He'd told Rory how he felt, how much he'd missed her. But confessing it to Connor was like absolution. Perhaps because Connor was the only real family Rory had left. If Sawyer was going to ask anyone's permission, ask their blessing on his relationship with Rory, it would be Connor's.

"But why *now*?" Connor persisted. "Why did you come back when you did?"

Sawyer considered this. "I don't know," he admitted. "I guess I just couldn't lie to myself anymore. I've experienced a lot in the last two years, but I've wasted a lot of time, too. I spent too much of it convincing myself I'd forget her eventually. I figured since we'd been together for so long, it would take a while to stop thinking about her. But I couldn't stop. She's still the first person I want to talk to when something happens. I can be in the middle of a conversation with someone, and the next thing I know, I've missed something they said because I was wondering what Rory was doing, right at that moment. There have been so many instances when I'm in the middle of a concert, look out over the audience and think I see her. And every time, I nearly stop singing because I try to get a better view and see if it's really her." He swallowed. "Without her...I've lost the music, somehow. Not just the melody but the lyrics, too. Everything I try to create just feels off."

"Well, it doesn't seem to have hurt your career." Connor's tone lacked sympathy.

Sawyer frowned. "It's not that I *can't* write songs…it's just that there's no heart in them. Not like there used to be when I was with Rory." He felt sheepish admitting this to Rory's brother, but he figured he might as well be honest. "I don't have anyone to sing for anymore, as strange as that might sound. The fans are great. Being a country artist is awesome. But when Rory isn't around, something's missing."

He took a step forward and raked a hand through his hair, wishing he could explain himself better. "Do you know I'd still reach for my phone on any given day just to call her?" His voice grew quiet. "And do you know how disappointing it felt when I realized I couldn't?"

"Not couldn't," Connor amended, his voice hard. *"Wouldn't."*

Sawyer hung his head. He couldn't argue with that. He'd had plenty of opportunities to call Rory, to come back to town, to reach out in some way. And he hadn't taken one of them. Until now.

"Connor, I'm not defending myself. I was wrong. The way I broke up with her was totally disrespectful. I was selfish. I made a mistake. But I'm here now. And I will do anything I can to win her back."

Connor shook his head. "You didn't see what it did to her. You didn't see how depressed she became." His voice dropped so low that Sawyer had to take a step closer to hear him. "There were nights I was afraid to let her go home to the apartment alone. I was afraid... she'd hurt herself," he whispered.

The words caused a sharpness in Sawyer's chest, cutting off his air supply. The thought of Rory harming herself because of him...it was more than he could stomach. He feared he might lose his dinner there on Connor's back porch.

"She went to a very dark place for a while, mate. And even when she came out of it, she was different. More serious. She doesn't laugh like she once did."

Sawyer's soul ached.

"It was hard for her when we were kids, after our dad first moved us from Ireland to the States. She didn't know where she belonged anymore. I'm not sure she ever did...until high school, when the two of you started dating. So when you dropped her, she lost her way. It was as if she didn't just lose you," Connor continued. "It was like she lost her hopes and her dreams, her life. I suppose, in a way, that's exactly what your leaving cost her."

Sawyer let this soak in as he and Connor stood in silence. A breeze lifted up, and he shivered. Connor's words had sobered him.

He'd known he'd hurt her. But he had no idea just how deeply. Neither of them spoke for several minutes.

Connor cleared his throat. "She's still wary, but I think she's forgiven you. She called to tell me you were coming tonight. Warned me not to say anything to you."

"I have a feeling you're going to disregard her request."

Connor eyed him sharply. "I'm her brother, Sawyer. If I don't watch out for her, who will?"

"I will," Sawyer countered without hesitation. "I'm not stepping out again. I'm going to make up for the last two years."

"And then?" Connor's voice held a challenge. "At the risk of sounding like my dad would have, I have to know...what are your intentions regarding my sister?"

Sawyer wanted to be offended. After all, he and Connor had known each other a long time. They'd been friends, not just because of Rory, but because they'd gone to high school together and had spent a fair amount of time in each other's company. Sawyer had always liked Connor, even admired him. But his question hurt. He knew he deserved it, but he'd never been challenged like this before. Both Connor and his father before him had liked him, had seemed to approve of him as Rory's boyfriend. Sawyer knew it was his own fault that trust had been broken, but he chafed at Connor's doubt just the same.

"I want to marry her," Sawyer announced.

He wasn't sure if that was the answer Connor had been expecting. His one-time friend watched him, his expression inscrutable.

"And I'd really like your blessing," Sawyer added.

Connor released a breath, muttered something and raked a hand over his face.

"Are you serious this time?"

"I'm serious," Sawyer answered. "I want to make her my wife, if she'll have me. I've waited long enough. We were high-school sweethearts, and she stayed with me while I was in the army, and then all those years on the road together. I know I messed up, but I want to spend the rest of my life with her, making up for that."

"Have you thought things through?" Connor challenged. "You're famous now. Practically your entire life is lived in the media's eye. And if you marry her, then by extension, Rory's will be, too. Your life, your relationship with her…it's not as simple as it once was."

"No, it's not," Sawyer agreed. "But Rory and I will find a way. I understand your concern for her. But she's stronger than you give her credit for. She always has been."

"I know that," Connor said. "I don't mean to imply she's weak." The tension drained out of Connor's expression. "I just want her to be happy. If you can give that to her, then I'm on your side. But if you break her heart again—"

Sawyer held up his hands. "Stop right there. You don't need to say anything else. I won't break her heart, Connor. I promise. I love her."

Connor relaxed, his shoulders sagging.

"In that case...you have my blessing."

Now it was Sawyer's turn to stand at ease. He felt a swell of relief, as if his absolution was complete.

"Thank you. That's good to hear."

Connor grinned. "You know, I have to admit...it's nice to see you haven't let fame and fortune go to your head."

Sawyer smiled in return. "Well, there are days when it's easy to get puffed up. But I think even though she wasn't physically with me, it's been Rory who has kept me grounded."

Connor arched an eyebrow. "How so?"

"Every time someone tells me how talented I am, I can just hear Rory in my ear saying, 'Oh, trust me, mate, he's not so great as all that.'" He put the proper Irish inflection into his words, mimicking Rory's accent perfectly.

Connor laughed loudly as the two of them headed back inside the house. When he reentered the living room, Sawyer immediately found his way to Rory's side. She looked up at his approach, her brow furrowed in question. She slid a quick glance at her brother, who was joining Harper, and then back to him.

"Everything all right?" she asked, obviously curious about why Connor had pulled him aside.

"Everything is fine," he promised, then leaned down to kiss her forehead. His heart swelled with happiness when she didn't pull back but rather looked up at him, her expression open and unguarded. "Everything is going to be fine."

IT WAS LATE when Sawyer headed back to his parents' home. While he'd been with Rory, he'd been able to avoid thinking of the news his parents had shared earlier that day. But once he was by himself, dark emotions of guilt and grief settled heavily on his heart. He knew the responsibility he felt was irrational. It wasn't as if his being home would have prevented the disease. But he couldn't help feeling as though he'd failed his family in some way. If he had been here, maybe they would have gotten the diagnosis sooner. Perhaps they could have done something to stave it off, to buy more time.

He supposed it didn't matter now. His father had Alzheimer's. And no amount of wishing or regret would change that.

He wrestled with his conscience during the short drive home. When he reached his parents' place, he pulled the truck into the driveway behind Chase's car and killed the engine. His mom had left the front floodlights on, and he navigated his way to the front porch by their glow. He let himself in with the spare key hidden beneath the cracked hydrangea pot next to the porch and stepped quietly inside the house. He'd barely locked the door when his mother's soft voice carried from the kitchen.

"There you are."

He turned to face her and noticed the kitchen light was on.

"I was beginning to get worried."

He wasn't sure how to react. He still felt slightly betrayed by his parents, but his sorrow and guilt were beginning to outweigh his anger.

"You didn't need to wait up," he finally said.

"I'm your mother. It's written in the mom's manifesto—no matter how old our children become, we wait until they're safely home before going to bed."

"There's a manifesto for this stuff?" He injected a teasing note into his tone.

She placed a finger against her lips, the glow from the kitchen behind her illuminating her head with a halo. "The bylaws forbid us from discussing it."

He couldn't help grinning. This was the same sort of silliness that had made his childhood so magical. His mom knew how to turn everyday conversations into something enchanting. But just like that, his mom's teasing became serious.

"I thought we could talk," she said. "I've made some tea, and there are butterscotch cookies."

He wasn't very hungry. But he knew the cookies were his mom's way of making up for how their earlier conversation had gone.

"Okay," he agreed. He wasn't sure exactly what else his mother wanted to speak to him about. Was it just a rehashing of his father's diagnosis? If so, he didn't know if he had the strength to hear the words a second time. But he supposed, after bearing this burden alone for so long, she deserved his ear. So he followed her into the kitchen without protest.

CHAPTER NINE

FIFTEEN MINUTES LATER, Sawyer nibbled at his third butterscotch cookie. Though he had little appetite, the sweet, butter-rich dough melted in his mouth, tempting him to eat more than he should have. Besides, it gave him an excuse to pause before answering his mother's questions about his evening and his attempts at winning Rory back.

"I think we're getting there," he finally responded, "but it'll take some time."

His mother nodded and seemed to know better than to press the issue.

"I suppose I'll have to make another batch of those tomorrow," she commented as he polished off the last bite of cookie.

"How about chocolate chip this time?" he suggested. This drew a smile from her, but it was a sad one.

He felt cookie crumbs catch in his throat and coughed to clear them. Was this what conversations were to be like now? This cloud of

every word they refused to say hanging over
their heads?

"It's good to have you home," she said.

"It's good to be back," he admitted. "I stayed
away too long. I'm sorry for that."

She waved a hand. "You were following
your dream, and you have to know how proud
both your father and I are of you. I confess, I
called up all the family when you won Artist
of the Year."

He felt a flush of pleasure at his mom's
praise. "Thanks."

"Mind you, they'd all been watching the
award show anyway. Your cousins in Virginia,
Aunt Margie's boys, they invited all their
friends over to see it. The guys were placing
bets on you winning. Margie said they made
out like bandits." She chuckled, and he sensed
she was delaying the inevitable. He felt a stab
of worry, made worse by knowing that she'd
already kept one huge secret from him. Was
there more?

He reached across the table to draw her
hand in his. His touch seemed to startle her
because she stopped talking and looked at
him with wide eyes. He noticed several addi-
tional fine lines around her mouth and tem-
ples that he hadn't remembered seeing before.
How long had they been there? Were they the

result of what she'd been through, worrying over his dad?

Again, he felt the sting of self-reproach. Why had he stayed away so long? He should have found time to come back sooner, or called more. How hard would it have been to send a text or an email from the tour bus once in a while?

He closed his eyes and tried to stop these runaway thoughts. When he opened them again, his mother's expression had softened to one of sympathy.

"I'm sorry we weren't more sensitive to how you'd react."

He let go of her hand and ran his own through his hair. "It was just a lot to take in all at once."

"Not only that, but you felt…left out?"

He nodded, relieved that she understood.

"And guilty," he added.

She cocked her head. "Guilty? Whatever for?"

He sighed and slid his hands down from his hair and over his face, scraping his palms over his cheeks. "For not being here. For not checking in more often. I should have known what was going on. You shouldn't have had to wait this long to tell me."

"Oh, Sawyer." She shook her head. "Being

here wouldn't have changed anything. Your father would still have this disease, whether you'd checked in or not."

"I know," he admitted, choking slightly on the words. He took a minute to rein in his emotions, then asked, "How did you find out? I mean, I know he was tested and everything. But before that…when did you first notice something was wrong?"

She looked past Sawyer, as though watching her memories take place at some point behind him. "It started with little things," she began. "On the weekends, I would make him breakfast, but at lunchtime, he'd ask what we were having for breakfast. Then one day—one day, we were out shopping at the new hardware store, and they asked for our email address to sign up for their mailing list. He couldn't remember it, which I thought was odd but not alarming. Then later that day, we stopped at the market, and when we got back in the car, he said we still needed to go to the hardware store." She shook her head. "I think the scary part was that he didn't even seem confused at that point. He simply had no recollection of where we'd already been."

He tried not to wince. Without the knowledge of his father's diagnosis, he likely would have dismissed all this as absentmindedness. But knowing about the disease made his mother's words positively chilling.

"Friends would call, and by the time he hung up the phone, he couldn't remember the name of who he'd just spoken with. I found out later that one afternoon on the way home from work, he called Chase because he couldn't remember how to find his way back here." The lines scoring her forehead deepened. "He convinced Chase not to say anything to me, but several weeks afterward, he told me about it. He said he told Chase he was just so overwhelmed with stuff at work that he'd had a momentary memory lapse."

She closed her eyes. "Then he began to misplace things in the strangest ways. I found his reading glasses in a flowerpot. His travel mug in the DVD cabinet. And then there were the notes."

"Notes?"

She nodded. "He started writing things down. Reminders of where things were kept, such as 'car keys on hook by front door.' Or 'socks in third drawer of dresser.'" Her eyes filled with tears once more. "And then I found a notepad with names. At the top were ours. 'Wife—Olivia. Oldest son—Sawyer. Youngest son—Chase.'" She sighed raggedly. "That's when I confronted him and insisted he see a doctor."

"And they ran tests?"

She gave a brief nod. "It took some time to reach the appropriate diagnosis because the doctors had to rule out so many other conditions. We visited several specialists before they finally realized what it was."

A new thought occurred to Sawyer, a glimmer of light in the darkness. "We need to get a second opinion. They might be wrong—"

"We did get a second opinion."

"Then a third—"

"That, too. We saw a specialist at Johns Hopkins, and his colleagues concurred on the diagnosis. It began with blood work and a lot of cognitive testing to check his memory and mental skills. They also ran a cerebrospinal fluid analysis along with a urinalysis. Then an MRI to check for a brain tumor or evidence of a stroke. After a PET scan and more neuropsychological testing, it was finally confirmed that your father's issues stemmed from early onset Alzheimer's."

"But surely there are treatments, ways to manage or delay the deterioration. Drugs, alternative therapies. He can change his diet, take some supplements or vitamins. If he exercises more and does some activities to assist with memory... Wasn't Chase trying to teach him sudoku? He can do more puzzles like that, to keep his mind sharp."

Her hand touched his, stilling the tide of his words.

"Of course. He can do all those things... In fact, he already is. He's on the most current course of treatment, I'm making sure he's eating appropriately, and we have routines in place to keep him active. But Sawyer, you have to realize... Alzheimer's has no cure. And the treatments, at best, will only minimally delay the progression of the disease."

A lump of emotion caught in his throat, and it kept him from speaking.

How long? The question drummed in his head. *How much longer will I have my father?* And then, *How much longer will he even know who I am?*

He leaned back, overwhelmed with the questions ricocheting around his head.

"Sawyer."

The heaviness in his mom's tone forced him to focus on her.

"There's something else."

He tensed. What else could there be? He immediately jumped to the worst conclusion.

"Please don't tell me you're sick, too."

"No, no." She waved a hand as though to brush

away the idea. "It's…well, there's a possibility…" She drew in a breath as though to gather courage. "The thing about early Alzheimer's is that it's hereditary."

He blinked, the words not sinking in immediately.

"Hereditary? You mean like, Dad got it from Grandpa?"

"Most likely. Your grandfather died much younger than your grandmother, and she never exhibited any symptoms in her life."

"Oh." He sensed his mom waiting for something, as though there was still one puzzle piece yet to snap into place. It didn't matter where his father had gotten the disease from, did it? Except…

That's when he realized what she was trying to tell him.

"You mean, Chase and I could have it?"

Her eyes filled with tears as she softly replied, "There's a possibility that is the case. It all depends on whether you have a gene mutation inherited from your dad."

He could no longer sit still. He stood and began pacing the kitchen. "That's impossible. I'm *fine*. Chase is *fine*. We've never had any memory problems or confusion or anything that would indicate we have *Alzheimer's*." He spat the word out for the foul thing it was, a sharp and bitter taste on his tongue.

"Not yet," his mother whispered.

And for some reason, that caused his emotions to explode. "You're being ridiculous! Why do you always have to assume the worst?"

"Sawyer, I'm not—"

He lifted a hand, cutting her off with the gesture. "It was bad enough you waited to tell me about Dad, and now you drop a bomb like this on me?"

"Keep your voice down—"

"I can't keep my voice down!" he shouted. "My father is dying, he's literally losing his mind, and now you're telling me that I'm next?"

"I should have waited to tell you until you'd had more time to process everything," she muttered, more to herself than him.

"Because that's worked out so well up to this point?" His voice was laden with sarcasm. He knew that none of this was his mother's fault. But this double blow made him want to lash out at someone, anyone.

"Sawyer, please," she begged. "It's not as if this is easy for me, either. Do you know what it's like to read through brochures about nursing-care facilities, knowing that it's something you're not considering for the distant future but for sometime in the next couple of years?" The tears that had filled her eyes began to overflow, one by one, until there was a steady stream.

"I'm losing him," she said, her voice a strangled sob. "I'm losing him one neuron at a time. It's like watching sand slip through an hourglass, knowing that each grain is precious. Each one is another day or month or even year that we won't have together. And then, on top of that, is the knowledge that I might experience it all over again with you and Chase." She met his eyes squarely, her own watery but fierce. "You are not the only one losing something. I am losing my family, one by one."

She reached for a napkin from the tabletop holder, tugged it free and dabbed at her eyes.

Her speech had drained the last of Sawyer's fight as he realized how selfish his reaction had been. His mother was right. This disease had slipped in, uninvited and unexpected, to steal the man she'd loved for more than half of her life.

And now, it might well steal her sons, too. Not suddenly but slowly, each day an agonizing death of watching and being able to do nothing.

Perhaps she carried the heaviest burden of all.

He went to her then, kneeled beside her at the kitchen chair and wrapped his arms around her. She fell against him, buried her face in his shoulder and cried, so loudly that now he was the one who feared she might wake the rest of the household.

His own eyes filled, but he blinked away the tears. He could not save her from the rest of it, but he could give her this—the chance to unburden herself without his father seeing. He rubbed her back, as he remembered her doing for him as a child. His shirt grew damp as her tears saturated it, but he didn't fidget, didn't so much as shift positions. He simply let her cry out all her anger and frustration, her grief and disappointment, until she sagged limply, and he knew she'd been drained of emotion. Only then did he pull back, tipping her face toward him and kissing her forehead.

"You can do this, Mom," he reassured her. "You can get through this."

He had nothing else to offer her but those words.

She didn't appear convinced, but she nodded anyway and used the crumpled napkin to pat beneath her eyes.

"It was hard not telling you," she said, "but I wanted to spare you as long as possible."

He understood what she meant because now

he realized the full weight of this disease, that it wasn't just after his father.

It was after him, too.

SAWYER WAS STILL in a dead sleep the following morning when his phone began vibrating. It took him a few minutes to wake up, and sometime while he was struggling toward alertness, the phone went silent. But its vibration had broken the heavy blanket of his slumber, and though he tried to return to its embrace, tendrils of worry kept him from falling back into his dreams.

Following his conversation with his mother the evening before, he'd insisted she go to bed and leave him to tidy up the kitchen. She'd protested, but he walked her to the stairs and watched her go up. Though she said she didn't mind cleaning up, he could tell she was exhausted—emotionally as well as physically. He couldn't imagine how she'd been coping the last several months with such a burden on her shoulders. Once more, it stirred feelings of guilt that he hadn't been there for his family when they needed him.

So after he put her to bed, he stayed up and tidied the kitchen. Then, still not tired, he sat in front of the television for a couple of hours, though he couldn't remember now what programs had aired. He'd simply been trying to distract himself, looking for some way to shake off the apprehension and fear that dogged him.

It had been bad enough, learning his father had Alzheimer's. But now, according to his mom, there was a risk he and Chase had it, too? He couldn't begin to comprehend what that meant for his future.

He was an up-and-coming country music artist, with a lifetime of potential ahead of him. And now, there was a possibility it would be cut short because of some mutant gene that would eat away at his cognitive function? It was more than a bad dream, it was a total nightmare and not just because of what it meant for his professional life.

No, all of that paled in comparison when he thought about Rory. What kind of future could he offer her now? After all his promises that he would be there for her, he now had to accept that those were vows he might not be able to keep. How was he going to tell her about this? How could he look her in the eye, after all they'd been through, and tell her there was a chance he would leave her again, not of his own will but because of some defective DNA that would eat him alive from the inside out?

And what about his promise to Connor that he'd cherish Rory every day of his life, that he'd never leave her again? If he ended up with Alzheimer's, just how much time did he even have left? He could only imagine how quickly Connor would withdraw his blessing once he learned about Sawyer's possible condition.

These thoughts had chased him into a restless sleep until sometime before dawn, when his body had been too exhausted to wrestle with his mind anymore. He'd finally succumbed to a deep and dreamless slumber... until his phone's vibrations pulled him from it.

Rolling over, he reached for his phone to check what he'd missed. There was a voice message from his manager. Although it was still the weekend, Perle didn't believe in taking Sundays off. He put the phone on speaker and tapped to listen.

"Hey, sugar, how are things up north? Getting in touch with your Yankee roots again?"

He made a face as he sat up in bed. Perle had northern roots of her own, though most wouldn't know it from the impeccable Southern accent she put on.

"Listen, darlin', there are a lot of interview opportunities that have come up since your Artist of the Year win. Give me a ring to let me know when you'll be back in town so I can set some up."

He frowned at this. He hadn't given Perle

a time frame for his trip back home, but he'd only been in town several days, and he wasn't ready to return to Nashville just yet. Not when he was finally beginning to win Rory back. And especially not with what he'd just discovered about his father, Chase…and himself.

He needed time to sort things out, especially in his own head. He had to come to grips with his father's diagnosis, to find out what could be done to help his family, and if anything could be done to help himself. And he still had to tell Rory his news, though he had no idea how to. Nashville, and his career, seemed very far away at the moment.

While he'd been considering all these things, Perle had been rambling on in the voice mail, naming several opportunities, including a performance on one of late night television's most watched talk shows. He ignored the list of interviews, climbing out of bed as he waited for Perle to wrap up the message.

"And those are just the highlights. Didn't I tell you this was only the beginning? Finish up your visit and give me a call—we need to get you back in the studio once we do some of these interviews. 'Bye, darlin'!"

After Perle's grating Southern drawl filled his ear, the silence following her voice mail was palpable. He should call her back, to at least let her know he planned to stay in town another week or two, or maybe more, but he knew she'd press for a firm commitment on his return. And that wasn't something he could give her. Not yet.

He pocketed his phone in the back of his pajama bottoms and went downstairs. The sun shining through the kitchen window told him the day was well underway. There was a note from his mom, pinned beneath the bottom of his dad's favorite coffee mug.

Your dad and I are running a few errands. Chase is meeting some friends. There are leftover pancakes in the fridge, just warm them up in the microwave. Hope to see you later today.

She signed the note with a string of hearts and the word *Mom*. Sawyer pondered how much had been left unsaid. Maybe it was his imagination, but he sensed her grief in between every line of text. He knew his mother well enough to recognize that last night's conversation likely weighed on her as much as it did him.

Out of habit he opened the fridge door and scanned the shelves until he found the pancakes. But his stomach was too twisted into knots to consider eating. He opted for a cup of orange juice instead, carrying the glass to the corner of the living room that held his parents' computer. He logged on to a browser and performed a search.

Hereditary early onset Alzheimer's.

A flood of links loaded in seconds, displaying everything from support group forums to DNA graphics, fact sheets and frequently asked questions, magazine articles and family interviews, hospital pages and testing facilities. He felt the juice begin to sour in his stomach and pushed aside his glass after only a preliminary sip. Squaring his shoulders, he dove in, opening several links in separate tabs, reading as fast as the pages could load.

An hour later, his head was pounding, and his back was stiff from leaning forward in the chair for so long. His eyes felt strained from scanning lines of text, and his stomach was torn between delayed hunger and ongoing nausea. He clicked out of the remaining websites and carefully cleared the browser history to erase the evidence of his research.

Leaning back in the chair, he ran his hands over his face. Everything he'd read confirmed what his mother had told him, as well as offering up more bad news.

Terminology he'd not previously known

about was now branded into his consciousness: amyloid plaques, which were clusters of sticky protein fragments that built up between nerve cells; neurofibrillary tangles of fibrous proteins called tau that strangled the brain; presenilin-1 and -2 along with APP, the gene mutations responsible for the disease. And Aricept, Exelon, Razadyne: the most common drug treatments for those with early onset dementia…

Of all the things he'd read, however, one fact stood out more sharply than the rest. Some people developed the disease as early as their thirties and forties. Sawyer had celebrated his thirtieth birthday last year while on tour in Australia. He was still in the prime of his life, and he had to consider that he might already be facing the end of it. If he had the mutated genes, even if he didn't develop symptoms until his dad's age, that still only gave him…what? Maybe twenty more years of good health?

Twenty years.

His plan was to commit to Rory for a lifetime, to grow old with her, to sing songs about her. His career was just beginning. He had everything before him. And now, in less than twenty-four hours, he'd learned that the best of his life might be behind him.

No. He shook his head sharply, his headache thumping at the movement.

That was the worst-case scenario, though, right? He might never develop the disease. He and Chase might both escape it.

But then, what if one of them did and the other didn't? Sawyer would give anything to spare his brother what might come. But if Chase didn't have the gene and Sawyer did, how would he feel about that? Of course, he'd be relieved for his brother…but he knew that jealousy would eventually set in. If one of them got to live out their life in relative normalcy while the other one wasted away, one neuron at a time, then he knew that would be a burden on both of them and their mother as well.

He put the computer to sleep and pushed back in his chair.

Enough. He had to do something to get his mind off things. Rory was working at the restaurant right now, and he didn't feel up to contacting any of his other old friends in town. He didn't know how soon Chase or his mom would be back, but he feared when they returned, the conversation would become uncomfortable.

He decided he'd put his free time to good use. His dad had begun remodeling the garage as a workshop. Maybe Sawyer could help advance the project by picking up where his dad had left off.

He stood up and headed for the stairs to rifle through his dad's clothes and find some paint clothes to wear.

SAWYER DIDN'T KNOW how long he'd been working in the garage when Chase's voice cut through his reverie.

"If you keep going like that, you're going to sand that drywall straight through to the studs."

Sawyer started as his brother stepped into the garage. He fixed his attention on the patch of drywall he'd been sanding in preparation for painting. Chase was right, he'd nearly sanded a groove into the wall—he'd been so distracted by his thoughts that he hadn't paid much attention to what he was doing. So much for trying to stay out of his own head.

"At least I'm working for free," he offered, but the words fell flat, lacking the lighthearted inflection he'd intended.

Chase didn't say anything—he simply picked up a spare piece of the sandpaper and began tackling another section of the wall. Sawyer decided that working without conversation was fine with him, so for a while, the two of them sanded in silence and then vacuumed down the walls to clear them of drywall dust. It was maybe another thirty minutes, and several smooth feet of wall space, before Chase spoke again.

"Mom said she told you. About the Alzheimer's being hereditary."

Sawyer swallowed, uncertain how to reply. He moved to the bucket of water he had prepped and soaked a sponge in it before scrubbing the wall again.

He sensed Chase watching him, but didn't respond.

"There's a test the doctors can do with a blood sample. It tells them if a person has the mutant gene that causes the disease."

Sawyer scoured the wall with far more force than necessary. Streaks of gray water ran in rivulets down the sanded surface. He didn't look at Chase.

"It's a way to know, Sawyer," Chase said, his voice low. "We could find out if we're going to get it."

"What if I don't want to know?" Sawyer snapped.

Chase was so quiet that Sawyer finally turned toward him. His brother looked... disappointed, and Sawyer felt a wave of remorse. It was frightening enough for him but how much more so for Chase? His kid brother hadn't even graduated from college yet, and now he might have a time bomb hanging over his head. Would it be so bad to do the test? To know if they were fated to end up with the disease? But then, if he learned he had the Alzheimer's gene, it would be like a death sentence, living every day just waiting for the symptoms to strike.

Sawyer softened his tone. "Wouldn't it be easier *not* to know? How could you face each day, knowing that the disease was there, preparing to surface? It would be like living with a sleeping dragon."

Chase leaned against the wall, oblivious to a smudge of stray dust that marked his shirt as he did so. "I've been reading about it. As soon as Mom and Dad told me, after you left yesterday, I got online and started asking questions in some of the EOA forums."

Sawyer cringed. "You were talking to strangers about this?"

Chase made a face. "The people in these forums know what it's like. They have loved ones dealing with the disease—friends, family, spouses, children. And a lot of them are also victims of the disease. I mean, who better to tell you the truth than someone who is living through this nightmare?"

Sawyer had to bite his tongue to keep from

berating his brother. He understood Chase's need to connect with people who understood what he was going through, but Sawyer wasn't ready to open up to anyone about it yet. He could barely wrap his own head around it, much less start asking coherent questions of anyone else.

"Everyone has a different opinion," Chase went on, "but that's what I wanted—to get multiple points of view. I've only had a few responses on the forum but given what I've read, I think…I want to know."

Sawyer sighed and tossed the sponge back into the bucket. It landed with a gentle splash and sloshed from side to side in the liquid. "Why?"

"Because then I can plan ahead. I can think about the future, prepare for it. It's like going into battle. If I know I'm destined to develop Alzheimer's, I can make my plan of attack, research my care options, treatments, decide if I want to have children, knowing I probably won't be around long enough to see them get married and have children of their own."

He stopped there, and Sawyer turned away, unable to consider this last statement.

"Knowing won't stop it, but it gives me a fighting edge. I still get to plan my life before it takes away my ability to recognize it."

It was a fair point, Sawyer had to concede, but he still wasn't convinced.

"You'd be living with a death sentence."

"Aren't we living with one anyway? Besides, there's always the chance we won't have the gene, that we'd be lucky enough to be passed over. And then we could live our lives without that cloud hanging over our heads."

"And if we're not that lucky? If we learn that it's inevitable? Chase, there's a reason no one knows their own future. I think the knowledge of it…breaks a person. If we find out that we're destined to have Alzheimer's, how would we function each day, knowing that the end is creeping closer with every minute?"

Chase pushed off the wall and took a step closer to Sawyer. "But what if it's a gift, in some twisted way? What if knowing what's coming allows us to cherish every day more than we would otherwise?"

Sawyer exhaled sharply. "There's no way you could call that a gift."

Chase shook his head. "Sorry. You know what I mean."

Sawyer bent over the water bucket and wrung out the sponge. He moved to the wall and began washing it clean once more. "No, I don't know what you mean." He tightened his grip, his knuckles turning white with the effort. "I can't see any reason, any *sane* reason, to take that test. I don't want to know, Chase. I'd rather live my life just like I've been doing, without knowing when my time is coming."

"But you don't have that luxury anymore, Sawyer," his brother replied. Though the words were harsh, his brother's tone was not. If anything, it was tearfully sympathetic. "We lost that the day they told Dad he had Alzheimer's. We don't get to pretend it can't happen to us."

A lump rose in Sawyer's throat, and he clenched his jaw to keep the emotion from rising any further. He let his arms hang at his sides, water dripping from the sponge and onto the floor. "I'm still trying to come to terms with this. It's bad enough, considering what this means for Dad. I need more time before I start thinking about what it means for me."

He began scrubbing at the wall again, his movements turning more aggressive as he spoke. "They should have told us," he practically growled. "How could they keep it a secret all these months?"

"I kind of get it," Chase argued. "They didn't want their problems intruding on our lives. I mean, you have your career. And I have college."

"But it's not just their problem. It's yours and mine, too. It's not just Dad's life. It's ours."

"You're right. But when you think about it, they had a point. Could you really have done everything you've accomplished in the last year if you had this hanging over your head? You're a star, Sawyer. You're famous. That takes some concerted effort and a lot of focus. They wanted to let you chase that dream for as long as you could without burdening you."

As much as it still frustrated him, Sawyer knew his brother was right.

"We deserved to know, but Mom and Dad were just trying to gift us with as much time as possible."

Sawyer grunted. He could have still argued his case, but he knew it was a losing battle. In the end, his parents had only done what they had out of love for their sons. He supposed their motive counted far more than keeping things secret did.

"I'm sorry. It's just a lot to process."

"I know." Chase eyed the unfinished wall. "So…you still want some help out here?"

Sawyer was humbled at Chase's offer. In spite of this darkness hovering over them, his kid brother seemed to be handling things with remarkable maturity.

Sawyer tossed the sponge at him, and Chase caught it.

"You know, sometime when I wasn't looking, I think you grew up."

His brother smiled, but Sawyer couldn't help noticing a touch of sadness there.

"I guess, after a while, we don't have a choice."

Sawyer dropped his head. "No," he said, "I guess we don't."

CHAPTER TEN

RORY DELIBERATELY KEPT her pace slow as four-year-old Kitt toddled after her around the backyard of the Moontide Inn. Her best friend, Erin, watched from several yards away where she kneeled by the flower bed, gouging holes in the dirt to transplant her begonias now that summer was almost upon them. Though Rory could have easily outpaced Kitt's short legs, it warmed her heart to see him stumble after her in an attempt to catch her in his grasping fists.

She let him overtake her on the steps of the gazebo, collapsing in a heap as he tried to tickle her in an imitation of what she did every time she caught him after a game of chase. She laughed and squirmed, and he giggled with delight as he thought his little fingers had found their mark in her rib cage.

"Oooh, it t-i-ic-c-ckles!" she exclaimed, and Kitt giggled all the harder until she turned the tables and reached out to grab him. He squealed in surprise as she wrapped her arms around him, dragging him down with her and planting kisses all over his sandy blond head and down to his cheeks. His weak protests for her to stop lacked conviction, since his smile was evidence of his delight.

"Stop it, Rory!"

She stopped momentarily, and his breathless chortles became spasmodic until she suddenly started tickling him instead. His squeals started up all over again.

"Give me a kiss, and I'll stop!" she teased him.

"No!" he declared, but he was grinning widely.

"One kiss, and I'll stop," she offered while she tickled beneath his chin.

"Okay, okay," he agreed. "One kiss."

She stopped tickling but rather than kiss her, he started tickling her in turn. His touch was featherlight, but she pretended he'd one-upped her just the same.

"Kitt!" Great-Aunt Lenora called from the bed-and-breakfast's back door. "Your breakfast is ready!"

Both Rory and Kitt collapsed at the same time, wordlessly calling a truce.

"Come on inside now and give Rory some time with your mom," Lenora urged.

"Coming, Lenny!" Lenny was Kitt's pet name for Aunt Lenora. He was the only one who referred to her this way since she wouldn't allow anyone else to call her anything but Aunt Lenora. Even guests who stayed at the B and B were urged to call her by her familial name. She was really Gavin's great-aunt, but as long as Rory had known her, she'd been Aunt Lenora to the whole of Findlay Roads.

Kitt scrambled to his feet but before he could run away, Rory grabbed his hand. "Hey, I still didn't get that kiss," she admonished.

He made a face but impishly stepped forward to plant a sloppy kiss on her cheek. Then he tugged free and scampered away before any more demands could be made of him. Rory lay there a second longer, sighing as she rested against the steps of the gazebo and looked up at its whitewashed dome. She felt...carefree.

It had been too long since she'd felt this way—unburdened, unencumbered, as if she was finally free to enjoy life. She'd like to think it was her morning with Kitt, playing with Fisher-Price trucks in the backyard and then racing around the lawn. But while the little boy never failed to lighten her mood, she knew it wasn't just her best friend's son who had instilled this lightness of being into her.

It was Sawyer—having him back, knowing he still wanted to be with her. The last two years of feeling as though her life was out of focus, as though she was out of sync, were gone. It was as if she had finally awoken from a long sleep and was no longer living in a fog. Life made sense again. She felt rerooted, anchored by the knowledge that her soul mate had returned to her.

Though she still hadn't agreed to reestablishing their relationship to its former level, she felt the promise of the future just the same. She wanted to be sure, wanted to know that Sawyer's heart was true in this relationship. And she needed to have some idea of what their future would look like. Would she stay in Findlay Roads, keep working for Connor? Or would she move to Nashville and find a job? But what about when Sawyer was touring? She was well-acquainted with life on the road, but was that what she wanted? She'd spent half her life traveling between gigs with Sawyer, but it wouldn't be the same if he was a headlining artist, and she was just tagging along. Could she be happy with that? How could they blend their two separate lives into one? There was a lot to think about.

But despite all the questions, she had a good feeling about Sawyer. It had taken some time, but he'd come back to her. And as long as he was sincere in his wish to be together, then she felt like it was all going to work out for the best.

"Did you fall asleep over there?"

Rory stirred at Erin's question. "No. Just thinking."

"Mmm. I assume that thinking has something to do with a certain country musician."

Rory sat up and eyed her friend across the grass between them. "Maybe," she admitted, uncertain just how much to share with Erin. They'd been best friends for years, at first just the girlfriends of Sawyer and Gavin, who were also best friends. But as time moved on, they began hanging out even without the guys. And when Sawyer and Gavin joined the army at the same time, they'd supported each other through their boyfriends' training and deployment. Then, when Sawyer had left the army to pursue music with her, Gavin had re-enlisted. Erin had shared her concerns over the years about her husband being deployed for so many months at a time. As Erin had confided in her, so Rory had kept in regular touch while she and Sawyer traveled the country, chasing their dream.

In the past two years that she'd been back in Findlay Roads permanently, her and Erin's friendship had deepened even further. Erin had grown more restless in the last year as

Gavin's most recent deployment was drawing to a close. He hadn't made the decision yet on whether he'd reenlist for another term. Rory knew Erin was hoping he wouldn't. But at the same time, she didn't want to put too much pressure on him to give up what he loved. Erin had entrusted her with some very private emotions, but Rory didn't know if she was ready to reciprocate.

Pushing off the gazebo steps, she stood and brushed off the seat of her jeans. She tightened her ponytail as she moved across the yard to sit beside her friend. Erin continued to work on the border surrounding the inn's back porch.

Rory tugged a blade of grass free and ran her thumbnail across its surface.

"I was a little surprised you brought Sawyer to Connor and Harper's the other night," Erin remarked.

"He came with me to the Harbor House Youth Center that morning and helped out with the kids."

Erin sat back on her heels. "Really? That was nice of him."

Rory shrugged a shoulder. "I kind of ambushed him into it. I didn't tell him we were going until we were there."

Erin laughed. "Smooth, Rory."

Rory grinned. "But he was amazing, Erin.

He was so good with the kids. He wasn't, I don't know...stuck up or anything. I expected him to be arrogant or maybe standoffish. But he jumped right in, and he made a total goofball of himself several times. He's still Sawyer. Maybe even better. I think he's grown into himself. He seems really comfortable with who he is."

"And you? Is he still comfortable with you?"

Rory dropped the piece of grass and picked at the smudge of green it had left beneath her nail. "Seems like it. I think he's more comfortable with me than I am with him. I don't know, it just takes some getting used to him being back."

Erin placed her dirt-stained hand over Rory's. "Are you happy he's returned?"

Rory met her friend's eyes. "So much that it scares me," she admitted.

Erin squeezed her fingers in encouragement. "I think that's a good thing." She paused. "I'm proud of you, you know."

Rory arched an eyebrow. "Really? Whatever for?"

"It takes courage to choose love, especially from someone who hurt you once. I know you, Rory. And I've watched since you came back, how heartbroken you were and how you, I don't know...lost yourself a little. But I also think you learned how to be *you*, without Sawyer. I don't want you to lose that again."

"Lose what?"

"Your heart. Your fire. You had both with Sawyer, but it took you a while to have them *without* him. You let yourself be taken over by what you lost. Don't let that happen again, no matter what. Okay?"

Rory nodded, understanding what Erin meant. She went to a very dark place in her head when Sawyer left her. After so many years together, she'd had no identity without him. But then there had been the kids and the youth center and her own music, and somehow, she'd managed to find herself in the midst of that darkness.

"I used to be so jealous of you."

Rory's attention snapped back to Erin's face at these words. "You were?"

Erin nodded. "You and Sawyer were living such a romantic life, traveling all over together, playing music and having adventures. You were creating memories when Gavin and I were doing our best to sustain our marriage through emails and care packages and Skype chats." Erin drew a breath. "I hope you give him another chance, Rory. He came all the way back here for you. That's pretty romantic, when you think about it."

Rory couldn't help feeling a flush of happiness. Erin had a good point.

"If we're talking about jealousy, I should tell you that I've always envied you and Gavin, too."

Erin's eyes widened in surprise. "You have? You never told me that."

"Yeah. I mean, even though Gavin is gone a lot of the time, he's…constant. His love for you never falters."

Erin paused in her movements and looked at her friend.

"You don't have to wonder about Gavin being committed to you. You can tell, every time he comes home that you're his safe place."

Rory grew alarmed as Erin's eyes filled with tears. "Rory, that is possibly the most beautiful thing I've ever had someone say to me." She brushed at her eyes, leaving smudges of dirt beneath her lashes. "The next time I'm feeling lonely and sorry for myself without Gavin here, I'm going to remember you said that."

Rory sniffed, feeling a mixture of embarrassment and pride. "I guess, when you think about it, we're both pretty lucky."

"I think you're right."

Erin wrapped her arms around Rory, and the two embraced for a short moment before Rory pulled away.

"I better go. My shift starts in a half hour."

They said their goodbyes, and Rory offered a wave as she headed for her truck. Erin had given her a lot to think about. Having Sawyer back was everything she'd wished for, but her friend was right—she didn't want to lose herself, all the strength she'd gained, by committing to Sawyer once more. But she also knew she didn't have to. She'd found herself, but Sawyer had found her again, too.

She was hoping, this time, it would be forever.

RORY THOUGHT SAWYER would be pleased with her suggestion, so his hesitation raised doubts within her.

"You want to just drop in on them?"

The question left her feeling a little embarrassed. "Well…yeah, I guess. Is that a problem?"

He paused longer than necessary, and she felt a twinge of awkwardness. They were on their way back from a romantic dinner, and she felt as if she'd suddenly cast a pall on their entire evening. She wasn't sure what she'd done, though. Why would her suggestion to swing by his parents' place cause him to frown as he was doing right now?

"My…parents?" he asked.

"Yes. The ones who raised you, gave you your first guitar, rented a billboard to advertise your first album when it was released? You remember them, right?"

Perhaps her sarcasm wasn't necessary, but his reaction nettled at her. And the way he was looking at her, as if she'd said something horribly offensive...

"I'm sorry, Sawyer, it's just that I haven't talked to them in ages," she went on. "And you said Chase is home for the summer, right? I was thinking it might be nice to see everyone again. I've been avoiding them since...you know, I moved back to town." She drew a deep breath. "The truth is, I miss them. Olivia's always been like a second mom to me, and after my dad passed away, Ford said that if I ever needed a fatherly shoulder to come to him. It's time I paid them a visit."

When he didn't answer, she experienced another wave of doubt. "I mean...if that's okay."

Sawyer was almost too quick to respond this time. "Yeah, of course it's okay. Why wouldn't it be?"

She opened her mouth to reply, to point out that he didn't seem too keen on the idea, but then she closed it again. What if Sawyer's parents didn't want to see her? Did they disapprove of his being back in a relationship with her? Maybe that's why he'd reacted so strangely. But then, she'd always gotten on great with his family. She couldn't imagine that having changed. Unless they were offended with her for avoiding them the last couple of years. She'd seen them on the rare occasion, offering a brief hello, and then moved on before things could become awkward. Perhaps her behavior had insulted them.

"If you think it's better not to—"

"I said it was fine."

She swallowed. His words weren't exactly terse, but they were slightly clipped. Something was definitely agitating him. He'd been acting off for the last few days now, and more than once during their date, she'd had to say his name to get his attention. Whatever was on his mind, he didn't seem inclined to share it with her, and that stung. Was he having second thoughts about the two of them? Did he regret coming back to town?

She remained silent so long, mulling over these questions, that he must have realized how his words sounded a moment before. His hand reached across the seat and touched hers. He offered up a smile.

"I know they'll be thrilled to see you again. They've been asking about you."

"Oh. Okay." That seemed like a good sign.

Then why was Sawyer obviously so ill at ease?

Twenty minutes later, seated in the Landry living room, Rory was still trying to work out the answer to that question. But in addition to her concern over Sawyer, she felt a certain uneasiness around his mom, as well. She and Sawyer were exchanging looks every couple of minutes while Rory and Ford munched on cookies and chatted amicably. She didn't understand where the tension was coming from, but something was definitely amiss. Did it have to do with her? She could only assume it did, which left her feeling embarrassed and slightly out of place in the home she'd once considered second to her own.

"Do you still have that guitar strap Sawyer got you?" Ford asked.

Rory nodded. "I do." She didn't add that she hadn't used that particular strap in some time due to the painful memories associated with it.

"I hear you play at the Lighthouse Café every Friday night," Olivia said, finally joining the conversation. "I would love to see you perform there sometime."

Rory warmed at his mom's interest, feeling some of her uncertainty melt. "That would be lovely. I'd enjoy seeing you in the crowd."

Olivia smiled at her, and Rory relaxed a

bit more. Perhaps she was imagining all this. Maybe it had just been so long since she'd visited with Sawyer's family that she was seeing things that weren't there.

There was a pause in conversation as Sawyer reached for another one of his mom's cookies. She tried to convince herself she didn't notice any rigidity to his shoulders as he leaned forward. Before the conversation could resume, she heard the front door open.

"Chase?" Olivia called.

"It's me, Mom."

Seconds later, Sawyer's younger brother stepped into the living room. When he caught sight of Rory, his eyes widened. She assumed it was surprise, given that it had been a long time since she was last in the Landry home.

"There you are," Ford said to his youngest son. "It's about time you got home. Look who came to visit? Sawyer and Rory are home for a bit."

Something about the words didn't quite make sense, but Rory didn't dwell on it. She was too busy watching Chase's reaction, trying to see if the same strain his mother and brother exhibited would be evident in him.

"Hey, Rory. Long time, no see."

"Hey, yourself," she greeted. She stood and moved to give him a hug. Sawyer's younger brother had grown up considerably in the last couple of years. He looked to be as tall as Sawyer now, but his physique lacked the definition his brother's did. Likely because Chase had always been a bit more of a bookworm than Sawyer. But she could see where college girls would find him appealing. He was handsome, with an edge of intelligence in his eyes.

"How are your classes going?" she asked.

"Good," he replied. "They're going really well, actually."

"That's great."

"Do you need help unloading the Christmas tree?"

Rory's head snapped around at this completely unexpected question from Ford. She felt the rest of them staring, the feeling of shock nearly palpable in the room. Ford was looking at Chase, his expression completely relaxed, as if he had asked his son about the weather. Her gaze snapped back to Chase.

"The—the what?" Chase asked. His voice had dropped low, the color leaching out of his face.

Rory's head swiveled back to Ford to see his response.

"The Christmas tree?" he placidly repeated. "Sawyer and I can help you bring it in." He shifted his attention to Rory. "It'll be so nice to have you and Sawyer home for the holidays this year."

Rory blinked several times, feeling as if she'd walked into the middle of a play and didn't know the context of the scene.

"You guys got a Christmas tree?" Her words sounded ridiculous. Why would they be putting up a Christmas tree in May?

Ford looked slightly offended. "We always get a tree, Rory. It's been too long since the two of you made it home for Christmas if you can't remember that."

Rory opened her mouth and then realized she couldn't think of a thing to say. She closed it again and let her eyes survey the room, turning from Ford to Olivia to Chase, and then coming to rest on Sawyer. Her heart twisted at the pained expression on his face.

"Dad," he murmured, "it's May. Not December."

Rory didn't turn her attention from Sawyer. He looked incredibly uncomfortable, almost as if verging on tears. To her shock, Ford laughed.

"I think I know what month it is, son. Your mother's been baking cookies all day for the Christmas Eve social at church."

Something was terribly, terribly wrong.

"Sawyer?" she queried in uncertainty.

"Why do you all look like you just saw the

Ghost of Christmas Past?" Ford chuckled at his own joke, which made the entire situation even more painful.

"Dad," Chase said, his voice cracking with emotion. "It's not December. It's May. I'm home from college for the summer."

For the first time, Ford seemed to hesitate. "College? You're not even out of high school yet."

"Oh, no," Olivia whispered. "No, no, no."

Rory wanted to help, but she didn't know how. She could only look from one family member to the other. It was as if Ford was having a mental breakdown. Or else they'd found themselves in some sort of bizarre time vortex.

And then, unexpectedly, Chase took charge.

"Well, I don't think it matters how old I get, I'll never get tired of Mom's cookies."

He moved forward to snatch one off the plate and then sat down beside his father. "Want one, Dad?" He held out the plate, and Ford took one with a grin.

Olivia and Sawyer seemed flummoxed, but Ford was positively serene. Whatever emotions were going on beneath the surface, Chase now appeared calm.

Unable to keep the question to herself any longer, Rory asked, "What's going on?"

Olivia didn't appear to have even heard her.

She was too busy watching Ford with an expression of loss and distress. Rory focused her attention on Sawyer.

"Sawyer?"

He met her eyes, and the emotions on his mother's face were mirrored on his own.

"I think you and I better have a talk."

CHAPTER ELEVEN

SAWYER RECOGNIZED THE confusion in Rory's face. It looked to be a mirror of the emotions he'd experienced when his parents had told him the news. She paced the back porch while he forced himself to stand still, watching her.

"What do you mean, he has Alzheimer's? He's way too young for that, isn't he?"

Sawyer shook his head. "It's called early onset or younger onset. It's when symptoms develop before the age of sixty-five. It happens in less than five percent of the population."

He watched as she stuck her thumbnail in her mouth and chewed the tip of it thoughtfully. He'd seen that little quirk of hers on more than one occasion. It was an action she did whenever she was trying to work through something in her head. Her brow furrowed as if a thought occurred to her.

"Alzheimer's is fatal, isn't it? There's no cure."

"No." Sawyer swallowed painfully, knowing there was still more to tell her. "There's not. But you don't die from the disease itself. It just weakens you so that the smallest infection ultimately ends your life."

"So your dad is still going to die?"

"Eventually."

"How long do they give him?"

Sawyer scratched the back of his neck. "It's difficult to say. A few years. But it's more than just a death sentence. It's…" He closed his eyes, trying very hard not to think of this in terms of his own life. "It's the loss of identity, of memories. Of losing the people you love, one by one, knowing you'll forget them—that you'll probably even reject them at some point because you don't remember who they are. And not only that, but there's also the loss of your dignity. You forget things, like where you live or how to do simple tasks, like tie your shoelaces. You start neglecting your hygiene. You forget where you put things." He opened his eyes to find Rory staring at him with a mixture of horror and grief. "You lose yourself in addition to everything else. Honestly, Rory, I think death is probably the least of it. In fact, maybe it's a blessing by the time it comes."

His chest ached as he wondered how to reveal what he needed to say. How could he tell her? How did he tell the woman he loved, the one person he wanted to spend the rest of his life with, that this might be his sentence, too?

"Rory," he whispered, his voice ragged with sorrow. "There's more. And it's worse."

Her eyes widened, as if in disbelief.

"How much worse can it be?" she asked.

He swallowed, hard. "Maybe a lot," he replied. Drawing a breath, he exhaled it slowly. He didn't know how to voice the worst of it aloud.

"Will you sit with me?" He gestured to the porch steps and waited until she moved toward him. He took her hand, and together, they sat down. He wasn't sure how long he sat there, running his thumb over the length of hers. She didn't press, didn't say a thing. She let him find his words in his own time. He was reminded, all over again, of why he loved her. Because she was patient. Supportive. Loving. Kind.

"The thing about early onset Alzheimer's..." He drew in a breath and held it for several seconds. After he spoke the words, his relationship with Rory would change forever. "Well, it's hereditary."

"Hereditary? Like, you could pass it on to your children."

He gave a short nod, waiting for the meaning to hit her. He felt it when she realized what this meant. She jerked slightly beside him, her hand twitching in his even though she didn't pull it away.

"And you might get it, too," she whispered. She swallowed hard. "Do you… Have you been diagnosed…?"

He shook his head. "There's a chance I won't have it. It all depends on these mutated genes and whether they were passed on in a person's DNA."

That was the moment she pulled free, stood up and stepped in front of him. "Sawyer." He didn't react, didn't so much as breathe.

"Sawyer, look at me. Please."

He met her eyes and experienced the full weight of her determination. "This does not mean you'll get Alzheimer's."

He dropped his head again. "I might already have it," he said. "There are three different gene mutations that cause the disease. Chase and I could have been born with any one of the three, and that would mean there's a one-hundred-percent chance we'd develop Alzheimer's."

"You're jumping to conclusions. You don't know that you have these genes…do you?"

"No," he admitted. "But, Rory, think about it. It's familial. There are three spots in my DNA that might curse me with this. What are the odds I'm going to escape it?"

She kneeled in front of him, her hands wrapping around his. "Hey, don't get ahead of yourself, cowboy. There's no way to know what will happen in the future."

"Actually...there is."

She frowned. "What do you mean?"

"There's this test." He sat back, breaking the contact between them. "They can do a DNA test to find out if Chase and I have the mutated genes. It would tell us if we're destined to end up like my dad."

Rory rested on her heels, arms at her sides. He could see her working through this, trying to absorb what it meant.

"You'd be certain then, whether you'll end up with it."

He nodded, watching her carefully for some sign—something to tell him what he should do.

"Sawyer, that's... I don't know. It's a lot to think about."

"I know it is."

She didn't say anything else, and he could tell she was deep in thought.

"How long have you known about this?" she suddenly asked. He didn't miss the suspicion in her tone. "Did you already know, when you came back here?"

"No," he replied, his voice firm. "I just found

out. Well, shortly after I came back anyway. But my parents have known for some time."

"And they didn't tell you?"

That familiar stirring of resentment coupled with guilt churned in his stomach. "No. Apparently, they wanted to give me time." He couldn't prevent the bitterness that leaked into his words. "I guess they thought they were doing me a favor, letting me pursue my career before I found out it might all have been for nothing."

She clicked her tongue. "How is it for nothing? You've made your dreams come true."

Something in her words set off a spark inside him. He jumped to his feet, brushing past her to pace the lawn in front of the steps.

"But for how long? If I have this—this disease inside of me, how long do I have to be a country music artist? How long before I start forgetting things—the lyrics to my songs, or how to play the guitar? What if I'm onstage someday, and the words suddenly leave me? Or I forget where I am and what I'm doing?" All the fears he'd built up in the days since his parents had shared the news with him began to spill out. "What if I'm doing an interview, and I can't remember what I'm supposed to say? Or something crazy happens, like I wander off after a show and can't find my way back to the tour bus?"

He began hyperventilating, his throat closing as he constructed more scenarios in his head.

"Sawyer, calm down."

Rory was on her feet, trying to keep up with his frantic pacing. She finally stood in front of him and held out her arms, placing her hands on his chest to make him stop moving. Once he did, she wrapped her arms around him, and he, in turn, grabbed her in an embrace.

"What if I forget my family? What if there comes a day when I don't remember my mom or Chase? What if my dad is gone, and I can't even remember he existed?" he whispered. And then, the worst burden of all. "What if I lose you, Rory? What happens if I can't remember who you are?"

The words left him feeling trapped. His whole life had come down to a second chance with Rory, to bringing her back into his life. What if he lost her all over again?

Her reply was muffled against his chest. "You're not going to forget me, Sawyer. You're not."

But despite the conviction in her words, Sawyer knew that such a thing was beyond her control.

SAWYER PRETENDED NOT to notice as Rory reached out and stole a fry from his plate. Despite the delicious entrée, he could only pick at his food. He'd lost his appetite over the last few days, ever since bringing Rory home to visit his parents, and his dad had confused the seasons.

Following that particular scene, they'd scheduled another appointment with his dad's neurologist. He confirmed what they should have seen coming—that the disease was progressing, and these symptoms were to be expected. The doctor gently warned them that these sorts of episodes would gradually become more frequent.

Sawyer's dad, for his part, had remained quiet about the entire affair. Chase had played along in the moment, which was apparently something he'd read about—not to try and convince someone with Alzheimer's that they were wrong. But later, his mom had told his dad what happened. Though Sawyer suspected his father was embarrassed, he also sensed his dad was mentally preparing, knowing that such mistakes would happen again.

And again. And again. Until it was routine.

Sawyer swallowed at the thought, his stomach twisting with discomfort. He pushed his plate away, causing Rory to look up. He'd been making a habit of visiting her while she was on her breaks at the restaurant. But each time he felt even guiltier than the time before. He was poor company these days, and he knew it. Though he'd promised to make the last two years up to her, he was doing a rotten job of it. He'd wanted to make her dreams come true… and now it looked as if he couldn't even hold on to his own.

"Hey," Rory murmured, pushing aside her own plate. "You doing okay?"

He forced a smile, though the look on her face told him it wasn't a very successful attempt.

"I'm fine. How's that steak?" He gestured to her half-eaten meal, but she ignored the question.

"You don't have to pretend, you know."

"Pretend what?" It was a stupid question. He knew exactly what she meant.

"Pretend that everything's fine, that you're not bothered about your dad and…you know, the rest of it."

Such a polite way to phrase his dilemma: the rest of it. The rest of it being the potential end of life as he knew it. He tried to shake off such a melancholy outlook, for Rory's sake.

"Let's not talk about it," he suggested, as he did every time she tried to bring it up.

She let out a quick breath, and he recognized the determination that came over her expression. She wasn't about to let it go this time.

"Sawyer, I don't think we can *not* talk about it anymore."

He shook his head, rather forcefully. "Sure, we can. We'll just pretend that everything is the same as it was before."

She frowned. "But it's not. And there's a chance it never will be. You can't ignore that forever."

"Maybe I can." Maybe he could avoid it right up until the moment he lost his mind. Then it wouldn't matter anymore.

But the look of disappointment she wore humbled him. She was trying, and he loved her for it. But he just couldn't think about it, couldn't talk about it.

"I spoke to my manager today," he said, trying to get her to change the subject. "She's working on scheduling me some studio time. I told her… I was thinking…maybe you'd want to perform some backup vocals for me. Maybe even play some guitar."

He was pleased when she blinked several times. "Really?"

"Yeah." He swallowed a rise of guilt. "It's what I should have demanded in the first place.

We're partners. I shouldn't be making music without input from you."

Tears filled her eyes, and he felt even worse. Why hadn't he done this already?

"I would love that," she said. "Thank you."

He leaned forward, across the tabletop, and planted a quick kiss on her lips. "You are more than welcome."

They sat for a few minutes longer, and he just enjoyed having her near him.

Until she spoke up again.

"We still need to talk about the possibility of you having Alzheimer's," she stated.

Her persistence nipped at his patience. "Keep your voice down," he said, with a touch of irritation. "Do you know what could happen if someone overheard?" He gave a quick look around. They were on their own at the moment, secluded in an unused portion of Callahan's outdoor dining area. But he was still uncomfortable with Rory voicing this thought aloud. Perhaps more so because speaking it reminded him it was true, rather than any real fear of someone overhearing.

Rory looked none too pleased at his admonition. "Sawyer, I understand the need for discretion, and if you want to talk about this somewhere more private, I am more than happy to do so. But we *are* going to talk about it."

There it was again. Her Irish bullheadedness.

"No," he declared. "We're not."

Annoyed, he pushed back from the table and stood up.

"Maybe you should get tested."

He scowled, wishing she'd let it rest.

"Why? So that I can see the end coming all the more quickly?"

She stood, though she was several inches shorter than him and had to look up to meet his eyes. "You don't even know if you have any of those mutated genes. What if you're worrying for nothing?"

"And what if I'm not?" he countered. "What will I do if I know for certain? My life will become a nightmare. Every time I enter a room and forget why I went in there, I'll think it's starting. When I try to find the right word and can't, I would have a panic attack. If I know it's bound to happen, then every innocent slipup, every moment I blank on something, I'll think it's the beginning of the end. How can I live like that?"

"Would it be any worse than how you're living now? It's eating you up inside."

"You wouldn't understand," he muttered, turning away.

"How can I, when you won't open up to me about it?"

The ache in her voice caused him to turn back. He saw then how wounded she was by the wall he'd built around this topic.

"Rory," he murmured, coming back to the table. He moved around it to gather her into his arms. "Rory, I'm sorry."

She leaned into him, her arms coming around his waist. Her touch made him want to weep. What sort of life was he asking her to live, sticking around for someone who might not even remember her name in another ten years?

"I know you mean well," he said into her hair, breathing in the gentle fragrance of her shampoo. "But I just don't know how to talk about this. I feel like no one could possibly understand how it feels."

She pulled back enough to look up into his face. "Then help me understand."

He traced the back of his knuckles over her jaw. Sweet, steadfast Rory. She was making a real effort. Maybe he owed it to her to try a little harder.

But how? He didn't know how to tell her what he was feeling, at least not without scaring her. It was as if he was living in two worlds. In the one, not much had changed. He still had a future full of possibility with Rory by his side. He was going to keep making music, marry Rory, start a family, take care of his parents. He'd be there for his dad no matter what happened, and then, when the worst came, he'd make sure his mom was looked after. Give her grandkids to ease her grief. If he had to lose his father, the world owed him that much, didn't it? The chance to live his own life.

The other world, however, was a living nightmare. He would lose his father. Then himself. He might lose Chase. Everything he'd worked for would be forgotten. And then, he'd lose Rory.

And that was the worst of it. How could he tell her that his greatest fear was leaving her alone again? Leaving her in a much worse state than he had before. No, he couldn't explain it to her.

No matter how much she pleaded.

She must have recognized she was getting nowhere because she sniffed and then pulled in a deep breath.

"If you won't talk to me then I think you should try talking to other people who are going through the same thing."

"Now you sound like Chase."

"I don't think that's a bad thing. Chase is a pretty smart kid."

He couldn't deny it. "He's been trying to convince me to attend a support group with him."

"That sounds like a great idea, actually."

Sawyer wasn't sure he agreed. "I don't know, I think the entire experience would be too depressing. I'm not sure I want to hear all the struggles these other people are going through."

Rory spoke gently, but the words still cut. "Not even when they're the same struggles you're facing?"

He winced before he could school his expression. She tightened her grip around his waist.

"What could it hurt? You can go and see what other people have to say. Maybe it will help you find a way to cope, or give you some insight on whether you should have the DNA test."

He hesitated. He still wasn't sure it was a good idea. He knew it didn't make sense, but he had some weird logic that by ignoring the disease, it would ignore him, too. It was almost as if he was hiding from it. Visiting a support group would announce his presence, and what if the disease came looking for him then? It was a childish superstition, but Sawyer was having a hard time shaking it.

"Sawyer," she said, waiting until he really looked at her before continuing. "You know you're not alone in this, right? I'm here. And your family has each other. Maybe, if you see how other people have coped, it will remind you that you can, too."

Though Rory's words held a degree of logic, he didn't know if he believed them. He couldn't imagine ever coming to terms with all of this—letting it become a part of his daily life and routine.

But he knew he couldn't escape the determination in Rory's eyes. If she and Chase joined forces on the idea of attending a support group, he might as well just give in and agree to go. There'd be no dissuading them. And if it was something that would ease a bit of the strain that had arisen between him and Rory, he'd do it.

He released a breath and knew she recognized his defeat by the way her eyes lit up.

"Fine. If you want me to try a support group then I'll try one. Just don't expect any miracles, Rory."

Since she stood almost a foot shorter than him, she tilted her head back to kiss the tip of his chin.

"Having you back is my miracle," she stated.

And he was reminded that she was so much better than what he deserved.

CHAPTER TWELVE

RORY AND CHASE chose the support group together. They managed to find one forty-five minutes away in Towson that advertised several members with EOA as well as the more common form of Alzheimer's. The group met on the third Saturday of every month, so they were lucky enough to be able to attend a meeting that weekend.

Sawyer considered insisting that Rory stay behind, but he knew he'd never make it through the entire meeting if she wasn't with him. So he didn't put up much of a fuss when she got someone to cover her shift at the restaurant in order to go with them.

They arrived in Towson in plenty of time and found the meeting place without trouble. The group met in a large room at a local community center. The minute Sawyer walked in the door, his nose wrinkled at the antiseptic smell of bleach and cleaning products. The floor was covered with rough, industrial carpeting in an indistinguishable shade of gray-green. Construction paper artwork covered the walls, a riot of color against the bland beige paint. There was a table off to the side, loaded with a platter of cookies, a basket of croissants and a coffee urn. There was no other table in the room, just a large circle of a dozen or more chairs. Sawyer felt uncomfortable at the sight of it. It put him in mind of group therapy, where everyone shared their "feelings." Of course, maybe that's exactly what this was.

He stopped short of the circle as Rory and Chase took another step forward. There were a handful of people already gathered, along with a petite, silver-haired lady at the center. She took note of their arrival and moved to greet them.

"You must be Rory," she said, extending a hand, which Rory took in her own. "I'm Joan, we spoke on the phone. We're so happy you've decided to join us today." She directed her attention at Chase, who moved toward her, arm extended to accept her handshake and introduce himself. Then it was Joan's turn to focus on Sawyer. He shifted uncomfortably, still standing a step behind Chase and Rory. As she looked at him, he waited for recognition to dawn. It was what he'd been dreading the most—having people realize who he was. But Joan either possessed a consummate poker face or she had no idea of Sawyer's celebrity status. She simply stood, smiling at him with an open and welcoming expression, and waited for him to speak.

"I'm Sawyer," he finally said, and nodded in her direction. He didn't offer her his hand as the others had.

"It's a pleasure to meet you, Sawyer," she said. "Rory tells me you and your brother have a relative who was recently diagnosed with early onset Alzheimer's."

"Yes," Chase said. "Our dad."

Joan's face fell. "Oh, I'm sorry to hear that. First learning about the diagnosis can be one of the most difficult parts of the disease. What made you decide to seek out our support group?"

Sawyer tuned out Chase and Rory as they elaborated on their reasons for being here. It didn't really matter to Sawyer what they said. He'd come here as a favor to Rory, nothing more. He didn't expect to get much out of it.

Joan shared a few details about the group, how they'd formed and how long they'd been meeting. She gave a quick overview of some of the members and their situations with the disease. A lot of them were caretakers for older parents, although she mentioned a few who were Alzheimer's patients themselves. She also confirmed that they had two other members who had loved ones diagnosed with EOA.

As Joan spoke, he scanned the rest of the group briefly. Most of the people in the circle were in conversations amongst themselves. There was one guy, however, who was staring at Sawyer pretty hard. He knew he'd been recognized. The thought made him wince. The last thing he wanted was an autograph session in the middle of this thing.

"Sawyer?" He turned to Rory, realizing the conversation had gone on without him.

"I'm sorry, what was that?"

Rory didn't seem put out that his attention had wandered. "Joan was explaining how the meetings work."

"We're a pretty informal group," Joan said. "We open by introducing any new members, and then we go around the room, taking turns and sharing our hardest struggle in the last month as well as our greatest joy."

"Sounds simple enough," Chase said.

Joan nodded. "It's a beneficial format for us. It gives us the opportunity to share what we've learned, be honest about the challenges of Alzheimer's, and find the good in the day-to-day."

"You can find good in it?" Sawyer asked, knowing his tone oozed skepticism.

"Oh, yes," Joan said. "Those in our group who have been diagnosed with the disease have a saying—'I've got Alzheimer's, but Alzheimer's doesn't have me.' We use that as a reminder that the disease is a part of us, but it doesn't define who we are. We are still fighting."

Sawyer thought it was a stirring sentiment. He just wasn't sure how realistic it was.

"You are more than welcome to speak up, ask questions, or share with the group, but it's not required. First-time visitors are often overwhelmed, having only recently learned that they or a loved one has been diagnosed with the disease. So it's perfectly fine to just observe."

This put Sawyer at ease. It was enough that he'd come; he didn't feel like sharing his feelings with a bunch of strangers.

Joan's attention shifted, and when they followed the direction of her gaze, he noticed a couple more people entering the room.

"Why don't you go ahead and have a seat? There are refreshments over there." She pointed to the table with the cookies and other items. "And feel free to mingle. We're a pretty friendly bunch."

They all murmured their thanks, and then awkwardly found seats in the circle. Sawyer noticed the guy who'd been eyeing him tapping on his cell phone. He didn't seem interested in Sawyer's presence anymore, which allowed Sawyer to breathe a little easier.

Several of the group members came over to introduce themselves, and they spent the next few minutes exchanging polite conversation. A younger woman studied him carefully, then said, "You look so familiar. I feel like I know you."

He smiled but didn't give her any encouragement. "I have one of those faces."

She shrugged, seemingly content to let it go. He was grateful for such a small group. The more attendees, the greater chance he'd be recognized. While it had become a standard part of his life, he didn't much feel like being Sawyer Landry the Country Music Star today.

"All right, first, I'd like to thank everyone for coming." Joan stood in the center of the circle and drew everyone's attention with her welcoming words. The few people who'd been congregating by the refreshment table found their way to their seats. "I'd like to welcome a few new faces today." Joan gestured in their direction. "This is Chase, Rory and Sawyer." She turned toward another couple that appeared to be a mother and daughter. "And this is Bella and Anne. I trust you'll make them feel welcome."

Sawyer drummed his fingers on his leg as Joan cleared her throat. "Let's start by sharing some of our struggles in the last month."

They began with an older gentleman two seats to Chase's left. His wife had recently reached the point in the disease where she had to be moved to a nursing care facility.

"Nights are the worst," the man, who introduced himself as Bill, explained. "The two of us used to stay up late together, watching the news and then reading. Even when things got bad, she was still there with me. Now, the house feels empty. Quiet. She hasn't died, but I've already lost her. I don't know how to mourn for her."

Several others expressed their understanding and sympathy. One lady talked about the grief process and how it applied even when the spouse hadn't yet passed on. The next person was closer to Chase's age. His grandfather had been diagnosed a year ago, and the older man's mental state was rapidly deteriorating. Because he was currently without a job, he had taken on a lot of the caregiving for his grandpa. He talked about how much it hurt when his grandfather lashed out at him.

"I try to remind myself it's not *him* saying

all these hurtful things. It's the Alzheimer's. But some days, it feels so personal."

There were murmurs of commiseration.

"We used to be so close. My parents worked a lot when I was growing up, and I ended up at my grandparents' most of the time. Gramps would do everything with me. We built model trains and went fishing. We'd work on his truck together. And now, half the time, he doesn't know who I am."

A couple of people spoke up, offering encouragement and talking about their own experiences with loved ones who were approaching this point. One man talked about how frightened he was to reach this stage, worrying his family wouldn't know how much he loved them.

Joan encouraged him to begin writing letters to his children and grandchildren, so they could have moments with him, even when his memory began to decline.

They circled the room, story after story. Sawyer felt frustration building within himself. Why had Rory thought this would be a good idea? He was overcome with despair for these people's suffering, yet inside he was also screaming at them all. He knew it was mean and self-pitying, but he couldn't help feeling most of them were lucky. While they were either a victim of the disease or loved someone who was, none of them were both patient and caregiver. What about him and Chase? They were going to watch their father wither away, only to, perhaps, become victims themselves one day.

They had nearly finished the circle. The last in the group was a woman who looked a little younger than him and Rory. She introduced herself as Madeline. She was petite and pale, but her expression was fierce. When she spoke, her voice had a smoky quality to it, with a sharp rasp that made her sound as if she'd been crying.

"In this past month, my struggle has been…" she trailed off, her jaw flexing with emotion. "Everything." She paused, clearly weighed down by her emotions. Her shoulders were stiff, and she leaned forward in her seat. "I am so *angry* with everyone. Everything. God. People who don't know what it's like to see a loved one succumb to such a horrible disease."

She ran a hand through her pixie-style red hair. "My husband is dying. He is thirty-eight years old, and he doesn't even remember how to work the microwave. He keeps forgetting the name of our son. How do I explain to my little boy why his daddy can't remember who he is?"

She scoffed, and the sound itself was laced with bitterness. "I'm watching my twelve-year-old become the man of the house while his dad regresses to a child. I caught my little boy the other day, showing his dad how to check his email. That night, I made macaroni and cheese for dinner. It was always my husband's favorite, but he spit it out and told me he hated macaroni and cheese. I tried to tell him that wasn't true, that he's always loved it, but he threw his plate on the floor like a toddler throwing a temper tantrum. What kind of example does that set for our son?"

She bit her lip, as if trying to contain herself. But the words wouldn't stop. "There are days when I hate him," she whispered, her tone bereft. "And then I feel so guilty because it's not his fault. He didn't ask for this. He watched his mom die from this disease when he was a teenager, and when he learned he had it, too, he was inconsolable with grief. This is not what he wanted for himself, or for us. I *know* that. But I need someone to blame. And I don't know who else to be mad at."

She dropped her face into her hands. "Some days, I think it would be a relief if he would die."

The words were muffled, but they echoed

in the stillness of the room. A shiver snaked its way up Sawyer's spine.

This. This was the cold truth. It wasn't platitudes or mantras or a balance of the good within the struggle. This was the everyday reality of living with Alzheimer's, especially the early onset kind. And he shuddered when he realized that Madeline's husband was less than ten years older than him. Coldness crept into his extremities. What if this was his fate?

And then, an even worse thought—what if this was what he was condemning Rory to? He shifted uncomfortably, the metal chair squeaking with the movement. The sound broke the tension, and Joan began speaking. Several others joined in, and he could tell by the tone of their voices that they were encouraging, commiserating, advising.

But he didn't hear their words. Not a one. He was buried too deep in his own fear and dismay. Sinking beneath the vision of a future he dreaded.

How could he ask Rory to marry him if this was what life would become? What kind of marriage was that? And what about children? They'd always planned to have kids one day. How could he condemn a child to a life without a father? Or worse, only a few years with one before memories were lost and forgotten, before the roles were reversed and Sawyer became the helpless child?

He felt sick. And because he couldn't focus on the others' words, he watched Madeline very closely. She was still hunched over, her eyes glazed. Whatever they were saying to her wasn't penetrating. She'd given up. He found no hope in her expression, no lift in her spirits. She was a defeated woman.

And all he could see then was Rory. Rory in this position. Rory, having lost her spark and fire to a man who had become a burden. Him. He did not want to become her baggage, her charity work, the thing that drained the life from her.

He stood to his feet abruptly, only vaguely aware that he'd pulled everyone's attention from Madeline to himself. But he couldn't breathe. He had to get out of this room with its antiseptic smell and cloud of false hope.

"Excuse me."

They were the only words he managed before pushing past his metal chair and heading for the door.

SAWYER REACHED THE HALLWAY, his breathing sharp and shallow. He still couldn't find his breath, and he felt nearly panicked with effort to reach fresh air. He turned a corner and realized he'd gone the wrong way.

Chase had led them to the meeting room, and Sawyer only vaguely remembered the way they'd come in. He tried to focus and stumbled back in the direction of the room, moving past it without a glance inside. He rounded a corner that he hoped would take him to the exit and thought he heard the door to the meeting room swing open.

He made it outside less than a minute later and immediately took in huge gulps of air as he struggled to compose himself.

And suddenly he was the center of a storm.

There were reporters—at least three of them, each with a cameraman. They descended with microphones and volleyed questions at him.

"Sawyer Landry, can you tell us what you're doing here today?"

"We received a tip that you're attending an Alzheimer's support group. Do you have a family member who is struggling with the disease?"

"Is this part of a charitable contribution on your part?"

"Why else are you in Towson?"

He'd never had a problem with the media before. He accepted they were a part of his life now, that anywhere he went there was the chance he'd be photographed or intruded upon.

But he hadn't expected this. Why hadn't he expected this? They were in his face with cameras and microphones, pressing for answers. He'd been caught off guard, and he cursed himself for not anticipating such a scenario. His face was well known these days. Did he really think he could come and go without being recognized?

He thought about the guy in the group, the one watching him covertly who was later absorbed in his phone. Had he tipped off the local news stations?

"Mr. Landry, are you making any other appearances today?"

"What brings you to the area?"

"Hey!"

He'd been frozen up until this point, paralyzed by the unexpected assault of questions. But when he heard Rory's voice cut through the commotion, her tone sharp and angry, he snapped to attention.

"Mr. Landry has nothing to say," she announced, placing herself between him and the reporters.

"Can we get your name, miss?"

"How do you know Mr. Landry?"

"Can you tell us what you're doing here today?"

She ignored them and faced him instead. "Chase is going to get the car." She grabbed him by the hand and began to lead him away, but the reporters followed.

"Just one statement, Mr. Landry, to let our local readers know why you're here."

"That's none of their business," Rory snapped.

If he hadn't been so dazed, he might have laughed at her irritation. But he didn't have an ounce of humor in him at the moment.

"I'm here on a personal matter," he said as he continued walking. "It's nothing that would interest your readers."

"I highly doubt that," one of the reporters returned.

She was probably right. If word got out that he might be an Alzheimer's patient, he imagined it would be big news. At least on a slow celebrity-news day.

"Come on, Sawyer, give us a clue! We're big fans!"

He chafed at this. Fans or not, wasn't he entitled to some privacy?

No, he realized. He wasn't. He'd given that up when he became a headlining act.

He abruptly stopped walking. It was so

abrupt that Rory's hand jerked free of his as she continued her forward momentum. He turned to face the reporters, suddenly feeling as if none of it mattered. The world would find out soon enough.

"My dad has Alzheimer's," he announced. The words silenced the reporters for the span of about five seconds.

"When was he diagnosed?"

"What impact do you think this will have on your career?"

"Is your father here with you today?"

He ignored all the questions.

"He has a rare form of Alzheimer's called early onset. My family and I are making the necessary determinations for the future. I'd appreciate some privacy during this difficult time."

With that, he started walking again, pausing when Rory hesitated. Then, together, they started moving toward the curb. Chase pulled up seconds later. The reporters followed, still asking questions, begging for statements.

But he was done. He'd given them enough fodder for their news stories.

He opened the door for Rory, and she climbed inside. He followed.

"Drive," he said to Chase.

"What are they doing here?" he asked.

"Just drive."

He was grateful when Chase didn't argue. They pulled away from the reporters, who were still shouting their questions, and headed for home.

CHAPTER THIRTEEN

NO ONE SPOKE much on the drive back to Findlay Roads, and the silence began to wear on Rory's nerves. She wasn't uncomfortable with quiet and especially not with Sawyer. But this silence was different. She felt it, like an invisible, impenetrable wall between them. The support group had gotten to Sawyer, and she feared the media encounter had pushed him over the edge. He'd turned into himself, blocking her out. She knew it would be useless to push him at the moment, especially with Chase in the car. And Chase must have felt it, too, because beyond asking his brother if he was all right, he'd only spoken a few words.

Rory did try small talk. She asked Chase and Sawyer if they felt the support group had been helpful.

Chase had only offered a tentative "I'm not sure yet" while Sawyer had sighed.

She didn't press him for more. Instead, she leaned back in the seat and looked out the window, watching the highway slip by and wondering what to do next.

She wanted to be there for Sawyer. She'd been hopeful about their future, even after he'd told her about the possibility of Alzheimer's. But if she was honest with herself, the support group had scared her. Some of the individual stories were beyond heartbreaking. Was this the life she was signing up for? Loving Sawyer only to have him forget her?

She nibbled on her thumbnail at that thought.

She couldn't lose him again. The first time had nearly broken her, and in that instance, she'd had her anger to carry her through. If he left her, mind before body, she didn't know how she'd deal with her grief. She might lose her own mind.

And then, what about children? She'd always dreamed of her and Sawyer as parents one day, but none of the daydreams had featured her as a single mom. And should she and Sawyer even let themselves try for children, knowing they might curse *them* with a disease that would shorten their life span? Most people didn't get to know their future, but what if fate was giving her a chance to get out, to protect her heart before she risked it again?

But then, the thought of breaking up with Sawyer, of sending him away, nearly tore her in two. To be with him meant living with the risk of losing him. But she knew she'd rather take that risk than a sure loss.

She turned her head, daring to look at him, but he was staring out his own window. She flicked her eyes to the rearview mirror and caught Chase looking at her. He quickly moved his eyes back to the road.

She felt a stab of dismay. She was so focused on Sawyer that it was easy to forget Chase was facing the same fear. He wasn't even out of college yet, and he already had to worry about whether he'd develop a fatal disease that would steal his life not long after he'd really begun to live it.

But Chase seemed to be handling things better than his brother. He had a practical outlook on the situation, recognizing that these worries might all be pointless. They didn't know for certain that either of the brothers had the mutated genes. Only the DNA test could tell that. She knew, from a private conversation with Chase, that he was in favor of being tested. But she also hoped Sawyer would agree to the testing, so they could go through it together.

But then, if they both learned they possessed the faulty genes, how could they possibly face the future knowing that three members out of their family would succumb to Alzheimer's?

Or perhaps worse, what if one of them had the disease and the other didn't? Would it place a rift between them? Would bitterness poison their relationship?

Rory had a bad feeling about it. They would have to be extraordinarily lucky for both of them to escape a positive diagnosis. Maybe one would be spared, but both?

She felt her mood slipping into darkness at these thoughts and tried to shake them off.

"Can we turn on the radio?" she asked and was surprised when her voice sounded almost hoarse with sadness. It was rough enough that Sawyer jerked from his fixation on the highway and glanced at her. She coughed lightly. "Please," she added in a slightly clearer voice.

Chase didn't reply but granted her request, punching the radio dial. Soft strains of a country ballad filled the car.

Rory didn't know if it was a good sign or a bad one that the voice streaming from the station was Sawyer's.

It all came crashing down on Sawyer the next day. He was in his parents' kitchen, pouring a glass of orange juice, when his phone rang. He reached for it with trepidation, worried it might be Rory. They'd parted awkwardly upon their return from Towson. Chase had dropped her off at the apartment, and their goodbye had been stilted as he said he'd call her.

The hurt in her eyes haunted him the rest of the day and into his dreams that night. He wanted to push her away, yet hold her. He needed her.

He was afraid to need anyone right now.

A quick check of caller ID filled him with both relief and disappointment. It wasn't Rory calling, but rather his manager.

He clicked to receive the call.

"Hey, Perle."

"Hello, Sawyer." Her tone was flat, lacking its usual vibrancy. He belatedly realized it was the first time she hadn't affected her faux Southern accent. "What were you thinking?"

"Excuse me?"

"Don't you dare play dumb with me. What's going on up there?"

He took a sip of orange juice, trying to quell his uneasiness at her tone.

"I'm visiting my family. I'll be back in Nashville soon enough."

"Cut the crap, Sawyer. What were you doing at an Alzheimer's support group in Towson yesterday?"

The orange juice turned sharp in his mouth. The reporters. Of course. He hadn't even thought to check today's headlines.

"Some local news station got you on video, announcing your father has some sort of dementia. The AP wire picked it up, and now it's being broadcast on every cable channel with an entertainment news ticker. When did you plan to clue me in to this? I'm just your manager, after all."

He prickled at her words. "It's a private matter. Between my family and me."

"Well, not anymore, sugar." Perle's Southern accent had gradually returned to her voice. "If it was so private, you shouldn't have made a statement to some nobody reporter. You should have come to me so we could have released this news to maximum effect."

A spark of anger lit, and he quickly moved from the kitchen and toward the hall that led into the garage. He didn't want to have this conversation within earshot of his parents.

"This isn't a press release, Perle. This is my *life*."

He closed the door to the garage, breathing in the cool, musty smells of concrete and drywall.

"Your entire life *is* a press release, darlin'. If you haven't realized that yet, you better wake up and smell the bacon."

Previously, he'd found Perle's use of clichés amusing. This one fell flat.

"I understand that, but this is nobody's business but my own."

Perle sighed dramatically. "Celebrities at your level don't have that luxury. Like it or not, your life is on display. It's free game for any tabloid or blogger. You don't get secrets anymore, sugar. I wish you did. Sorry."

The apology put him over the edge. One word that was supposed to make everything better. What a weak and pathetic attempt at consolation.

"Why do people think their sympathy makes a difference? I don't *care* if you're sorry. What good does that do me? Your *sorry* doesn't fix anything. It's not a cure. And my dad doesn't have dementia, by the way. He has *Alzheimer's*. The kind that strikes people when they're still young. The kind that gets passed down through generations. The kind that can kill you before you reach forty. The kind that I might very well have right now without even knowing it. So pardon me if your *sorry* doesn't do much for me."

Perle was silent for so long that some of Sawyer's ire deflated, and he began to regret speaking so harshly to the woman he owed so much to. But it also felt good to yell at someone, to let out the anger he'd had on a slow simmer the last few days.

"Listen, it's just been…rough on this end," he said.

"I can tell," Perle offered, her tone cool.

He didn't say anything. He didn't know what else to say, other than to apologize. And somehow, he didn't feel like saying he was sorry for wanting the world to leave him alone while he sorted things out.

After a time, Perle sighed again, but this time it sounded more genuine. "Are you telling the truth, about possibly having Alzheimer's? Or are you blowing smoke?"

He leaned his forehead against the garage wall and closed his eyes. "It's the truth." He elaborated a bit, telling her about the mutated genes that caused the disease and how there was a real possibility he'd inherited them from his dad. He didn't have that many illusions about his relationship with Perle. They got along well, and he appreciated how she'd helped in launching his career. But he recognized that they weren't friends, and by telling her this, he might be jeopardizing their working relationship.

"It sounds to me like you have a lot to figure out."

He released a breath, somewhere between a scoff and a sigh. "Yeah. I'd say you're right."

"Then tell me how you want to handle this.

My phone's been ringing off the hook with questions and interview requests. I can compose a formal press release, if you tell me how much you want the world to know."

He was both surprised and touched. Perle knew the power of leverage, and this kind of news was certainly something she could exploit in order to elevate his notoriety. But by asking how much she should share, she'd just given him the right to control how far he let the rest of the world in. He was grateful to her for that. They spent the next several minutes going over the details of what to announce and how to present it.

"You know this is going to gain you a whole new level of exposure," she said once they'd wrapped up the conversation.

"I know," he admitted.

"You sure you're ready for it?"

He considered this, remembering what it felt like to have the reporters in his face yesterday, how threatened he felt by their interference. He thought about Rory. Was this something he should discuss with her first? Should he ask her opinion or how she felt about such a private issue being paraded before the public?

As much as he wanted to get her input, he wasn't sure it mattered. His life wasn't exactly his own anymore. And as much as he wanted

Rory in it, he was beginning to realize that might not be best for her.

"Sawyer? I want to make sure you're okay before we proceed with this."

He straightened and leaned his back against the wall. "I'm not sure I have much of a choice."

His uneasiness only increased when Perle didn't deny it.

IT HAD BEEN three days since Rory saw Sawyer. It was the longest time they'd gone without seeing each other since he'd returned to Findlay Roads. They'd communicated by text and one phone call, and Rory had done her best to give him space. But without the constant contact, doubts had crept in. What if she and Sawyer weren't meant to be? Their paths had diverged so dramatically that maybe it was a sign they should let their past be the past. With the added threat of Alzheimer's, she couldn't shake the idea that fate was trying to tell her something.

Now she was driving to the welcome-home party for Gavin, who had arrived in town on army leave to participate as a groomsman in Connor's wedding. She and Sawyer could have gone to the party together, but he hadn't suggested it, and she didn't want to ask him. So they were attending separately. That in itself didn't bode well for them.

Sawyer's life was so different now. In the last seventy-two hours that had become abundantly clear, beginning with the reporters who had assaulted them following the Alzheimer's support group in Towson. At the time, her focus had been on Sawyer, and she hadn't had the opportunity to consider how strange the situation was—how far removed it was from the kind of existence she and Sawyer had once lived.

But the next day, after she'd read the local headlines about Sawyer's presence at the support group, her mind had begun to spin. Was this the life she wanted for herself? She'd seen how painful it had been for Sawyer to confront those reporters. Even worse, she had witnessed their utter disregard for his requests for privacy. She couldn't imagine such an intrusion into her personal space. But if she committed to Sawyer, this could become a daily occurrence for her.

She didn't know if she was ready for it. Despite being a performer, she'd always been a private person, and that trait had grown in the past two years. The idea of her life, and her relationship, on display left her uncomfortable. She wanted to talk to Sawyer about it, to unburden her reservations and have him reassure her. She needed him to tell her they were in this together, that he would guide her through the strangeness of this new world.

But Sawyer was already burdened by the situation with his father. She felt selfish and small that she craved his attention and comfort when he was facing so much. She ached for how he suffered and wanted to console him. But he hadn't reached out to her. He'd placed a wall around his heart, and she didn't know how to breach it. Or if she should even try.

There had been a time when she knew exactly what Sawyer needed without him asking. Now she was no longer certain. Maybe things had changed too much for them. Maybe he realized it, too, and that's why he'd been so distant the last few days.

Such a thought was so disheartening that she had to blink back tears. Seconds later, she was pulling into the parking lot of the Moontide Inn. The party was being held in the inn's spacious backyard. Connor and Harper's wedding ceremony would also take place there that weekend.

A quick scan of the other vehicles revealed that Sawyer hadn't arrived yet. Rory felt a moment's uncertainty. What if he didn't show up? But no, Sawyer wouldn't do that. Not to Gavin, who had been his best friend since high school. They'd gone through army basic and their first deployment together. Even though she knew the two of them hadn't been in touch much over the last couple of years, Sawyer wouldn't miss this.

She swallowed as she realized that she was confident Sawyer wouldn't bail on Gavin, but she couldn't say the same about whether he would on her. She shook her head at the thought. That was only her insecurity coming into play. Sawyer had asked her to trust him, to believe in him. She owed it to him to try. He'd had a rough time of it since he'd been back. She shouldn't project her own insecurities onto his behavior. After all, he was fighting to find his way through everything that had happened.

But even with this internal reassurance, a small voice of doubt raised its head.

What if Sawyer didn't find his way through and chose to cut her out of his life as a result?

CHAPTER FOURTEEN

SAWYER WAS LATE arriving to the party at the Moontide Inn. Though Erin had said it would be a small gathering, he still found himself nervous to face his friends. Perle had released their press statement, and there had been several articles about his dad's diagnosis. He read a couple of them, but the way the media had played to the worst-case scenario had shaken him. There'd been speculations on his early retirement, and one paragraph that had embedded itself in his very soul: "It is a sad consideration that Sawyer Landry's star might have winked out before it truly had a chance to shine."

He'd stopped there, not allowing himself to read any more. But the weight of those words had stayed with him, taunting him. It had sent him into a dark funk that he'd been unable to shake. Even now, as he stepped up onto the porch of the inn, he felt weighed down by a cloud of gloom. He was sad and uneasy, hesitant about facing Rory after their last three days apart and not in the mood for a party.

He even entertained the notion of heading back home. He could always stop by and see Gavin later, when things had died down. But before he could really consider this option, the door swung open and his best friend stood before him.

"Well, it's about time. I thought I was going to have to hire some paparazzi to camp out on the lawn to lure you here. I didn't think you'd show without an audience, now that you've gone and made yourself a household name."

And just like that, Sawyer's spirits experienced a little lift.

"Shows how much you know about us celebrities. We always arrive fashionably late."

Gavin threw his head back and laughed, and Sawyer's heart warmed at the sound. Everything might have changed, his entire world upended, but there were some things—and people—he could still rely on. Gavin was one of them. Without any further ribbing, his friend drew him into a hug, slapping his back so hard that Sawyer coughed.

"Geez, dude, how much are you bench-pressing these days? You're like Iron Man."

Gavin responded with a firm punch to the arm.

"Ow!" Sawyer declared with fake dramatics and rubbed at his bicep.

Gavin wrapped his arm around Sawyer's shoulder as he led him inside. "Seriously, bro, I'm glad you could make it. I was beginning to think you weren't coming."

"I wouldn't miss it," Sawyer said, and in that moment, he realized it was true. It had been too long since he'd seen Gavin. And being around his old friend might be exactly what he needed.

He was suddenly really glad he had come. Unable to resist, he asked, "Is Rory here yet?"

He and Gavin made their way from the front of the inn toward the back doors that led out onto the lawn area.

"Yeah, she arrived like twenty minutes ago." Gavin slid him a glance. "I heard you two broke up, before you moved to Nashville."

Sawyer didn't know what to say to that. Though he'd been in touch with Gavin once or twice since he'd moved, he'd never elaborated on what had happened between him and Rory.

"Yeah, that was a stupid decision on my part—one that I'm trying to fix."

Gavin nodded in approval. "At least you can admit you were wrong. That's a start." They stopped by the back door, and his friend faced him.

Sawyer shifted uncomfortably. "I appreciate the vote of confidence, but you don't know the half of it."

Gavin cocked his head. "You mean the Alzheimer's deal?"

Sawyer's jaw dropped. "How did you know about that?"

Gavin rolled his eyes. "I read, you know." He pretended to puff out his chest. "I'm a man who keeps abreast of current events."

Sawyer arched an eyebrow. "That, or a tabloid junkie."

Gavin grinned. "It passes the time when I've got nothing better to do." He let the smile slip. "Honestly? Erin told me. She saw it on some celebrity news site. Why didn't you tell us?"

He looked away. "I just found out. My parents told Chase and me not long after I arrived in town."

Gavin was quiet for a second, and Sawyer couldn't look at him.

"So, is it true what they're saying? Your dad has this early onset Alzheimer's, and there's a chance you do, too?"

He forced himself to look at his friend. "Yeah. It's true."

Gavin's expression filled with sorrow. "Man, I'm sorry. That's…rough."

"Yeah."

"How are you holding up?"

Sawyer hesitated, not wanting to admit how desperately he was hurting. But this was Gavin. Next to Rory, there was no one he trusted more. "Not so good."

Gavin placed his hands on Sawyer's shoulders, forcing his friend to look at him. "Hey, don't let this take you down. I watched you fight for your dreams for years, you and Rory. You spent all those hours on the road, and you played in some pretty crummy places. No way is some disease going to beat you. You've got this, Sawyer. You know that, right?"

It wasn't exactly the pep talk he needed, but it was enough to rally him. He felt some of the gloom lifting from his mood.

"Remind me again why we haven't talked in so long?"

Gavin released him with an eye roll. "Beats me. Unless you've forgotten how to Skype. Of course, when you're touring the world all the time and winning awards..."

"Yeah, yeah." This time, it was Sawyer who punched him. "Don't make me out to be some diva. I'm not the one who freaked out when he found a scorpion in his bunk."

"That was not any old scorpion! That was like the Scorpion *king*."

As they stepped out the back door and toward the party, Sawyer had to admit—it felt good to laugh again.

RORY COULDN'T REMEMBER when she'd last felt so at ease. It was as if time had spun backward with her and Sawyer, along with Gavin and Erin, together again. They lingered long after the rest of the party had broken up and gone home. There was a copper fire pit in the backyard that they'd all gathered around, seated on wicker chairs with plush cushions. Kitt had exhausted himself following his dad around all afternoon and now he was curled up on Gavin's lap, sleeping soundly, his tiny hand tucked into Gavin's larger one. It was a heartwarming sight. When she stole a glance at Erin, she could see her friend must have been thinking the same thing by the way she gazed adoringly at her two guys.

For Rory, it was enough to be holding Sawyer's hand as he and Gavin chatted softly, catching up on all they'd missed in the last couple of years. Rory remembered many nights like this one, the four of them hanging out— talking, laughing, dreaming together. It was both amazing and reassuring to know that they were still some of the most important people in her life, even after all this time. And even more so since Sawyer had come back.

"...decided I'm going to get out after this deployment."

Rory roused herself to listen to what Gavin was saying. She watched as he shared a glance with Erin.

"We've talked about it, and I think it's time I come back here and settle into civilian life. Kitt's getting older, and he needs me around. Erin, too. Plus, Aunt Lenora can't keep up this pace forever. She's pushing ninety. She'll be needing more help in the years to come."

Rory felt a swell of happiness. "You're coming home? For good?"

Gavin nodded. "That's the plan. Soon as this enlistment is up."

"Gavin, that's grand." Rory knew how much Erin missed her husband when he was deployed. And Gavin was right—Kitt needed his dad around, especially as he grew older. She was happy for her friends. But then, a small spark of jealousy flared within her. How blessed Erin was, to have a devoted husband like Gavin, a darling boy like Kitt and a happy future ahead of them.

As quickly as this thought arose, she smothered it. Erin had earned the right to happiness. She'd waited a long time on Gavin, throughout his army career, raising Kitt practically on her own. They deserved a shot at a promising future.

Gavin and Erin continued discussing their plans while Rory studied Sawyer with lowered lashes. For the first time in days, he seemed at ease. One hand held onto hers while his other held a can of Sprite. His shoulders were relaxed, and it was as if the worry that had hounded him had evaporated. She wished so desperately that it could always be like this. But then, maybe that was the point—to enjoy these moments as they came, to treasure and store them up against the hard times.

These were the type of memories that could carry her and Sawyer through whatever dark days they might face in the future. Through his father's illness, through wherever his career took him and through the possibility of him developing Alzheimer's. As long as they had each other, friends like these and nights like this one, they could weather anything.

But then she remembered that the moments like these were the ones that Sawyer would lose. He wouldn't have them to carry him through. They would disappear, one by one, like dandelion seeds scattered on the wind.

She suddenly tightened her grip on his hand so hard that he glanced in her direction with a concerned frown. But she didn't want to steal the moment from him, this time when he could be at ease with his friends. So she smiled, making every effort to imbue her face with warmth. He smiled back, even offered a wink, and her heart fluttered as he turned his attention back to Gavin.

She watched him for what must have been two whole minutes before she looked away and caught Erin staring at her. She tried smiling, and Erin offered one in return, though it didn't quite meet her eyes.

Rory had the feeling that Erin knew exactly what she was thinking.

If Sawyer had Alzheimer's, then how many more moments like these did he have left?

SAWYER HADN'T KNOWN how to react when his mom came to the garage to tell him Connor was here to see him. The last thing he'd expected that morning was for Connor Callahan to knock on the door. Sawyer had experienced a moment's uneasiness as he put down the paint roller and wiped his hands on a rag. Had Connor come to tell him he didn't want him near his sister anymore, given the media attention of his family's situation?

If he had, Sawyer wasn't going to argue with him. He had a right to protect his sister, and allowing her to continue in a relationship with a potentially dying man wasn't exactly a brotherly move.

Sawyer finished cleaning his hands on the rag and tossed it onto the workbench before heading through the garage door that led into the main house. He found Connor in the kitchen, discussing the merits of Wüsthof knives with his mom.

They both looked up as Sawyer entered the room.

"Hey," Connor greeted him.

Sawyer gave a brief nod in greeting.

"It's a lovely day outside," his mom said. "Why don't the two of you go out on the porch?"

Bless his mom for trying to give them some privacy. He gestured toward the back door, and Connor preceded him. Neither one spoke until they were outside. Connor took a seat in one of the lawn chairs, but Sawyer was too restless and chose to stand.

"I wonder how the girls are getting on," Connor began.

This innocent remark only threw Sawyer more. Harper and her bridesmaids were away for the day in Annapolis for Harper's bridal shower. He'd made plans to see Rory the following afternoon, after they returned to town.

"I'm sure they're enjoying themselves,"

Sawyer offered, feeling awkward. What was Connor doing here? If he'd come to tell Sawyer to back off, he just wished he'd speak up and get it over with. No need for small talk. He'd rather hear it straight out.

"Did Rory tell you they're taking Harper to some sort of mystery dinner theater? Apparently it's been on her bucket list for years."

"Hmm." It was the most Sawyer could muster by way of reply. Rory had told him about the outing, but he hadn't asked many questions. He'd been too deep in the mire of his own thoughts, as he recalled.

Connor seemed to finally sense his uneasiness. He leaned back in his chair and tapped his fingers on the armrest.

"Hard to believe I'm getting married in a couple of days."

Sawyer perked up at this. "You're not nervous, are you?"

Connor shook his head. "Not a bit. I can't wait to make Harper my wife. With the restaurant's success, we've had to postpone our wedding plans too often. I am nothing but ready to marry her."

"She's a good woman."

Connor agreed. "That she is. Keeps me on my toes." He grinned. "Plus, Molly adores her."

Sawyer didn't know what else to say. It was

obvious Connor was head over heels in love with his bride. Like so many things these days, seeing his friends' happiness only served to punctuate his own unhappiness. How had his life unraveled so quickly? He'd had a plan. Come back to town, win Rory's heart and get back to Nashville with the promise of her joining him at some point...as his wife. Now, he could barely sort out what to do when he returned...and his heart was twisted with indecision on whether he should be subjecting Rory to his problems. He suddenly couldn't stand it anymore. If Connor had come here to tell him to break things off with Rory, then so be it.

"You can just say it, you know."

The other man looked surprised. "Say what?"

Sawyer sighed. "I won't hold it against you if you've come to tell me to leave Rory alone."

Connor straightened, his expression startled. "What?"

Sawyer hesitated. "That's not why you're here?"

Connor looked appalled. "Not at all. Why would you think that?"

Sawyer ran a hand through his hair and took the seat next to Connor's. "But don't you know? About the Alzheimer's?"

Connor's expression softened. "Aye. I know."

"Then… I assumed you came to tell me to cut Rory loose, to let her live a life without a man who's a burden to her."

Connor looked out over the backyard. "She chose you, Sawyer. Who am I to get in the way of that?"

Sawyer was both touched and grieved by the statement. Yes, she had chosen him. But she had made that choice before she knew what she might be in for.

"I just thought, after the way I left her before, that you'd see this as another black mark."

Connor's gaze was pitying. "You didn't bring this on yourself, Sawyer. This isn't your doing. And besides, from what I understand, you don't even know if this is something you'll be facing in the future."

"No," Sawyer said, "but the odds aren't exactly in my favor."

"They weren't in your favor for becoming some big music star, and yet you've managed that, haven't you?"

A corner of Sawyer's lips twitched. "I suppose that's true."

The two men were silent for a moment.

"Listen, I'll be straight with you. Am I concerned about my sister? All the time. But she's a smart woman, and I trust that she knows enough about herself and what she wants to decide who she loves. And she loves you. For better or for worse."

Connor's use of marriage vows startled him. Better or worse. Sickness and health.

"I do love her, Connor. I promise you that."

"I know. I mean, I was pretty well certain until yesterday, when I saw you with her at the Moontide, and then I knew for sure."

Sawyer was surprised that Connor had been watching them. He hadn't noticed. He wondered exactly what Rory's brother had seen to make him so certain Sawyer loved his sister. They hadn't wandered very far from each other's sides during the party. And he'd held onto her hand for much of the time. It was as if she was his anchor, holding him level, while the future was a clawing monster threatening to drag him under.

"So, if you didn't come here to tell me to back off," Sawyer said, "do you mind my asking what you're doing here?"

Connor blew out a breath. "Can't two mates just get together for some bonding time now and again?"

Sawyer arched an eyebrow, and Connor laughed.

"Okay, so I do have another reason for coming." He breathed in a deep breath. "I wanted to ask if you'd stand up with me, at my wedding, along with Gavin, Weston and Rafael."

Sawyer's jaw dropped. Of all the things he thought Connor might say, this was at the very bottom of the list.

"You want me to be one of your groomsmen?"

"Yeah. I do. I had an old friend lined up, a mate from my culinary school days. But he backed out. Can't get away from his restaurant. Harper and I were going to just double up the bridesmaids—place Rory and Erin with Gavin, but then I realized...you should be up there with us."

Sawyer was touched, though not entirely understanding. "I'm honored, Connor. Seriously, I am. But...why?"

"Because you're family," Connor responded. "You were family before, and I figure that you and Rory will be making it official at some point. You'll be my brother, even more so than you've been in the past. And I want you standing there with us when Harper and I take our vows."

Sawyer was overwhelmed by Connor's generosity in asking him to be part of his wedding. Even more than that, by entrusting him with Rory.

"So what do you say?" Connor prompted. "Will you stand up with me?"

"I'd be honored," Sawyer responded. "You don't know how much that means to me."

Connor gave a short nod. "Then since you're officially a part of the wedding party, I hope that means you'll come out with us for my stag night tonight. I'm not sure what all the lads have planned, but Gavin's in charge so it should be a good time."

"I wouldn't miss it. Thanks."

Connor stood. "Well, now that's sorted, I'd better be getting back to the restaurant. I've got a lot to do before Harper and I head off on our honeymoon."

"Of course. I imagine you're pretty busy." He rose to walk Connor out.

"Yeah, but the way the restaurant's been the last couple of years, that's always the case."

Connor waved to Sawyer's mom as they headed back through the house and to the front door. When they reached it, Sawyer paused.

"Connor, I just have to say…thanks."

"Nothing to thank me for. You make Rory happy. Other than the last two years, you always have. I know you always will." Connor reached for the door handle. "See you at the stag party tonight. I'll have Gavin text the details."

"See you then."

"YOU HAVE GOT to be kidding me."

It didn't matter what Harper said, the expression on her face told Rory everything she needed to know. Harper was thrilled with her bachelorette party.

"Seriously? We're seriously doing this?"

"You said it's something you always wanted to try," Tessa reminded her.

Harper squealed with delight and extended her arms to try and encompass all of her bridesmaids into a group hug.

"Best bachelorette party *ever*!" she declared.

Rory laughed and snuck a glance at Paige's face. Though the mystery dinner theater hadn't been Paige's idea, the three of them had finally managed to bring her around.

"We decided that with your restaurant background, you might enjoy this particular scenario," Paige added, speaking as if she'd been on board since the beginning.

"I love it," Harper enthused. "I love it!"

Erin had been the one to find the program after Tessa had brought up Harper's longtime wish to attend a mystery dinner theater. Paige had taken care of securing a reservation at the Cena Mortem Theater in Annapolis, though they'd kept Harper in the dark as to their destination until they arrived. Now, seeing her reaction, Rory would say they'd chosen well.

The dinner theater storyline included a food theme, which they'd all agreed was something Harper would enjoy. The mystery's plot concerned an up-and-coming television chef who was performing the first taping for his new cooking show. But when the chef is poisoned during a taste testing, it's up to the audience to determine who killed him.

Harper really got into the story. She, along with several other audience members, asked pertinent questions, took notes and composed theories on who the murderer could be. Rory had to admit, the entire thing was great fun. Not only was it entertaining, but the food was also excellent.

It was so much fun that she couldn't help wishing Sawyer was there to experience it with her. She thought that maybe this would be a fun date for them sometime, an opportunity for him to indulge in a fantasy world and forget the grief that weighed on him in real life. Her introspection must have been evident because Erin leaned over and whispered in her ear, "It's okay to let yourself enjoy this. You don't have to feel guilty. Sawyer would want you to have a nice time."

And that was it, she realized. She felt guilty. She didn't feel she had a right to a moment's reprieve when Sawyer was struggling. She knew that wasn't logical, but she couldn't help it. More than anything, she wanted Sawyer to be all right. She wanted to find some way to ease his worry. But there was nothing she could do. She wondered if he'd changed his mind on having the DNA test done. They hadn't discussed it. In fact, they'd avoided all references to Alzheimer's in their recent conversations.

"She's been stabbed!"

Rory nibbled on her thumbnail as she turned her attention back to the theater. The actors performing the scene were gathered around the "dead" body of the producer, adding another murder to the plot.

Suddenly she ached to see Sawyer. She needed him to know how much she loved him, that she would stand by him no matter what.

It was then that she realized she'd made her decision a long time ago. No matter what happened, she wanted to be a part of Sawyer's life, and him of hers. Whether he had Alzheimer's or not, she wanted them to face the future together.

She suddenly couldn't wait. She had to tell him how she felt. Perhaps he'd begun to doubt her, to doubt himself. Maybe his recent turning into himself was to protect her, as well as him. In any case, it didn't matter.

This was her strength, she suddenly realized. Even if Sawyer had once given up on them, she had still loved him. Though she'd tried to hate him and made every effort to harden her heart, she had loved him through it all. When he'd come back, at first she thought she had to protect herself, to erect a wall that he could not climb. And then, just when he'd found his way through to her heart once more, he'd learned about his dad's diagnosis and his possible future as an Alzheimer's victim.

Once she stripped away her doubts, she could see the truth for what it was. She loved him. She always had, and she always would. She had conquered her heartache and was stronger because of it. Maybe Sawyer didn't recognize the strength she possessed, but she did.

Alzheimer's or not, she was with him. If that wasn't what he wanted, so be it. But as long as he needed her, loved her, she'd be there for him.

The revelation came so forcefully that she rose to her feet. Fortunately, almost everyone was absorbed in the show and didn't notice. Erin, however, shot a glance in her direction, her expression questioning.

She leaned down. "I'm fine. I just have to make a phone call."

Her friend's brow furrowed, but she didn't ask for details. She merely nodded and gave a little shooing motion with her hand. Rory didn't need to be told again. She slipped from the room just as they were starting to name the possible suspects.

SAWYER HAD TO ADMIT, he was having a great time. Gavin's idea of a paintball-war bachelor party was great. It was the most fun he'd had in ages. He and Gavin were already several points ahead of the other guys, but no one was worried about keeping score. They were way too focused on seeing how many times they could pop each other with the paint pellets to keep a close tally.

Connor, as the groom, had become their main target. He wore multiple splatters on his vest, but no one was cutting him from the game.

Sawyer was taking a momentary breather, hunkered down behind a shelter of stacked steel barrels, when his phone rang. He pulled it from his pocket and checked the caller ID, a smile playing around his lips as Rory's face appeared on the screen.

"Hey," he answered. "Shouldn't you be in the thick of murder plots right now?"

Her reply stunned him.

"I love you."

"What?"

"I love you," she repeated, her accent slightly pronounced, probably due to the rise in emotion in her voice. "I can't remember if I've said it since you came back. I was afraid to, at first. It felt like it would give you too much power over me, but I realized I don't want to hold it back anymore. So I had to tell you right away. I love you."

The words were an arrow, directed straight at his heart. "I love you, too," he declared. "I never stopped."

"Neither did I. I just…buried it, for a while."

They were silent for a few seconds. Sawyer could hear the other guys laughing and hollering some distance away. He ignored them.

"I know you're scared."

Her words were so soft that he pressed the phone closer to his ear.

"I'm not scared," he argued, but he knew it was a lie.

"Yes, you are. You're afraid that your life is over. But Sawyer, you don't know how much time you have left. None of us knows that. How is this any different?"

He felt a touch of irritation at her question. "Because *I* know how things will play out if this happens."

"You don't."

"I do. What happens if I start to forget things? What do I do if I can't remember who you are anymore?"

There was a pause on the other end. That short gap confirmed Sawyer's fears. He wanted Rory to be able to tell him he was being ridiculous, but he knew he wasn't.

"Sawyer, you're borrowing trouble. We don't know you're going to get Alzheimer's."

"We don't know that I won't. Is that really what you want? To watch me forget you, forget me, forget all the things that make life worth living?"

"I love you," she stubbornly declared. "No one said we get everything we want when we choose to love someone."

"But if you have that choice, Rory, are you sure you want it to be me?"

"Maybe I *don't* have a choice. Maybe I can't help loving you. Maybe I never could."

He leaned his head back against one of the barrels, his emotions twisting in confusion. He wanted her. He needed her. But because he loved her, he didn't know if he could ask this of her. He didn't think he could ask it of anyone, much less the woman who had already poured so much of her life into his.

"Sawyer?" she whispered.

"Sawyer! Where are you hiding at?"

Gavin and the guys were calling him.

"I love you," he said. "I love you more than you know, Rory." He couldn't make her any promises about the future. All he could offer her was that one, simple truth. He loved her.

"Sawyer—"

"The guys are calling me. I have to go."

"Can we talk about this more when I get back?"

"I don't want this ruining your night." *Or your life.* "You just focus on having a good time with Harper and the girls."

"But—"

"I better go. The guys are waiting."

He ended the call before she could respond, and then he put his head in his hands and let the weight of worry settle on his shoulders once more.

CHAPTER FIFTEEN

"SORRY, PERLE, BUT I'm not interested."

His manager scoffed. "Sawyer, darlin', you best quit burying your head in the sand. This is no different than the press release. People are going to start reporting on your situation whether you like it or not. At least, if we take the bull by the horns, we have some say on how and when the news gets out."

Sawyer pinched the bridge of his nose and tried to keep his tone even. "I don't want to talk about it."

"Sorry, sugar, but that's no longer an option. The word is out, and your fans want details."

He knew she had a point. Booking him on a national talk show to discuss his father's diagnosis was probably a smart move. It would bring more attention to him and his music. He supposed, looking at it from Perle's perspective, all of this was a potential gold mine. Even though it bothered him, he knew Perle was right. He couldn't keep trying to hide from the world. His reality had changed. At some point, he would have to change along with it.

"What are the details?"

Perle filled him in on the when and where of the interview. He'd have to fly to Los Angeles for the taping of the show.

"Which brings me to my next point," Perle said. "When are you coming home, Sawyer?"

His gut reaction was to retort *I am home*, but he knew that wasn't fair. Perle had been more than patient during his hiatus in Findlay Roads. He couldn't stay here forever, at least not without giving up on his career as a Nashville star.

"I'm in a wedding tomorrow," he announced, buying himself more time.

"Not your own, I trust? Because I'd want to sell the photos—"

"No," Sawyer interrupted, his heart aching at the thought. "No, not mine. A friend's."

"So you'll be back in town on Monday?" she persisted.

His first thought was of Rory. How he'd say goodbye. How he'd explain. He wasn't sure where they stood anymore, him and her. He wasn't sure about anything.

"Yeah, something like that."

"I need you back here, Sawyer," she insisted. "I understand your need for a break, but it's been weeks. We have studio time scheduled, and we need to coordinate with the guest artists who will be performing on your next album."

"I know, I know." When he'd first come to Findlay Roads, he'd been looking forward to more studio time, getting back to the heart of the music. He'd been hoping to get inspiration from Rory and the promise of a new beginning with her. It was hard to believe how much he'd lost in such a short time. "I'll be back sometime next week."

"I'm going to hold you to it, darlin'." She launched into another agenda item, reviewing some deal she'd landed for one of his singles to be featured as the theme song of a new television show. In some distant part of his consciousness, he recognized that it was a boon, but he had a hard time wrapping his head around the details. Everything felt foggy and that made him worry that his mind was somehow compromised, and that this was only a hint of what was to come.

"Listen, Perle, that sounds great, but I've got to run. Email me everything I need to know. I'll shoot you a text when I'm back in town."

She began to protest, but he rushed her off the phone with the promise to check in soon. When he ended the call, he placed his face in his palms. It was comforting, in a way, to know that good things were still happening for him.

But what about the future...and Rory?

What would happen when he left Findlay Roads and returned to Nashville? What kind of life could he offer Rory now? For all his fame and fortune, he couldn't promise her any sort of stability. Asking her to love him felt selfish. And how could he ask her to give up everything—her life in Findlay Roads, her job, her proximity to family—to move to Nashville and...what? Be a witness as he started to lose himself? Become his nurse and caretaker? That was never the life he planned for himself, and it certainly wasn't a life he was prepared to offer Rory.

SAWYER WAS SITTING outside when his dad found him. He hadn't bothered to dress after his phone call with Perle so he was still wearing his pajamas. He'd gone outside after their conversation, dragging a lawn chair out beneath the oak tree in the backyard. It was the same tree he and Chase had climbed as children, the one his dad had attached a handmade swing to so they could sway back and forth beneath its branches in the summer breeze. The swing was gone now, but Sawyer still saw it in his mind's eye. He became obsessed with the image, trying to recall every detail. It had been painted a royal blue, but the color had faded with time. The paint began peeling, and beneath it were chips of pale yellow wood. There had been some sort of trim on the edges, but he couldn't remember if it was orange or red. His drummed his fingers on the lawn chair's armrest as he tried to recall such a vague and forgotten detail. Orange or red? They had played on that swing for hours at a time. Why couldn't he remember the color of the trim? It was an inconsequential detail but one he felt he should know. He dug his fingernails into his palm and squeezed his eyes shut.

Red. It had to have been red. His dad had an old workbench in the garage that he had painted with the same color. Definitely red.

But what if it hadn't been?

"Sawyer?"

He opened his eyes, surprised at the sound of his dad's voice. He'd been so caught up in trying to pinpoint the memory that he hadn't heard his father approach.

"Oh, hey, Dad."

"Hey there."

His dad started to sink to the ground but Sawyer got up and insisted he take the lawn chair instead. Sawyer settled himself on the ground and did a quick inspection of the older man from the corner of his eye. He found it strange that his dad didn't look that different. If he studied hard, he could guess that his skin was a bit too pale, and his eyes a little bloodshot...but other than that, he still looked like Ford Landry. He wondered if that would change, as time went on. If the disease would immobilize his dad's countenance like it would paralyze his mind.

"How are you feeling this morning?" Sawyer asked.

It was an awkward question. It wasn't as if his dad had stomach pain or a fever or headache.

"I'm all right," his dad assured him. But Sawyer wasn't reassured. He wasn't all right. He'd never be all right again.

But Sawyer didn't want to say this aloud. So instead, he just said, "Good."

They sat in silence for a bit longer.

"Your mom told me you're going to be a groomsman in Connor's wedding, and that you'll be paired with Rory."

"Yeah." After his conversation with Rory, he wasn't sure how he felt about that anymore. When he had first come back to town, he couldn't have imagined anything better. Now, he worried Connor would regret asking him.

"I've missed that girl."

"Me, too," Sawyer admitted and then experienced a moment's panic, wondering exactly which point in time his dad was talking about. Did he know they were in the present day or was he living in a past where Sawyer and Rory had been on the road for a while?

"So, what are you gonna do about it?"

Sawyer blinked. "What? What do you mean?"

"You came here to win her back, didn't you?"

Sawyer felt a swell of relief at this question. At least they were living in the same moment. But he didn't know how to reply to the question.

"Seems to me you've been avoiding her lately."

Sawyer shifted uncomfortably on the grass, surprised that a man with Alzheimer's could be this observant.

"I know I embarrassed you in front of her the other day, son."

Sawyer's attention jerked to his father's face. His eyes were clear but there was a hint of sadness in them.

"Your mom told me what I did."

"It's okay, Dad. You didn't know."

Ford didn't respond right away. When he did, his words were thoughtful. "This disease is a funny thing. It steals in subtle, immeasurable ways at first. Like forgetting the time of year and not even knowing you did until later, when someone tells you." He looked right at Sawyer. "You're right, I didn't know. But I wish I had. I'm sorry."

Sawyer felt tears rising and looked away. He didn't want his dad to see him cry.

"It's not going to get any better, you know," his dad said. "And I don't think it's going to get any easier, either."

Sawyer blinked back the tears and swallowed hard so he could face his dad once more.

"I know, Dad," he admitted.

"I've taken care of my will. I named you executor when the time comes."

"Dad—"

Ford touched a hand to his son's head, as if bestowing a benediction on him. "I'm not out of this fight yet, Sawyer. I don't intend to be for some time. But no one puts off death forever. And when it happens to me, I'll be ready for it." He drew a breath, removed his hand. "I've had a good life with a woman I love and two amazing children, who have made me so proud. My only regret is not telling you that more often." He waited for Sawyer to look at him and held his gaze. "I'm proud of you, Sawyer. More than words can ever say. I admit, I was a little uneasy with the way you did things for a while. All that time chasing your music, never settling down, you and Rory both traveling all around the country just so you could keep performing the songs you loved."

He nodded, his expression turning introspective. "But it turns out you were wiser than I was."

Sawyer's lips parted in surprise. These were words he'd never expected to hear his father say. "Wiser? You've always been the wisest man I've ever known."

"Pshaw." His dad scoffed. "You're the one who recognized how important it is to pursue your dreams. I'm the one with Alzheimer's, yet you're the one who knew long before I did that life is too short not to go after what you want. You didn't do things the way people expected, but you forged your own path. And look where it got you."

Sawyer hesitated. "You're giving me way too much credit. I didn't do things as smartly as I should have."

"The way you and Rory split up, you mean?" He gave a short nod. "I don't know a single person who doesn't have regrets in life, not even the ones whose dreams came true. The point is, you're trying to make things right. You came back for her, and I'm trusting you admitted your mistakes and asked her forgiveness."

"Yeah." For all the good it had done them. He'd won Rory's heart but feared he was destined to break it again.

"People go after a lot of things in life. I suppose you've seen your share of it while living in Nashville. We pursue fame, fortune and transient things that never last. Not enough of us pursue what really matters. Like love."

"Love."

"Love," Ford confirmed.

The word held bitter connotations for him now.

"Go after Rory," his dad said.

"I'm not sure that's the wisest thing."

"Why not?"

Sawyer raised an eyebrow in disbelief. "I'd think you, of all people, would know why. How can I ask Rory to marry me, knowing what might happen? If I love her, how can I do that to her? It would be like punishing her for loving me."

Ford fell silent, and Sawyer felt a twist of guilt. He hadn't considered how the words might sound to his father, who was already living with a disease that was only a possibility for Sawyer.

"Dad, I'm sorry. I didn't mean for it to sound like you're a burden or anything."

"But I will be."

"Dad—"

"Sawyer, it's okay. I know what the rest of you are facing. Sometimes, I think Alzheimer's must be harder for the people who watch you go through it. They lose you, everything that makes you who you are, in the most slow and agonizing death, while your outer shell remains. It's a double death. The loss of this person you love, your memories and moments, and then, in the end, the physical death. It is a cruel way to go, and not just for the person dying."

"And you think you're not wise?"

Ford offered up a sad smile. "I think facing your own mortality can make anyone a little wiser."

They sat in silence for a bit until Ford cleared his throat.

"Listen, son, I wanted to say… I'm sorry."

"Sorry? For what?"

Ford scratched the back of his neck. "I know what you'll say, and you're right. It's not my fault. This disease isn't something I chose. It's not what I want, for me or for my family. But somehow, I can't help feeling partially responsible for the position it places you and Chase in, knowing that one day…" He trailed off.

"We don't know what will happen, Dad." Sawyer spoke the words, even though they weren't much comfort.

"Perhaps not," Ford conceded, "but I see how it's weighing on you. And I just need you to know that if there was any way I could spare you this…I would."

Sawyer's chest tightened with sadness. "I know that. And I don't blame you for this. Neither does Chase."

Ford gave a brief nod of his head. "You're good sons. I love you both so much—" He broke off as his voice cracked, and Sawyer reached for him, grabbing his hand in his own.

"We're going to be here for you, Dad. No matter what the future brings."

It took Ford a minute to bring his emotions back under control. "I appreciate that. I do. But I've also made arrangements for long-term care, to minimize the burden as much as possible. I don't want you worrying about me all the time. You need to live your own life, Sawyer. Marry Rory. Keep making music. Cherish all of your days while you have them so that when they're gone, you have as few regrets as possible. Promise me that?"

Sawyer hesitated. He could only promise

his father so much. He wanted to marry Rory. He wanted to keep making music. But what if those choices were taken from him?

When he didn't answer immediately, his dad continued, "I need you to know that I don't have any regrets. Not a one. Life offers no guarantees, and uncertainty is no reason to give up on the things that make life worth living. If I had to live my life all over again, there's not a single thing I'd change."

Sawyer swallowed. "Not even now, seeing what Mom is going through?"

His question didn't seem to bother his dad. Ford looked hard at him. "Marriage isn't easy, even on the best of days. But it's a commitment. For better, for worse. Sickness and health. Your mom and I didn't take those vows lightly. We considered what the worse and the sickness might look like. We might not have imagined this, but we didn't commit to each other blindly, either."

"But if you'd known about the Alzheimer's before you got married. What would you have done then?"

Ford considered, growing sober. "I'm not sure I know, Sawyer. I don't know what either of us might have decided in that case." He rallied, drawing a deep breath. "But love makes all the difference, doesn't it? If you love someone, you don't give up on them. Rory won't give up on you. Ever. You have that girl's heart, you always have."

The words should have buoyed him, shored him up. But they only made him more melancholy.

"Don't cheat either of yourselves by worrying about a future that might never happen." His dad released a sigh, a signal that he had exhausted himself on the topic. He made one more effort, though, and added, "Make me that promise, son. Promise me you won't give up on yourself, or Rory."

Sawyer chose his words carefully, not wanting to make a vow he couldn't keep. "I promise that I'll live my life the best way I can, not knowing what the future holds." It was the most he could give.

"Good. Now, stop wasting time hanging around here. Go get that girl of yours and do something fun."

"You're just looking for an excuse to take a nap," Sawyer teased as his dad's eyes slid closed.

"You're right about that," Ford replied. "This sunshine is putting me to sleep."

Sawyer smiled, but he didn't move. He just sat there beside his father as he dozed, trying to embed this moment into his memory to hold against the days ahead.

RORY MET SAWYER'S gaze across the small distance separating them in the backyard of the Moontide Inn. Harper and Connor were listening intently to the minister as he explained when they'd be reading their vows and exchanging rings, but Rory had tuned out the instructions to focus on Sawyer.

Her feelings were conflicted as she looked at him. He wore a casual, button-down flannel-print shirt, and his hair was tousled as if he'd run his hands through it a dozen times. He was watching the minister with an intent expression on his face, hanging on to every word as if this was his own wedding rehearsal. Rory's heart lurched at the thought. She knew he'd been struggling lately, especially after their phone conversation during the bachelor and bachelorette parties. But she was still hoping for him to come around. She'd made her decision. She wanted to be with Sawyer, no matter what. She wanted to marry him and care for him, should it come to that. She'd done her own research on EOA. The disease could strike at any time, as early as one's thirties, which she knew was Sawyer's greatest fear, but also into one's fifties or sixties. Most cases developed when the patient was in his or her forties or fifties.

It still didn't give her and Sawyer enough time. But she would take every minute God gave them, whether it struck him at thirty-five or fifty-five or anywhere in between...or not at all. They'd already been luckier than most. They'd been high-school sweethearts and other than the last two years, they'd been with each other ever since. Maybe that luck would continue to hold, and Sawyer wouldn't develop Alzheimer's. But even if that wasn't the case and the worst should happen, Rory still chose him, still chose to love and cherish him.

"Then there will be the exchange of the rings..." The minister continued to walk them through the ceremony step-by-step while Rory and the rest of the bridal party waited patiently in their positions on either side of the bride and groom.

Rory's eyes didn't wander far from Sawyer, though Gavin occasionally distracted her. He was making faces and trying to get Erin to laugh, as she attempted to remain serious. With his typical charm, he managed to get Weston, Paige's husband, in on the antics with him, and Rory caught Paige rolling her eyes in annoyance. But it was difficult to become truly irritated with Gavin. He just had one of those personalities, goofy but sweet, where you couldn't help laughing along with him, no matter how silly he became.

Erin finally broke, bending over with erupting giggles, and the minister paused to look their way. Erin coughed.

"Sorry, sorry. By all means, Reverend, continue."

She shot daggers at Gavin for getting her in trouble, but he raised his hands as if to say "I didn't do anything wrong here."

Rory felt her lips twitch with a smile. Erin and Gavin were such an easygoing couple. They loved and supported each other, made each other laugh. She wanted that. She and Sawyer had something similar once upon a time. And she believed they could get it back. If he'd just put aside his fears and trust her, trust their relationship—they could weather whatever came their way.

Her focus shifted again, and this time, she found Sawyer's eyes on her. She offered him a slight smile, and to her relief, he responded in kind. Her heart soared. His smiles had been too rare lately.

I love you, she mouthed, for him alone.

Love you, too, he mouthed back, and a part of her melted.

The pastor's words interrupted her thoughts

as he said, "I will then dismiss the wedding party, who will go back down the aisle in pairs, first Erin and Gavin, then Rory and Sawyer, followed by Tessa and Rafael, and Paige and Weston. I will then announce the bride and groom." He gestured to the chairs set up in neat rows on the lawn. "And Connor and Harper will head toward the back."

They all relaxed and broke ranks to mingle. Molly brought Kitt over from where they'd been playing in the grass. The pastor continued to give an overview of what would happen next, but Rory only listened halfheartedly as she found her way to Sawyer's side. She didn't wait for him to say anything, but rather stepped right up and stood on her toes to plant a soft kiss on his lips.

He smiled, and in that moment, she sensed no tension in him, no worry for the future. She breathed an internal sigh of relief.

"Hey."

"Hey," he replied with a broad grin and then leaned down to kiss her in turn.

She forgot where she was and wrapped her palms around his neck, holding him to her. He'd been sparing with his kisses in recent days, and she ached at the loss of them. After two years without his touch, she craved it now more than ever, wanted to make up for the time they'd been apart.

She lost herself in the feel of him, the way his arms slid around her waist. His lips were gentle on hers, and his thumbs stroked her back until she shivered.

A whistle pierced the air, and both she and Sawyer jumped in surprise, pulling apart.

"Seriously, guys, do we need to send you two on the honeymoon instead of Connor and Harper?"

Rory blushed as she realized the attention they'd drawn. At least Gavin had managed to make a joke out of it, relieving most of the awkwardness.

"I am *not* giving up my honeymoon," Connor announced, placing a possessive arm around Harper's waist and drawing her in for a kiss of their own.

"Then these two will just have to get married and book their own honeymoon," Gavin countered, crossing his arms over his chest and raising an eyebrow at them.

"Sounds good to me," Rory said, low enough that it was for Sawyer's ears alone.

She slid him a glance, but his expression was unreadable. He did, however, take her hand.

"One wedding at a time, guys."

"I agree with that statement," the pastor said

and wrangled them all in once more to go over final details.

Maybe it was Gavin's teasing about the two of them going on a honeymoon. Maybe it was simply the atmosphere, being surrounded by loving couples. Or maybe it was just the feel of Sawyer's hand in hers.

But whatever it was, Rory chose to trust in him and their future.

SAWYER DROVE HOME with a lighter heart than he'd had in a while. After the conversation with his dad, the wedding rehearsal and dinner and his time with Rory, he was feeling a little bit better about the future. He was strong. His family was strong. They could get through this. There was no reason they couldn't. If Rory was willing to have him, then he wanted nothing more than to spend the rest of his life with her. He would hedge against the future. He would plan for it. But he couldn't live his life in anticipation of something that might never happen.

He felt confident about his decision the whole way home, even humming a few notes of a song he'd been working on in the weeks before he'd returned to town. A tentative bubble of happiness grew, expanding and filling him with joy.

As Sawyer pulled into the driveway, he noticed Chase's car wasn't there. He hoped his younger brother was out having fun. He had always been the more serious of the two of them, but this Alzheimer's diagnosis had made him even more so. Chase deserved a break.

Turning off the ignition, he exited the vehicle. He didn't even make it to the walk before the front door opened, and his mom appeared on the stoop.

"Is he with you?" Her eyes were frantic, her silvery blond hair standing on end. She wore a faded sweatshirt, one of his dad's, he realized, the Baltimore Orioles logo worn to a pale shadow of what it had once been. She had her arms wrapped around herself. His stomach dropped, all the happiness he'd been feeling disappearing in a puff of concern.

"What?" He didn't know what she meant, but he automatically knew the question was in reference to his father.

She quickly said, "Chase is out looking for him now. We've been calling you."

Sawyer reached for his phone but couldn't find it. Had he left it at the restaurant, after the rehearsal dinner? No, he remembered letting Molly play with it while they were still at the Moontide. He'd forgotten to take it back from her. It must still be at the inn. He mentally berated himself for being so careless, placing himself out of touch from his family yet again.

"Mom, slow down. What's happened?"

"It's your father," she answered, confirming his worst suspicions. Her expression was pinched with fear. "He's missing."

CHAPTER SIXTEEN

CHASE HAD ALREADY called the police, and they had units on the lookout for Ford. Sawyer wanted to go out and join his brother in the search, but his mother was manic with worry. He was afraid to leave her on her own. He'd used the house phone to call Chase for an update and to apologize for not having his cell phone on him. His brother sounded calm, but he also detected the faintest touch of worry in his tone.

Chase explained that they'd been in the garage, finishing the painting Sawyer had begun. Their mom was out at the store. Their dad had gone inside to clean some of the paint items, rinse out the brushes and the like. Chase had been so busy finishing up that he hadn't realized how long their dad had been gone until maybe thirty to forty minutes had passed. By the time he went inside to check on him, Ford was gone with no clue as to where he went. There was no note and the sedan was still parked along the street. Since Sawyer was driving the pickup they knew he couldn't have taken that. Chase's car was still in the driveway, and their mother had the only other vehicle, and she was still out running her errands.

Now she sat at the kitchen table, her head in her hands, her shoulders shaking slightly with suppressed sobs. The wall clock's ticking was the only sound in the room, and with every tick, the apprehension grew. Sawyer had never been so aware of time in his life. Every moment his father remained missing was a chance for something to happen to him. What if he became so disoriented that he walked in front of a car? What if he wasn't disoriented at all, but had left on some mission to spare his family what was to come? What if he'd merely stepped out of the house for something and then gotten lost and was simply stuck somewhere, unknowing of where he was…or even who he was?

Sawyer thought he'd go crazy with wondering.

He suddenly noticed the white plastic bags deposited by the refrigerator door. There was a pale puddle forming beneath one of them. He moved closer and realized his mother hadn't even bothered to put away the groceries she'd picked up. The ice cream, dropped on its side, had melted and leaked through the bag.

For some reason, noting this was a relief. It gave him something to do besides wait for word from Chase. He began gathering up the abandoned foodstuffs, placing them in the sink to rinse clean. He scrubbed a container of orange juice, washing off the ice cream's sticky residue, and ran water over a bag of grapes until he was satisfied they were clean. He drew a sink full of water to wash some of the other items and then left them to dry on the counter while he used paper towels to swipe the ice-cream puddle off of the floor. He filled one of his Mom's glass serving bowls with soapy water to scrub the tile clean. It was only as he was finishing up that she stirred from her sorrow and noted what he'd done.

"Oh, no. Oh, Sawyer, I'm sorry." She was suddenly beside him on the floor with a clean towel, drying up the leftover water.

"It's okay, Mom, I've got it."

"No, it's not okay. It's not." She was trembling, from her fingers to her shoulders and down her torso. He experienced a moment of alarm.

"Mom." He tried to take the towel from her, but she kept a tight grip on it. "I told you I got it. It's fine."

"No." She pushed at him, and he was so surprised that his balance gave way. He toppled to the side as she kept trying to dry the remaining drops of water. "No," she repeated, "it's *not fine*. Nothing is *fine*. Nothing will ever be fine, ever again, do you understand me?"

It was only then that he sensed the break in her. The trembling became a convulsion as she bent over, forehead to the floor, and finally released her anguish. She sobbed onto the tiles, her tears wetting the surface he'd just cleaned. The sounds coming from her were horrible, grief-stricken wails, and he wondered just how long she'd had to hold all this inside her.

He moved then, easing himself back to a sitting position and bending over to wrap his arms around her. He didn't try to make her stand up, and he didn't try to make her stop. He just let her cry as he covered her back with his chest to remind her that he was there.

Shudders wracked her, and he felt each one vibrate through his midsection. He had to bite the inside of his cheek to keep from releasing his own tears. Right now he had to be strong for her.

When the sobs finally eased, he backed off and sat on the floor, resting his back against the fridge. His mom straightened, still sniffling but without the level of grief he'd just witnessed.

"I'm sorry," she apologized, her voice thick.

She cleared her throat. "I'm sorry you had to see that."

He didn't say anything. He was sorry, too, but not for the reasons she believed. His sorrow was for all of them, for the suffering they were in the middle of and the suffering to come. If anything, he was grateful for his mother's outburst. He had a feeling she'd needed it. But it also rattled him. Because his mother was one of the strongest, most stalwart people he'd ever known. She'd nursed both her parents through cancer. She'd miscarried twice before she conceived Sawyer. She was strong. Unbreakable. Seeing her like this shook him to his core. If his mom, of all people, could break…what chance did the rest of them have?

So instead of replying to her apology, he reached over and took her hand. She shifted to sit beside him, placing her back against the refrigerator and leaning into him. Her head came to rest on his shoulder. Neither of them spoke.

It was several minutes more before the phone rang, and they both scrambled off the floor to answer it. His mom reached it first, grabbed it off the hook and answered, "Chase?"

He watched her expression carefully, waiting to see what sort of emotion revealed itself. After a beat, relief stole over her features, and he felt himself release a sigh, his shoulders relaxing.

Still clutching the phone, she met Sawyer's eyes.

"He found him."

IT WAS WELL after midnight by the time they got his father tucked into bed. His mom went with him. Sawyer knew she didn't want to let him out of her sight again. He and Chase sat at the kitchen table after their parents had retired. Despite the late hour, Sawyer didn't think he could sleep. Not because he wasn't tired—he was exhausted. But rather because there were too many thoughts circling in his head.

Besides, Chase looked like he needed to talk, and after everything his kid brother had been through, he had no intention of leaving him on his own. Instead, he salvaged what was left of the melted ice cream and blended it into a milk-shake concoction. He squeezed in a fair amount of chocolate syrup and thought of Rory as he did. It always worked for her and her brother, so why not him and his?

He placed a glass in front of Chase, who sat at the kitchen table with a weary expression and bloodshot eyes.

Sawyer was curious, but he didn't want to push. When Chase brought their dad into the

house, it was obvious they were both emotionally drained. So their mom took over, is-
suing directions to get her husband into bed.
Chase didn't give them details, and they didn't
ask. But Sawyer wondered what had happened,
why their dad had disappeared and how Chase
had found him.

He took a sip of his milk shake, but the
sugary sweetness was more than his stomach
could handle at this late hour. He pushed it
aside. Chase didn't even touch his.

"He was at someone's house."

Sawyer straightened as his brother spoke.
"You mean, he was with someone?"

Chase ran a hand over his face, his exhaus-
tion evident. "Sort of. They took him inside
after he kept insisting it was his home."

Sawyer tried not to wince but failed. "Whose
house was it?"

Chase shrugged, obviously weary. "I don't
honestly know. They said he started pounding
on their door earlier this evening, and when
they answered, he kept telling them that this
was his home. So they finally let him come
in, and they fed him. They said he just seemed
more confused the longer he was there. He
didn't have any identification on him, no wal-
let or anything. So they tried calling around
to hospitals and nursing care facilities, but no

one was missing any patients or residents. Finally, they called the police, and that's how I found out where he was."

Sawyer sighed. "How far had he gone?"

"About two miles from here. The strip of houses along Carrick."

"Near the fire station?"

Chase gave a short nod.

"How in the world did he end up over that way?"

"He walked, as far as I could tell. I'm not sure where he thought he was going."

Sawyer considered. "Home, I guess. But why would he leave home to look for home?"

"I don't know, Sawyer." Chase slumped forward, resting his elbows on his knees. "I should have checked on him. I don't know why I waited as long as I did. I just didn't think. I mean, it never occurred to me that something like this might happen."

Sawyer reached out to place a hand on his brother's shoulder. "It's not your fault."

"Then whose fault is it?" Chase looked up, his eyes desperate. "If not mine then whose? Dad's? He can't help that this disease is stealing his mind. And it's not Mom's responsibility to watch him every second. You were away, and he was in my care. I should have been more responsible."

"Chase." Sawyer's tone was firm. "This is not your fault."

Chase opened his mouth to protest, but Sawyer forged ahead.

"This is no one's fault. It's not yours, or Mom's, or Dad's, or mine. You can't assume responsibility for things beyond your control."

Chase leaned back, breaking away from Sawyer's grip. "I should have kept a better eye on him," he insisted.

Sawyer wanted to protest further, but he could see that nothing he said tonight would make any difference. Chase was determined to shoulder the blame for what had happened.

"The important thing is that you found him," Sawyer insisted. "Listen, you've had a long night. Why don't you head to bed?"

Chase shook his head. "I'll never be able to sleep."

"You should still try. Things will look better in the morning. I guarantee it."

It wasn't the truth. He couldn't make any such promises. But he hated to see his brother agonizing over what had happened. Chase still hesitated.

"I've decided, Sawyer. I'm going to have the DNA test done. I—I have to know. I can't live like this, uncertain about whether I'll end up like Dad or not."

Sawyer understood, but at the same time, his stomach pinched at the thought. "What will you do…you know, if you have the mutated genes?"

"I don't know," Chase admitted. "But knowing has got to be better than always wondering about it."

Sawyer wasn't so sure he agreed, but it was a decision they each had to make on their own.

"I'll go with you," he decided. "Not to have the test, but just to be there. For moral support."

Some of the tension in Chase's shoulders eased. "Really? I'd appreciate that."

"Sure. We're family, Chase. No matter what happens."

Chase nodded. "Family," he agreed. "No matter what."

Sawyer waited for Chase to leave the kitchen before he let the tears flow.

"He's on the way right now," Rory promised for the third time and ignored Paige's exasperated look by pretending to fiddle with ribbon wrapped around her bridesmaid's bouquet.

Connor and Harper's wedding was starting in ten minutes, and there was no sign of Sawyer. Rory had tried his phone so many times she'd lost count, but it went straight to voice mail with each and every call. Paige was nearly apoplectic.

"But *why* isn't he picking up?" she demanded. "He should have been here an hour ago!"

Rory didn't have any answers, and her own concern was growing with each passing minute. She'd tried the phone at the house, but that call had gone to an answering machine.

"I can drive over to his parents'," Gavin suggested, placing his back toward Paige so that Rory could focus on him. "I can see what's going on."

Rory recognized her own concern reflected in Gavin's eyes.

"The wedding starts in ten minutes. It won't make any difference."

Paige must have heard her because she caught a glimpse of the other woman throwing her arms up in the air. Tessa and Weston moved in to do damage control.

Gavin locked eyes with her, and neither of them said anything. Seconds later, Connor stepped up. Rory had to admit that he was devastatingly handsome in his suit and black tie. He'd been growing his hair out for a few weeks, so that now it curled around his ears. He looked rather like a dashing pirate. Harper was going to swoon when she saw him.

"Mind if I have a word with my sister?"

Gavin nodded. "I'm just going to wait out front of the inn, to see when he pulls up."

Rory rubbed her palms over her bare arms. The weather was perfect for Connor and Harper's outdoor wedding, but she couldn't help feeling chilled in her sleeveless bridesmaid dress. Erin was inside with Molly and Harper, adding finishing touches to the bride's hair and veil. Harper had known thirty minutes ago that Sawyer hadn't showed up yet, but none of them had told her he still wasn't here.

Rory nibbled on her lip, barely paying attention to her brother until he raised his hand and tapped her forehead.

"There. Right there."

She stopped fidgeting and stared at him.

"What?"

"That worry mark right there needs to go."

She blinked. "Aren't *you* worried? This is your wedding, after all. And Sawyer's just bailed on you."

Much in the same way he bailed on me two years ago.

"He hasn't bailed," Connor stated with such confidence that her jaw dropped.

"You don't think so?"

Connor shook his head.

Her brother's lack of concern was surprising. Part of her anxiety had been because she knew Connor had extended a hand of friendship to Sawyer, by asking him to be part of the wedding, and now, with his would-be groomsman nowhere in sight, he still kept his faith in Sawyer.

"Wh-why do you say that?"

"Because he loves you. And he'll be here. Not for me. Not for Harper. But for you."

Rory didn't know what to say. Her brother's words filled her up and gave her a hope she didn't know she'd been lacking.

"Are you sure?" she murmured.

"Without a doubt. I was angry at him for hurting you, but the way I've seen him with you since he came back…he's here for you, Rory."

"But, everything with his dad, and the Alzheimer's…" She trailed off, and Connor didn't say anything, not at first.

"I won't say I'm not worried about the two of you. If things turn out for the worst, you and Sawyer would be in for a tough road."

Rory drew a breath. "I know, but… I love him. No matter what. I love him."

Connor wrapped her in his arms and held her tightly against him. "I know. And I think you'd be far happier with him, no matter what happens, than you would be without him."

She returned his embrace by circling her arms around his waist. "I need him, Connor. No matter what we're facing, I need him in my life."

Connor pressed a gentle kiss to the top of her head. "I know, love. I know."

She surrendered then, just letting herself be held and feeling a swell of joy in knowing what her brother was gaining on this day. He would have Harper now. Some of Rory's responsibility for him, as his sister, had just transferred to her. But she was glad. Harper would love him to her dying breath. Rory had nothing to worry about on that score.

She pulled back a little to look at his face. "I'm happy for you, you know. You deserve Harper, the restaurant, all of it. You've worked so hard. I'm just…grateful how things turned out."

"Me, too."

They looked at each other for a moment longer, sharing things that only siblings can through words that didn't need to be spoken.

Seconds later, Gavin approached them.

"Sawyer just pulled up."

CHAPTER SEVENTEEN

SAWYER STRAIGHTENED HIS tie as Gavin met him at the front door of the inn.

"Cutting it a little close, aren't we, bro?"

Sawyer didn't reply. Gavin might have been his best friend, but he didn't think he could explain things, even to him. Fortunately, Gavin didn't press the issue.

Rory was waiting for him in the bed-and-breakfast's foyer. He came to a halt at the sight of her. She wore a knee-length turquoise dress that complemented her dark hair and fair skin. Her hair was pulled up with a braid winding its way around the crown of her head and ending in a coiled bun at the nape of her neck. A white daisy was tucked behind her ear. She was breathtakingly beautiful. So much so that he physically ached at the sight of her. Was she truly so lovely today? Or was it just his mind torturing him after the decision he'd come to in the wee hours of the morning?

Of course, she would appear even more beautiful on the day he'd decided to give her up.

Despite this, he stepped forward to brush a strand of loose hair behind the flower. She shivered beneath his touch, and he felt a line of heat wind its way up his palm.

"You're going to draw attention away from the bride," he murmured.

She smiled and ducked her head. "I'm glad you made it," she whispered and then lifted her eyes to catch his own. She seemed happy. His heart twisted as he realized he'd be taking that joy away from her soon. But he'd made his decision. This was what he had to do, for her sake more than his own. If he loved her, he had to let her go.

"It's about time you showed up!"

He watched Rory wince before he raised his head and focused his attention on Harper's older sister.

"The wedding starts in *five minutes*," Paige snapped. "So nice of you to make it on time."

He nearly laughed in the woman's face. His measurement of time had completely changed in the span of the last few weeks, and particularly over the last few hours after he'd witnessed how easily it could be distorted. His father had begun to jump back and forth, confusing the years, losing track of days and events. If that was Sawyer's future then he was going to start viewing time very differently.

"Well, you wouldn't have started without me, I'm sure," he teased, and he was pretty sure he might have seen steam coming out of Paige's ears. He ignored her and turned to Connor instead, as the groom approached.

"Everything okay?" Connor asked, directing the question at Sawyer. He expected Rory's brother to be irritated, if not outright irate, but he didn't seem in the least flustered by his late arrival.

"Everything's fine," he lied. "I'm sorry I'm late. I didn't mean to stress you guys out." That much was the truth. But after the late night, he'd overslept. They all had.

Connor waved a hand. "I didn't have any doubts you'd make it."

And then Connor looked at Rory, something unspoken passing between them. Sawyer wasn't sure what he'd just witnessed.

"Well, now that we're all here," Connor said, "does anyone have any objection to getting this wedding started?"

It was a perfect ceremony, in Rory's opinion. Though everyone else turned to look at Harper when the "Wedding March" sounded, Rory kept her eyes on her brother. And she knew the second Harper appeared because she saw it in Connor's face. His entire expression suffused with joy, his countenance glowing. He suddenly had eyes only for his bride, and his face conveyed love and awe. It brought tears to Rory's eyes, which she dabbed delicately with a tissue. Erin had warned her not to go smearing her makeup.

She shifted her attention to Sawyer and was surprised to find that instead of watching the bride, like everyone else, he was focused solely on her. She smiled at him, and he returned the gesture…but there was something sad in it. She was reminded all over again of the weight he carried. But she was ready now. No matter what the future held, they would face it together.

She knew, even without Connor telling her, that Sawyer loved her. She'd always known it, deep in her soul. It had just taken her a while to trust again. Perhaps that's why she'd never really let go. She had known, somehow, that he'd come back for her. And he had.

Alzheimer's couldn't keep them apart. Should it come for him, they would face it together. She would hold on to him as long as she could, fight for him with every breath. If the disease wanted him, it wouldn't claim him without a long and fierce battle from her. She longed to tell him that, but she couldn't, not right now. Harper was stepping up to the front, and Rory's gaze shifted as Connor stretched out his hand for her.

It felt as if the ceremony went quickly. Connor and Harper made their vows with Molly standing between them, and Harper spoke special vows just to the girl, claiming her as a daughter and making a promise to be the best mother she could. Molly beamed, and a part of Rory felt a tiny sting of loss. She would no longer be the first woman Molly looked to in the future. Harper would fill that role. It was as it should be, and Rory was glad for the kind of mother Harper would be. But she couldn't help feeling a strange little stab of grief just the same. It was the end of one thing and the beginning of something better. Change wasn't always bad, it was just different.

She released a breath as she felt Erin's hand reach for hers, squeezing lightly. Her friend knew how she felt. And she was grateful. She was surrounded by love, with everyone she cared for right here, in this moment while her brother committed his life to his soul mate.

This was the happiest she'd been in a long time.

SAWYER WAS HAPPY for his friends, but he couldn't help feeling a slight touch of bitterness. Everything about the wedding and the hours that followed had been perfect. The ceremony was beautiful. Connor and Harper obviously made a wonderful couple. Their love and commitment was evident in every word they spoke, every gesture they made and every look they shared.

At the reception, their affection was even more apparent. In fact, Sawyer felt surrounded by romance—nearly suffocated by it. Paige and her husband had barely left the dance floor. Harper and Connor were kissing every five minutes as the wedding guests dinged their forks against their champagne glasses. Gavin and Erin were seated next to each other, Gavin's arm draped tightly over Erin's shoulder. Not that Sawyer begrudged his friend. Gavin would be shipping back out in a few more days—he deserved every minute he could get with Erin during his downtime.

The rest of the guests were all paired off, dancing or drinking, laughing and loving. A wedding was not the place to be when your heart was breaking. But that's exactly where he'd found himself.

He stood apart, leaning against the wood-and-iron railings, watching the party and occasionally glancing out over the bay. Rory was on the dance floor, leading both Molly and Kitt in an awkward version of the "Macarena."

Kitt couldn't quite master the choreography, and Rory and Molly had to keep starting over with him.

He could only look at Rory for a few seconds at a time. It hurt too much otherwise. He wished he could go back by a month and never have returned to Findlay Roads. It would have been so much easier on both of them if he'd stayed away. He never would have tried to rekindle things if he'd known then what he knew now. It would have been far more merciful to let her go on thinking the worst of him, that he'd ditched her for fame and fortune.

He couldn't stay with her. He couldn't ask her to marry him. He couldn't condemn her to the uncertainty of the future. His mother's tears from the night before had haunted him through the midnight hour and into the light of day. He couldn't shake them. His father hadn't remembered anything this morning, but he'd been chastened when he'd heard what had happened. His dad's embarrassment was made worse by his mother's insistence that it was all right.

He had seen the grief she tried to keep hidden from his dad. He would not condemn Rory to that. He couldn't bear to think of her hiding her sorrow for him should they end up in the same situation.

He didn't doubt she loved him, which only

made this so much harder than he could have anticipated. Either way, he seemed likely to wound her. His options were to hurt her now, before too much damage was done, or later, after their lives became interwoven even more.

Better to cut things off while she still had a chance of recovering and moving on. She would find someone else, eventually. Maybe this time, it would be different. One day she would understand that he'd broken things off with her not because something better waited for him, but because there were better things out there for *her*. Surely that would bring some consolation and healing to her heart.

And if he could do that for her then perhaps he could find some measure of peace for himself, as well. To do right by Rory was the best legacy he could leave. She was the one. She'd always been the one. She'd been with him for so much of his life's journey, had cheered him on, had stood by him. The only way he could think to return the selfless gift of her love and friendship was to let her go.

He knew there was the possibility he'd never develop Alzheimer's. He could even have the test to be certain one way or the other, but he'd found he wasn't strong enough to do so. If he didn't have the mutated genes, it would be a relief…but what if he did? Then he'd live his entire life just waiting for symptoms to develop. He'd wake up every morning fearing that was the day he'd begin to lose himself, his memories, his mental cognition. He couldn't live like that, with the cloud of inevitability hanging over his head. At least, this way, he still had the hope that the disease would pass him by.

But he couldn't ask Rory to live like that. He wouldn't. Especially after the way he'd left her two years ago, placing his needs before hers. He wanted her to have the opportunity to escape a tenuous future and find a life that wasn't overshadowed by the threat of sickness and death.

And yet, letting her go hurt. It hurt so much more than learning his dad had Alzheimer's. It was far more painful than facing a future where he might have the disease. The worst thing he had to give up in this was Rory. But he loved her more than his own need. This time, he would do the right thing.

He felt tears rising and blinked rapidly to stop them. He was facing the water, his elbows resting on the rail, when her arms slipped around him from behind. He knew it was her, by touch alone. How many times had she embraced him just like that? More than he could count, and yet he held each memory precious because it was all he'd ever have of her now.

He shifted, turning so that she could find her way into his arms.

"You okay?" she asked.

There was no easy answer to that question. So he didn't give her one, but rather tightened his arms around her, drawing her close to him and pressing a fierce kiss against her temple. He could allow himself that much, couldn't he? Or perhaps he was being selfish once more.

"Why don't we take a walk?" he suggested, whispering into her ear.

She nodded, but he couldn't see her face. Did she suspect what was coming? If she did, he wasn't sure she'd have gone with him so willingly. He took her hand, and they made their way around the dance area and toward the steps leading down to the boardwalk fronting the restaurant. From there, they headed for the promenade. The dusk of the evening was waning into twilight, and the iron lamps illuminated the wooden walk before them. The breeze was coming off the bay, cool and strong, but it did little to chill the heat of disappointment churning in his gut.

They were quiet as they walked, and Sawyer kept the pace slow. He was in no hurry to have this conversation. He would cherish every second he had with Rory, knowing these would be the last. When they were finally some distance away from the restaurant and the reception, he knew the time had come.

Stopping, he turned to face her. She watched him, her expression curious and slightly concerned.

"Sawyer, are you okay?" she asked again, her voice a whisper nearly stolen by the wind.

"I'm leaving. On Monday."

"Oh." He watched her struggle with his news, trying to figure out what it meant.

"When will you be back?"

He didn't reply, and the first hint of doubt crossed her features.

"Sawyer." She said his name clearly, with a touch of force. "When are you coming back to Findlay Roads?"

"I don't know," he replied, which was the truth. He knew he'd be back for his dad, to help his family, but those details had yet to be arranged. "But when I do come back—" he drew a breath, his heart pounding double time as he forced out the words "—it won't be for us."

"But you will be back, right?"

It was as if she hadn't even heard him. He didn't think he could bear to say it again.

"Rory, I'm trying to tell you that…it's over." A knot of despair lodged in his throat, nearly stealing the words from him. "We can't do this again, you and me."

"You're joking, right?"

He shook his head. "I'm sorry, but we're done. For good this time."

A spark lit in her eyes, a flare of denial.

"What are you doing, Sawyer?"

"Look, this was a bad idea. I should have known better than to return here and try to get back together with you. We're just not meant to be. It was worth a try, but this—" he gestured between them "—you and me? It can't work."

"Why not?" she demanded, and he loved her more than ever in this moment. Because she wasn't going down without a fight. She wouldn't be cowed into submission, into giving up. He could see it in the way she squared her shoulders, as though preparing to do battle.

He had already made his choice. He wouldn't put her through this. But if there was anyone in the world that he could choose to fight beside him in this war, it would be her. She was so fierce, and her eyes blazed as she dared him to offer up the truth.

"Because your life is here, and mine is not. I have a career and friends in Nashville—"

"Stop." She took a step forward, jaw set tight. "If you're going to break up with me, at least come up with a better excuse than last time."

It was a fair enough request. He owed her more than that.

"Fine. The truth is that I can't do this, Rory. I can't worry about me and you, too."

"Worry about *me*?" Her tone was incredulous. "You're unbelievable. What in the world did I do wrong?"

Nothing, my love. Absolutely nothing.

"If we keep at this, you're going to have to move to Nashville. And you won't be happy there. You know you won't. How can I focus on my career and my music, if I'm worried about you being miserable?"

"You're creating problems that aren't even there. I'm happy wherever *you* are," she reminded him. "We were nomads for years, never staying in one place, always moving on to the next gig. I didn't need anything or anyone but you. You were my home. As long as I was with you, I was happy. Nashville won't change that."

Her words burrowed into his heart and soul, and he decided that he would fight for them. If the worst happened, and he developed Alzheimer's, these were the words he would fight to keep—that he had been loved so much.

"I can't do this," he repeated. "We had a

nice few weeks, and it was great to reconnect with you. But it's time to be realistic. This was a fool's game, from the beginning. It's all my fault. I shouldn't have come back here stirring things up. I think I was just feeling nostalgic. It was selfish, and I'm sorry."

She shook her head. "Are you telling me you don't love me anymore? Is that it?"

This was the hardest part. Because he could lie in so many ways to spare her the future. But he didn't think he could lie about how he felt.

"Rory," he began, trying to sidestep the question, "it doesn't matter what we feel. Because we just aren't meant to be."

"It does matter," she countered. "Because that's the entire point. You love me. I wasn't sure of it before, but I am now."

He felt a twist of frustration. Why did she have to make this so hard? "How? How do you know?"

"Because you're trying to break up with me to spare me if you get Alzheimer's."

He didn't know why he thought he could get away with this. She could see right through him. She had known him too long and loved him too well.

"Why can't you just walk away?" *For your own good, Rory. Please walk away.*

"Because I love you, too."

The words nearly undid him. She loved him, more than he deserved. She'd loved him through nearly two years of silence and self-ishness. She'd loved him as a boy, trying to find himself. She'd encouraged his passion for music, believed in him before he believed in himself. She'd waited while he was in the army and thrown in her lot with him when he came back and decided he wanted to start traveling the country, playing music wherever he could. She had been by him through so much, and he knew she'd be by him if the worst should happen.

But for once, he wasn't going to be the self-ish one in this relationship. Just this once, he was going to do right by her.

"Rory." His voice was hoarse, thick with emotion. "We can't be together."

"What if you don't even have the disease?" she persisted. "What if all this is for nothing?"

"If it frees you to fall in love with someone who deserves you, then this isn't for nothing."

"I already love someone who deserves me. Just like I deserve him. I'm not afraid, Saw-yer."

"But I am." It was a hard thing to admit, but there it was. He was scared beyond measure about the future and his greatest fear was see-ing Rory as his mother had been last night. "I don't want to live like that. I can manage this, if it's just me I'm worrying about. I can't do it if I have to worry about you, too."

"Then what will you do? Go back to Nashville, make your music and do like you did for the last two years, forget that I exist?"

"Yes," he countered, his frustration mounting. "Yes, that's exactly what's going to happen, and that's the point. There's a good chance I will forget you one day. I won't want to, and I'll hold out as long as I can, but eventually, my memories of you will be erased. And I don't want you to look at me when all I see in return is a stranger." He took a step closer, his words urgent. "That's why I'm doing this now before it's even harder."

She took a step back, tears filling her eyes. "You're a liar." Her voice was accusatory, low and hard. "You promised me you weren't going to leave me. You won my heart all over again, only to break it a second time."

"I know. And I'm sorry."

He could have said more, so much more. He could have told her that she would be the memory he'd hold on to the longest. She would be the reason he kept going, fighting off this disease for as long as he could, if it came to that. But he didn't want to stop the anger he saw rising in her. If Rory could find her anger, she could walk away. If she could hate him, she could let him go.

"You're going to be fine," he said, as much to assuage his conscience as to reassure her. "You're smart and talented and stubborn. You'll be all right."

She didn't respond. She just looked at him. The wind was pulling at her hair, dragging several tendrils free from her braid to flutter against her cheeks. She wrapped her arms more tightly around herself. He didn't know if it was the breeze off the bay or sadness that made her shiver.

"You really think it's so easy? Letting someone go?" she asked.

He swallowed. He knew that it wasn't. But what choice did he have?

"It's easier than trying to hold on to them, when everything falls apart."

She shook her head, her expression both pained and angry. "Shows what you know. Love was never meant to be easy, something you walk away from when times get tough. Those who talk about true love like it's something out of fairy tales or movies, who think the path is smooth from the moment you find the person you're meant to be with—they're wrong. People forget that true love, *real love*, takes work. It's being with someone even when things get dark and ugly. That's when love becomes true." A single tear slipped down her cheek and then another. "I wish you'd been brave enough to believe that for us."

And with that, she turned and walked away, leaving him desolate and alone once more.

CHAPTER EIGHTEEN

SAWYER SAT BACKSTAGE, waiting for his segment on the *Morning View* talk show. The makeup girl had come around twice to pat the shine from his forehead. But it was more than nerves causing him to perspire. He'd felt this way ever since leaving Findlay Roads three days ago. It had been difficult to say goodbye to his friends, especially when Connor thanked him for being part of the wedding. It had been harder still to leave his family, but he promised to be back for doctor's appointments and decision making. Bidding farewell to Gavin had made him nostalgic for the simple lives they used to lead when they were younger.

And Rory. He didn't get to say goodbye to her, which he supposed was appropriate given that their ending had come when he'd told her they couldn't be together anymore. He'd seen her one last time, before leaving the reception. Her expression had been full of hurt, her gaze accusatory. That was his last image of her, and the one that had haunted him in the days since he'd flown to Nashville and then to L.A. for this interview.

"You're on in five, Mr. Landry," a producer's assistant wearing a headset informed him.

He shifted on his seat, wiping his palms on his designer slacks. What was wrong with him? He'd never minded these interviews before. In fact, he'd relished them, enjoying the opportunity to talk about his music and the future. But perhaps that was the problem. The future was so uncertain now, and he couldn't find any joy in speaking of it.

He suddenly ached for Rory, wishing she was there with him. She'd place a steadying hand on his arm, give him that smile of hers and let him know, without speaking a word, that he could handle this.

But he had to learn to manage without her. It was the selfless thing to do. And the last thing he wanted was to be selfish where Rory as concerned.

"Mr. Landry, if you'll follow me, they'll be introducing you after this break."

Sawyer stood and followed yet another production assistant into the wings. He waited, listening as the show's hosts, Camille and Kirk, listed his accolades by way of introducing him to their viewers.

"And most recently, the winner of American

Heartland Radio's coveted Artist of the Year award, we'd like you to give a *Morning View* welcome to Sawyer Landry!"

The production assistant gave him a nod, and he drew a deep breath, pushed back his shoulders and stepped out onto the stage. The audience applauded enthusiastically, and he waved in their direction, offering a smile that felt too false, too strained. He then shifted his attention to the show's hosts, gracing Camille with a kiss on the cheek and Kirk with a handshake, before they gestured for him to take a seat on the plush, gray suede couch. He seated himself and waited for the applause to die down. It took some time, and Camille and Kirk finally had to gesture for the audience to wrap it up.

At last, it was quiet enough to speak. He exchanged pleasantries with the hosts, thanking them for inviting him on the show and then talked about his recent award win. As he spoke, he continued to feel unsettled, fearful of missing a step in conversation, or forgetting a word or name, anything that hinted of Alzheimer's rearing its head and tripping him up.

But the interview seemed to be going well, and he felt he was articulate on the topic of his next album and upcoming plans for his musical career. It was then, however, that the topic shifted.

"Now, Sawyer, you just recently announced to the world that your father has been diagnosed with early onset Alzheimer's," Camille began, her voice softening in sympathy.

He swallowed hard, but a knot of grief still remained lodged in his throat. "Yes, that's right," he replied and noted the gravelly catch in his voice.

"Now, for our audience members who aren't familiar with this disease, it's a form of Alzheimer's that develops much earlier in life," Kirk explained.

Sawyer nodded. "I've been told it's much rarer than the more common form. It strikes only about five percent of the population."

"And it's hereditary, which means that you might inherit it from your dad," Kirk added.

Sawyer had known this would be a topic in the interview. In fact, it was part of what had gained him a coveted spot on this couch. Having won Artist of the Year didn't hurt, but throw in the Alzheimer's angle, and he was a hot commodity for an interview. Or so Perle had told him.

"That's correct," Sawyer replied, making every effort to keep his voice steady.

"How does that make you feel," Camille

asked, "seeing your dad going through this and knowing you might be next?"

The studio audience had hushed, and the air felt weighted with anticipation of his response.

"It's scary," he admitted, trying to separate his emotion from his words in that moment. "But you can't live your life in fear of the future. And there is an option to get tested and find out if I have the genes that cause the disease."

"Is that something you plan to do?" Camille asked.

Sawyer shook his head. "I've decided I'm better off not knowing. It's difficult, thinking that it might be a part of my future. But for me, I think it would be worse if I was certain of it. It would consume my thoughts. I'd be waiting, day by day, for the symptoms to strike."

It occurred to Sawyer that this wasn't so different from what he was doing now. If he had chosen not to have the test in order to live with the hope that he might not ever develop the disease, then why was he still so focused on it?

"Now, in your awards speech, you thanked someone named Rory. We've come to discover that she was your girlfriend and musical partner for years, and that you two recently reconnected."

A prickle of heat washed over Sawyer's skin.

He hadn't anticipated this. Rory wasn't supposed to be up for discussion. But then, he'd named her publicly at the AHR awards and had been seen with her by the reporters at the Alzheimer's support group. He'd done absolutely nothing to keep their relationship private. He should have expected that her name would be dragged into this eventually.

The two large flat screens on either side of the interview area lit up with images of him and Rory from years past. He felt sick to his stomach. How had they gotten hold of these photos? He didn't even recognize some of the pictures. They must have been sent in by friends or fans or people who had seen them perform at some point.

A more recent image appeared, one of him and Rory onstage at the Lighthouse Café. Obviously, someone in the audience had been taking photos. Sawyer had never even considered the possibility.

"From the people we've talked to, the two of you have only very recently reestablished your relationship. Did she know about the Alzheimer's diagnosis when you reconnected?"

His chest felt tight. It was difficult to find air. "Um…well, no. I didn't even know about it at the time."

Camille clucked her tongue in sympathy.

The sound grated on Sawyer's nerves. "How does she feel about all this? I imagine this sort of thing could put quite a strain on a relationship."

Sawyer thought about the question. He probably should have told them the truth—that he and Rory were no longer together. But he couldn't find the words to speak it aloud. Maybe because the truth was that Rory had handled all this far better than he had. She wasn't the problem. He was. He was frightened and not just of losing himself to Alzheimer's. He was scared of putting her through it, too.

"Sawyer?"

His mind had wandered, and he hadn't answered Camille's question.

"I'm sorry...what did you say?"

Camille flicked a quick glance at her co-host. Kirk cleared his throat and jumped in.

"We were just wondering how Rory feels, knowing that you might end up with Alzheimer's one day?"

"I guess that's something you'd have to ask her," he said. But as he spoke these words, he felt a hitch in his chest. He wouldn't answer this question in Rory's stead. How she felt was up to her. But then, hadn't he made all the decisions for them by himself up to this point? He'd taken away her right to choose by forcing her out of his life, all in the name of protecting her. But was that love? Not giving her the opportunity to love him for whatever time they had left? She'd been right, after all. The Alzheimer's wasn't a guarantee.

So why was he living as if it was a done deal?

"I can't speak for Rory," he said, "but I can tell you that she's a strong person. One of the strongest I know." He felt emotion force a lump into his throat. "She's loyal and loving, and she has this Irish stubborn streak that drives a man insane." His lips twitched. "But that's part of where her strength lies. She doesn't give up easily."

She'd never given up on him. Not once.

"If there was ever a person you wanted to stand beside you, come what may, she'd be the one."

Camille had tears in her eyes, and he heard several sniffles in the audience.

"That's a lovely testament to how special this woman must be. It seems like you love her very much."

He suddenly realized how much of himself he'd revealed on national television.

"All of this sounds like a song on your next album," Kirk said, giving him the chance to lead into a discourse on some of the songs he had planned.

But even as he spoke about what his next hit single might be, Camille's words repeated in his head.

It seems like you love her very much.

He couldn't deny how much he loved Rory. But love just wasn't enough.

"THAT WAS FANTASTIC," Camille raved at the end of the show. "One of the most touching interviews we've ever had. Wouldn't you agree, Kirk?"

Kirk was punching away on his phone, obviously having tuned out of the conversation as soon as the show wrapped up. "Hmm? Oh, yes, amazing stuff. So glad you could join us on the show, Sawyer."

"Thanks," he automatically replied, "it was a pleasure being here."

Camille faced him, offering an eye roll in Kirk's direction. Her co-host had already turned his attention back to his phone. "Don't mind him. I swear, he even showers with that thing."

Sawyer's lips quirked upward. He didn't mind Kirk's inattention. In fact, he couldn't wait to say his goodbyes and call for a car to take him to the airport. The interview had been a positive experience but a draining one.

"We'd love to have you back again in the future, Sawyer. Can we contact your manager about setting something up?"

"Of course, that would be great."

"Wonderful." Camille leaned in and placed an air kiss on his cheek. "You know, you've got something."

He gave her a questioning glance. "Something?"

"You know. Not just the 'it' factor but something more. I think that wherever you go or whatever you do, Sawyer Landry, you're going to be a success."

It was an odd statement, especially on the heels of the issues they'd discussed on the show.

"Um, thanks. I appreciate that."

Camille's smile was genuine, but before they could chat further, his phone rang. It was probably Perle checking in.

"Excuse me, I should take this."

Camille pointed a thumb in Kirk's direction. "It's okay. I'm used to it."

Sawyer gave her a nod and thanked her again before answering his phone as he stepped toward his dressing room.

"Hello, this is Sawyer."

He expected to hear Perle's voice on the other end of the line. He hadn't even looked at the caller ID because he'd been so certain it would be her. So he was stunned to hear Rory's voice in his ear, her words thick and garbled as if they had a bad connection. He couldn't understand a word she said, though he recognized the rich tone of her voice. It immediately made him miss her, an ache that went deep into his soul.

"Rory? What? I can't understand you."

There was a pause on her end. A creeping dread stole over him. Rory wouldn't have called him after the way he ended things if it wasn't serious. Life-and-death serious.

"It's Gavin," she choked out, and though her voice was thick with emotion, he heard the words clearly enough.

"He's dead."

SAWYER HADN'T EXPECTED to find himself back in Findlay Roads so soon. But Rory's call had sent him racing back. As soon as he got off the phone with her, he'd called the airlines and changed his flight, rerouting it from Nashville and back to Baltimore. Chase picked him up and drove him back to their parents' house. His family offered their condolences but didn't press him to speak. It was too much in too short a time to learn he was losing his father, perhaps his brother and even himself, and then to lose Gavin on top of it.

It wasn't supposed to be this way. Sure, Gavin had been a military man, and there was always an element of danger in protecting his country. But that was the worst part—Gavin hadn't even died doing the job he loved so well. He'd been killed by a drunk driver, on his way to the airport to head back to the base. There would be no medals for him. In his death, he had become little more than a statistic.

And that, perhaps, was what angered Sawyer most of all. Because his friend had been more, so much more. To have his life cut short on the bad choice of a man who had chosen to get behind the wheel intoxicated was beyond a level of injustice that Sawyer could comprehend.

He was so angry on behalf of Erin and Kitt, the wife and child left behind. He had to curtail this emotion at the funeral when he saw them. Erin was remarkably poised for someone who had suffered such a devastating blow. He approached her in the receiving line, but when he stood before her, he had no words to offer. They looked at each other, conveying their grief in a silent exchange before he reached out and folded her into his arms.

"You were his world," he whispered and felt a shudder pass through her. "Don't you ever forget that."

When she pulled back to look at him, tears were brimming in her eyes. "You were his best friend," she replied. "Time and distance didn't matter. He never thought of you as anything less."

He nodded, his own eyes filling and overflowing. She didn't know how much he'd needed those words, how desperately he needed to be reminded that Gavin had never seen the last two years as a failing of their friendship. Because, for the rest of his days, Sawyer knew he would regret not taking the time to stay in touch.

"If there's anything you need, you or Kitt or Aunt Lenora, call me."

She nodded and squeezed his arms. He leaned forward and kissed her forehead. He knew he had to give others the chance to share their condolences. But for just one moment longer, he held on, knowing that this was the last link to his friend. After this, he truly had to say goodbye.

Erin let him stand there as long as he needed until the lady behind him cleared her throat. Only then did he pull away. Lenora and Kitt were off to the side, separate from the receiving line. The old woman sat in a chair since her arthritic knees wouldn't support her to stand for long. Kitt was leaning against her, his pale face somber. He was so young. Would he have any recollection of his father to cherish growing up? He suddenly felt an odd kinship with the boy. They both faced the threat of disappearing memories.

He went to him and kneeled down on one knee. Kitt shied away. He didn't know Sawyer that well. Sawyer had been gone for so much of the boy's childhood.

"Hey, Kitt."

He buried his face in Lenora's skirt.

"Your dad was my best friend." His voice caught. "I'm sorry, buddy. I'm so sorry."

He glanced at Lenora, her faded blue eyes filled with tears. "I'm sorry for your loss."

Lenora nodded and reached out a hand to rest on his head. "You won't forget him."

He blinked, wondering if she knew what she was saying.

"You were his friend, and you'll remember."

It was almost as if she was offering up something prophetic. He didn't know if it was her advanced age speaking or her grief, but he didn't disagree with her. Instead, he squeezed her twisted, arthritic fingers in his, and offered her the same kiss to the forehead that he'd bestowed on Erin. He stepped away from her and nearly ran into Rory, who had obviously been waiting.

He wanted to touch her, to wrap her in his arms and hold her. Let his grief and hers combine, let them hold each other up. But if he touched her now, he'd never let go. Rory's eyes were bloodshot, her face paler than usual. The dark sweep of her hair, brushed over her shoulder, only accentuated the dark smudges beneath her eyes. She was obviously as grief-stricken as he was.

"Harper and Connor wanted to fly back from Ireland, but Erin insisted that they not cut their honeymoon short."

He nodded in understanding. Erin would have plenty of support in the immediate days, but she would need her friends more than ever when the business of the funeral and settling Gavin's will died down.

"She asked us to sing."

He blinked. "She…what?"

"She asked us to sing for Gavin. At the graveside, when they inter the body."

He didn't know if he could keep his emotions in check to sing for his friend, especially if Rory was beside him.

"It was…a request of his."

"A request? But…he…"

She shook her head. "It was part of the instructions he had written up after his last deployment. He arranged the service of his funeral, should anything happen to him while he was overseas."

Sawyer felt grief clutch his chest. His friend had known that death was a possibility. He had lived with it, prepared for it, accepted it. It made Sawyer feel weak and cowardly in comparison.

"What song?"

"'The Parting Glass,'" Rory softly replied.

Sawyer swallowed hard. It was the most mournful but beautiful song he knew. Rory and he had only performed it a handful of times, the most important of which had been the night before he and Gavin had shipped out for army basic. The four of them—Sawyer, Rory, Gavin and Erin—had gone down to the shore for one last bonfire together. Gavin was the one who'd encouraged Sawyer to pull out his guitar and asked him and Rory to sing the song.

Of all the thousands of times he'd sung before an audience, dozens upon dozens of songs, he couldn't think of a single performance that would be more difficult than this one. But if his friend had asked it of him, if this was his last request, then Sawyer would do it.

"Are you up for it?" he asked Rory, focusing on her tear-filled eyes and the lines of grief carved around her mouth. He wished he could hold her, kiss every one of those lines away.

She squared her shoulders. "I can if you can," she said, a spark of resolve lighting her eyes.

There was that fire he knew so well, and he marveled at her strength. She was no quitter, his Rory.

His Rory.

But she wasn't his. Not anymore.

THICK GRAY CLOUDS had stolen across the sky by the time they reached the graveside for Gavin's interment. Rory thought the dismal weather was fitting. It was as if even nature mourned the loss of their friend. She held tightly onto Kitt's hand as Erin and Lenora each took a turn laying flowers on the coffin.

Her throat was tight with grief, and she didn't know how she would loosen it in time to sing the song Gavin had requested. She wasn't sure what weighed on her more—Gavin's death or seeing Sawyer again, knowing that she'd lost him as well. She supposed that was an unfair comparison. Gavin was gone, suddenly and far too soon. Sawyer still lived, even if he'd made it clear they weren't meant to be together. But the truth was, it all felt like too much loss. Her heart was heavy with it, her spirit weighted in the mire of grief.

She glanced down at Kitt, who had been so quiet ever since Erin told him about his father's death. She didn't know how much he comprehended or if the reality of death had sunk in yet. Gavin had been gone for a lot of Kitt's young life, and maybe this felt no different to him. But Rory sensed a somberness in the little boy that indicated he was more aware of what had happened than any of them realized. She made a mental note to check in on Kitt as much as she would on his mom in the coming weeks.

She realized Erin had taken her seat across from the grave and was searching for Kitt. Rory led him to her and then stepped back.

The officiating pastor took his place and spoke a few words about life and death and the hope of the hereafter. Some scriptures were read, and a prayer was offered. And then the service was turned over to her and Sawyer, for the final song.

She looked across the casket and caught his eye. No matter what had happened between them, they would come together, one last time, to do this for their friend. She stepped across the grass, and Sawyer met her at the head of Gavin's casket.

He had his guitar in hand. He must have picked it up somewhere between the funeral and the trip to the cemetery. He lifted the strap over his head and tested a few chords before he began playing.

The first few notes went straight to her soul, taking her back to the night she and Sawyer had sung this same song before he and Gavin had left for the army. She remembered her emotions that night, her gratitude and love for her friends, as well as her uncertainty for the future. She'd been young and unsure, so in love with Sawyer but worried about where this road would lead them. In all her wildest imaginings, she had never seen life leading them here, to the casket of their friend Gavin, who had loved so well and brought such laughter. She had never considered that someone with so much life and vibrancy would be the first of them all to pass on.

Her heart was so heavy, the ache in her throat so thick, that after several introductory chords, it was Sawyer who sang the opening lyrics of the song. She closed her eyes and let the sound of his voice soothe her ravaged emotions.

Of all the money that e'er I had
I spent it in good company
And all the harm I've ever done
Alas, it was to none but me.

And all I've done for want of wit
To memory now I can't recall
So fill to me the parting glass
Good night and joy be with you all.

Here was where Sawyer's voice finally
failed, turning throaty and cracking on the
final words. Rory drew her breath, gathered
her strength, and took up his place.

If I had money enough to spend
And leisure to sit awhile
There is a fair maid in this town
That sorely has my heart beguiled.

Her rosy cheeks and ruby lips
I own she has my heart enthralled.
So fill to me the parting glass
Good night and joy be with you all.

Rory opened her eyes and looked at Erin,
but her friend's gaze was focused on the coffin,
her lips buried in Kitt's hair as she held him
on her lap. Grief rose anew, but then Sawyer's

voice joined with her on the third verse, and she found the will to keep singing.

Oh, all the comrades that e'er I had
They're sorry for my going away
And all that sweethearts that e'er I had
They'd wish me one more day to stay.

The guitar's sweet chords stopped, and Rory paused as she looked at Sawyer. He had stopped playing, and tears were running down his cheeks. But both of them kept singing, joining together in a cappella harmony on the last four lines.

But since it falls unto my lot
That I should rise and you should not
I'll gently rise and softly call
Good night and joy be with you all.

She and Sawyer paused and then joined together, repeating the last line with finality.

Good night and joy be with you all.

CHAPTER NINETEEN

Sawyer knocked on the front door of the inn and waited. He had a plane to catch later that day, but it didn't feel right leaving without talking to Erin, to convey his condolences in private, without any other mourners around. He stared down into the bouquet of flowers he'd brought, a mix of blooms he'd picked up from a local florist. The colors were bright and cheerful, and it occurred to him that maybe he should have chosen something more subdued.

It was too late to go back now, as the door to the inn swung open. Kitt stood there, his eyes wide with curiosity.

"Hey, buddy."

Kitt abruptly turned and abandoned his post, but left the door wide open. Sawyer knocked again, stepped inside and called out, "Hey, can I come in?"

Erin appeared around the corner dressed in a pair of jeans and one of Gavin's old army T-shirts. She wasn't wearing makeup, and her face was pale, but her eyes were only faintly red-rimmed. He took that as a good sign.

"Hey, Sawyer," she greeted. "Come on in. I'm sorry about Kitt. He's been a little skittish ever since—"

Sawyer held up a hand. "It's okay. You don't have to explain." He held out his other hand with the bouquet. "These are for you."

She brightened at the sight. "Oh, thank you." She moved forward to take them from him, burying her face in the petals for a moment. "These are lovely. It will be nice to have a few flowers with color around here. A lot of the ones we've received are kind of...dull."

He instantly felt better about his choice of bouquet. Erin started moving in the direction of the kitchen, and he followed.

"Want something to drink?" she offered. "Aunt Lenora made iced tea this morning. Her special lavender-black-tea blend."

"Sure, that sounds good."

He entered the kitchen and sat himself at the table, waiting while Erin put the flowers in a glass of water.

"We're all out of vases," she explained.

She grabbed two more cups from the cupboard and filled them with tea from the fridge. She picked up a paper plate piled high with cookies and covered with plastic wrap and set it on the table along with their two glasses of tea.

"People have been bringing lots of food by," she explained. "We have more casseroles, cakes and cookies than we can eat."

She sat down across from him.

"I suppose you're heading back to Nashville soon?" she asked.

He reached for the tea, taking a sip of the sweet, cool liquid and enjoying the bite of black tea and the notes of lavender.

"I am," he confirmed as he set the tea back down. "But I wanted to stop in before I left and see if you needed anything."

"Thank you," she said, her tone genuine. "I appreciate that, but I think we have everything we need for the time being."

He nodded and reached for his tea again.

"We're going to miss you, you know."

He paused with the glass halfway to his lips, looking over its rim at Erin. Something in her tone said she wasn't just referring to her and Kitt. There was a lot of emphasis on the *we*.

"I'll miss you guys, too," he said.

She watched him a bit too closely for his liking, but he ignored the look and concentrated on peeling the plastic wrap off the plate of cookies.

"Rory's been coming by. She was here this

morning, playing with Kitt. She only left a short while ago. You just missed her."

"Hmm." His heart sped up at the thought of how close he'd come to seeing her again. He told himself he'd made his peace without her because that's what was best, but with his every breath, he knew that was a lie. But he wouldn't burden Erin with any of this. She had enough to carry now.

He expected her to press him about Rory, given his noncommittal response. To his surprise, she didn't.

"It's been a rough month, hasn't it?" Erin spoke the words as more statement than question, and they caused him to stop messing with the plastic wrap.

"Yeah," he agreed. "It has."

They were silent for some time, each with their own thoughts.

He finally found the courage, and asked, "Do you regret it? If you could go back, knowing that he would die and leave you a widow with a little boy…do you think you'd have made different choices, about marrying him? About falling in love?"

Erin stared at him, her expression fierce. "No. No, I wouldn't change a thing." Her answer was so firm, so vehement, that it surprised him.

"I didn't mean—"

"I know you didn't," she interrupted. Her expression softened a little. "I would have had far more regrets if he had died, and I had never been with him. I will take every minute of the life we had together and treasure it." Her eyes filled with tears as she held his eyes. "No one can take that away from me, Sawyer. No one. I will have the memory of every kiss, every dance, every joke to get me through this."

He was struck again with how selfish he'd been with Rory. Though he'd tried to break free of her for her own good, he was really only denying her the memories that he was so afraid to lose for himself. He never considered that those were the very memories that would sustain her, should the worst happen. He was the one who might develop Alzheimer's. Not her.

Erin wiped at the tears on her cheeks. Sawyer tugged a napkin free of the table's holder and handed it to her. She took it and soaked up the tears.

"You never know about death," she murmured. "You can plan for it, try to prevent it and pray for it not to darken your door, but it has its own timetable, and none of us knows when that is. The only weapon we have against it is how well we live until it comes for us."

Her words buried themselves into his spirit. "Gavin was fearless in that regard," he said. "He lived well."

"Yes, he did," Erin agreed, still watching him closely. "And I think the best way we can honor his memory is to keep on living as well, as much as we can manage."

He recognized what she was trying to tell him, and he knew she was right. He hadn't been living very well in the wake of all that he'd learned. He'd been running scared, letting fear dictate his choices. When would he stop and have a little more faith in himself?

And in Rory?

The first rays of hope began to break through. He could live his life, with or without Alzheimer's. He could live right up until it broke down his last defense and dragged him under. He could live how Gavin had, as Chase had pointed out—never taking a minute for granted. He had the ability to turn this thing on its head and use it to his advantage. Let the disease make him more aware. Motivate him to do the things he might have put off otherwise. Remind him to tell the people he cared about just how much he loved them.

He could make Rory his wife and fit a lifetime of loving her into whatever years he had left on this earth. And in that, he could honor his friend's legacy.

He raised his tea, holding it in the air until Erin lifted hers as well.

"Here's to Gavin. He was brave and true, a good friend, husband, father."

Erin tapped her glass to his, her lower lip trembling.

"To Gavin," she replied, "and to love."

Sawyer reached for her hand and squeezed it to let her know she wasn't alone.

"To love," he repeated.

RORY DIDN'T KNOW what to make of the invitation. She'd heard Sawyer would be performing a benefit concert in town. It was the beginning of a partnership he'd formed with a national Alzheimer's association, to be a spokesperson for funding efforts on their behalf. Or so she'd heard. Findlay Roads had been astir for the last two weeks with talk of the performances. Sawyer must have pulled in several favors because there were some pretty well-known acts being featured. The town had entered the height of the summer season, and the streets were filled with vacationers from DC, Baltimore, even New York and New Jersey. The concert was set to take place the following weekend, on the last Saturday in June. The event had been advertised everywhere, and Rory was pretty sure the tickets had sold out days ago.

But she held in her hand a special VIP pass for a front row seat with a handwritten note attached.

Please come.

Two simple words, and he'd signed his name. It was cryptic, mysterious and, if she was honest, it left her a little breathless. He'd asked her to come to the concert, arranged a special seat.

But why?

He'd gone into radio silence ever since leaving town after the funeral. She hadn't heard even a whisper from him, and when she casually asked Erin if she'd had word, her friend had only looked at her sadly and shaken her head. She didn't want Erin's pity, especially since her friend was going through the grieving process, so she hadn't asked again.

But she'd still wondered about him. There was little mention of Sawyer in the news at the moment. She'd broken down and started doing daily web searches on his name. He was back in the studio, from what she could tell. The most she found was information on his newly formed partnership with the Alzheimer's organization. She was proud of him for that last bit, recognizing that stepping up and becoming a face for the disease had likely been a scary prospect. But he'd conquered that fear to do what he felt was right.

She only wished he'd been able to do the same for the two of them. She shrugged off the thought and looked again at the invitation.

Please come.

Two little words, and he thought she'd come running? He didn't know her so well after all. She tossed the invitation in the trash and walked away. She tidied the kitchen. She reorganized her closet. She picked up a magazine and then threw it back down.

Then she went and retrieved the invitation from the trash, tacking it on the refrigerator along with his note.

Please come.

THE ENTIRE PARK had been cordoned off for the benefit concert. Sawyer was both impressed and humbled by the efforts of every person involved. The Alzheimer's association had organized the event, and the local chamber of commerce had assisted with the details of sectioning off the venue. There were rows of chairs, donated by various charities both in Findlay Roads and beyond, assembled to seat over two hundred people along with tickets sold for standing room only. Local police and firefighters were serving as security. Record label sponsors had assisted in providing the stage and equipment, and Sawyer was touched by how many of his musician friends had agreed to perform without commanding their usual fees.

All in all, the event was already a success. It had generated a substantial amount of buzz, and the tickets had sold out quickly. He was moved by what had been accomplished in so short a time.

"Looks like it's going to be a promising turnout."

Sawyer shifted to look at his dad, who stood with him behind the stage, watching as the ticketholders began looking for their seats. The concert was set to begin in the next half hour. Interspersed with the music, patients with Alzheimer's, both early onset and common, would be sharing their stories. His dad was scheduled as the first to speak.

"Looks that way. You nervous?" Sawyer asked.

His dad considered. "Ask me again in a half hour, when all those seats are filled."

Sawyer grinned. "You're going to do great."

His dad paused. "If I forget my words up there, just promise you'll come rescue me."

Sawyer grew serious. "It's a deal." He

paused. "You know I've got your back, Dad, right? Always."

"I know it."

They stood in silence a moment more.

"Sawyer... I have to tell you something."

"Yeah?"

"You've done good, son."

The words hadn't been what he was expecting. "Well, I think *we* did pretty good, putting this all together."

"No." Ford shook his head. "You did this. You took something dark, something you feared, and found a way to bring it into the light. No matter what this disease takes from us...you found your own way to fight back. Don't ever underestimate that. You're still a soldier, Sawyer. You're just fighting a different war. I wish Gavin were here to see it."

Sawyer drew a breath, feeling the familiar sharp pain that he always did when Gavin's name was mentioned. He didn't think he deserved quite the credit his father had given him, but it was true—he'd found his own way to fight.

Now all he needed was the one person who mattered most fighting beside him.

He looked out into the growing audience, his eyes zeroing in on the empty chair in the front, with the special reserved sign and her name. What if she didn't come?

"She'll be here."

Sawyer's gaze slid back to his dad's.

"She'll be here," Ford repeated.

Sawyer didn't reply, but he turned his attention back to that single seat in the audience and willed Rory to appear.

SHE WAS LATER than she'd intended. Although she'd never been one to fuss over what she wore, she'd changed outfits no less than four times, and now she found herself running late. She cursed her indecision, especially since she'd ended up choosing the green sundress, paired with white strappy-heeled sandals. She never wore heels. And it was obvious why, as she rushed toward the park and nearly tripped. She could hear a crowd in the distance, applause and the rumble of conversation. There was the screech of a microphone, and she could tell the event had already started.

She picked up her pace, still struggling in her heels, and finally grew so frustrated that she stopped and tugged them off, carrying them by the straps and ignoring the rough sidewalk beneath her feet.

It was a relief to dig her toes into the grass when she reached the park. She approached the cordoned-off entrance and presented the special ticket. She expected the handler to simply wave her through, but he studied her ticket for a long minute before gesturing to someone else. They came over, and he spoke words that Rory didn't hear.

The next thing she knew, she had a personal escort into the venue. She felt herself blushing as her private usher led her up the main aisle. It felt as if two hundred pairs of eyes were watching as she took her seat in front of the stage.

She turned to thank her escort, but he had already headed back up the aisle. Settling into her seat, she drew a breath, trying to still the rapid beating of her heart and enjoy the show.

The man onstage was talking about Alzheimer's and the program lineup for the evening. As far as she could tell, he was with the national Alzheimer's organization that had helped put together the event. Her eyes scanned the stage, but she didn't see a sign of Sawyer. She fought a little bubble of disappointment and had to remind herself that he'd make an appearance eventually.

She did her best to concentrate on the speaker as he listed facts and statistics about Alzheimer's. It seemed as if he would never cease speaking, and she tried to glance around to see if the rest of the crowd was growing as impatient as she was. Most people seemed to be listening with rapt attention, and Rory released a slow breath.

Still, it took effort not to fidget until the introduction finished, and she heard the words she'd been waiting for.

"And now, let me introduce the man who helped bring us all here tonight. Findlay Roads's own Sawyer Landry."

Rory sat up straighter, her mouth going dry with the anticipation of seeing him again. When he finally stepped onstage, her breath caught in her throat. He was dressed in a T-shirt with the Alzheimer's foundation logo and a pair of stonewashed jeans. He wore cowboy boots, and a white straw cowboy-style hat. The simple, casual look still left her breathless.

How was it that it had only been a few weeks since she'd seen him last, and yet it felt like an eternity? And then, her heartbeat sped up as Sawyer looked out into the audience…straight at her. His eyes fell on her face, and his entire expression brightened with a grin. For the space of a few heartbeats, it was just the two of them as the rest of the world fell away. And then, from her position in the front row, she heard the introductory speaker clear his throat, pulling Sawyer back into the present. He faced the rest of the crowd and introduced himself to a round of wild applause.

Sawyer didn't look at her again before he introduced the opening performer. But she soon found herself caught up in the music and the stories that were being told. After the first artist performed a couple of songs, Sawyer stepped back out onto the stage. Grabbing the mic, he held it for a long moment, as if struggling to find the words to begin. The crowd waited patiently, the atmosphere growing hushed as they anticipated what Sawyer had to say.

At last, he cleared his throat and began. "I have the extraordinary privilege of introducing our first speaker this evening. He is a man of wisdom, and someone I've admired my whole life. I could tell you some of his story myself, about the struggles of an Alzheimer's diagnosis, especially when you're young enough not to expect it. But he puts it into words so much better than I ever could, and I just hope that one day..." Sawyer broke off and turned away from the mic, and the muffled sound of him clearing the emotion from his throat could be heard. Rory clenched her hands in her lap, feeling his struggle as if it was her own. She wondered if that would ever change. Would there ever come a day she felt disconnected from him? Or would it always be like this, an invisible cord that bound them together, despite time, distance and silence?

Sawyer faced the mic once more.

"If the time comes when I'm facing what he's up against, I hope I can do it with half the grace and determination I've seen him exhibit. I'd appreciate it if you'd all give a huge round of applause to my dad, Ford Landry."

The crowd went wild, and Rory found herself whistling and cheering along. As Ford took the stage, he didn't head straight for the microphone, but rather for his son, engulfing Sawyer in a long hug. The sight moved the audience so much that almost as one, they stood to their feet, still applauding for the obvious bond between father and son. Rory was as moved as the rest of them, thinking that love like this was something Alzheimer's could never really destroy. It might take recognition, the ability to remember the simplest of skills and family memories, but it couldn't change how a person felt. And Rory felt certain that even once Ford no longer remembered the things that mattered most, he'd still be able to recognize the love his family felt for him.

It was several long minutes before the audience took their seats once more, and Ford began speaking.

Rory listened with rapt attention as Ford talked about what it was like when he first began experiencing symptoms. How at first, he chalked it up to forgetfulness, but then how he soon began to realize there was something more going on. She brushed tears from her eyes when he revealed how he'd started to keep notes to remind himself of people, places, everyday tasks or directions. And then he talked about his family, and Rory realized, with more clarity than she had before, exactly why Sawyer had held so much back from her.

"I've come to think of my Alzheimer's as a thief," Ford explained. "It's stolen its way into my life, into my house, into my marriage, and all my relationships. It plans to take whatever it can, and no matter how vigilant I am, I know that it will succeed." He drew a long breath, and the crowd sat, listening intently. Rory couldn't hear a single sound other than the distant lapping of waves on the bay, the rattle of the metal flagpole and the flapping of the American flag that stood in the center of the park.

"I wake up every morning now, and the first thing I do is seek out my wife. I look at her face, trying to etch it into my memory. And she looks back at me, unflinchingly, because she understands that she is my strongest weapon against this. I am using her to keep myself tethered to my mind and my memories for as long as I can. But as in any war, there are casualties, and I fear she will be the greatest. Because we both know that one day, I will look at her and not know who she is. On that day, I fear she will think we've lost."

There was a lump in Rory's throat. This was what Sawyer feared. Not only that he would lose her, but that she might one day also face life without him, long before either of them had intended. So he'd tried to cut things short, spare them both as much pain as possible.

Tears filled her eyes. Stupid, stupid man. Did he not know? She would rather take one day with him than a lifetime without him. She wasn't naive. This journey might be the most difficult they would ever make together. But all she had ever wanted was to be with him, no matter how short or how long that time might be. Look at Erin and Gavin. She doubted they'd expected to be severed from each other so soon. But she also knew that Erin had no regrets for loving Gavin as she had.

She tried to focus on Ford once more.

"The thing I need my wife to know, as well as all of you, is that we have not lost…as long as someone is still fighting. I am praying for a cure for this disease, but I doubt it will come in time for me." Ford gripped the mic, his gaze sweeping the audience. "But if you fight for me, after I cannot fight for myself, then I believe that one day…we will win." He gave a nod, as if approving his statement. "Thank you."

The crowd was on its feet once more, but Rory couldn't move. She sat in her seat, tears streaming down her face, and wished there was some way to get through to Sawyer, to let him know that she wouldn't give up on him, that she was strong enough to go through this with him.

Why had he asked her to attend today's concert? Why had he gone to the trouble of a front-row seat? Did he want her to witness these testimonies? Was he trying to drive his point home on why he'd broken up with her again? If he thought this would scare her away then how little he knew her. She wasn't afraid of the future. She was afraid of losing whatever time she had left with him.

She rode a roller coaster of emotion for the next hour, the personal stories bringing tears to her eyes and the music lifting her spirits. Sawyer made a couple of appearances during the concert, performing several duets with the other artists there. But he never held the stage for long, and she grew restless each time he disappeared again. What was she doing here? She believed this concert was a good thing, and she was enjoying it. But why subject herself to the frustration of seeing Sawyer when she didn't even know why he'd asked her to come? Did he have any idea how hard this was, to see him and know he'd decided they couldn't be together?

As the concert began to wind down, she grew even more restless, wondering if Sawyer planned to seek her out after it was over or if she should just head home. Perhaps she should duck out early, before the end. That way there would be no awkwardness or uncertainty.

But just as she had nearly made up her mind to leave, the man from the Alzheimer's association announced the final song of the event. He introduced Sawyer once more, but to her astonishment it wasn't just Sawyer who took the stage. Her jaw dropped as the kids from the youth center trailed behind him on their way to the front. They were all smiles as they zeroed in on her. It was obvious they knew where she was sitting and had been eager for this moment. And it was clear to her Sawyer had something else planned.

She leaned forward in her seat, her heart humming with hope. No way was she leaving the concert now.

CHAPTER TWENTY

SAWYER DIDN'T USUALLY experience a lot of nerves anymore when he performed. But today, he was twisted into knots as he made sure the youth-center kids each took their place. He couldn't look in Rory's direction, but from the way the kids were beaming toward the audience, he knew she was still out there.

It was only after they were all assembled, and his band took up their instruments, that he grabbed the microphone and looked for Rory.

"First of all, I want to thank you all for coming out and being a part of this event with us. As someone who has a personal link to Alzheimer's, I can't tell you how grateful we are for your support."

The words fired up the audience and a round of applause swept through the crowd. He raised his hand to quiet them, and gradually, the enthusiasm died down.

"I'd also like to share my heartfelt thanks for each of the artists who performed here today. They've given their time and talent to this event to raise awareness and funds for a worthy cause. I'd especially like to thank my friends here onstage." He gestured to the kids from the youth center. "These are some of the most talented kids I've ever met, and they're doing the honor of joining me in the last song of the evening."

More applause. Though his gaze had jumped around the audience, it kept coming back to Rory. She sat still and attentive in her seat, her focus unwavering on him. It gave him a boost of confidence. He cleared his throat.

"There's one more person I'd like to thank for being here." He shifted his guitar in front of him and strummed a few notes out of habit. "Not everyone is fortunate to have a champion in their life, someone who roots for them, cheers them on and believes in them no matter what." He drew a breath and let all of his attention fall on Rory. "I have been unbelievably blessed to have just such a person in my life." His fingers traced over the guitar strings, and behind him, his band played a few introductory notes.

"Rory Callahan."

Her eyes widened as he said her name.

"You were right. About everything." He felt a ripple of emotion, and he struggled to keep his voice even. "I'm afraid," he admitted into the microphone. The rest of the audience didn't matter. They fell away from his peripheral vision as he kept his attention on the only person he cared about in that moment. "I'm afraid of the future, of what might happen. But I'm more afraid to face it without you. You've always known that I speak better with music than I do with words. So that's why I wrote this song. For you."

He launched into the song's intro, shifting his focus for a moment to make sure the youth-center kids knew their cue.

I'm not too proud
I can say I was wrong.
I can't live this life
Without you along.
I don't know the future,
I can't see what's ahead.
But I know I want you,
I can't leave this unsaid.

The music lifted toward the chorus, the youth-center kids joining in with a background of echoing melody. He could feel the energy radiating from them, their pride in being part of what he was trying do here today, both with the Alzheimer's foundation and with Rory. Es-

pecially with Rory. When he'd told them his
plans, they were eager to contribute.

So I'm starting to believe
And I'm learning to crawl.
Because of you I know
Love does conquer all.
Times will get tough,
Without a doubt, I know.
But you're the only one
Who will never let go.

He couldn't look at Rory anymore. He feared
if he saw her reaction, he'd break down before
seeing the song through. He launched into the
second verse.

Love has no explanation,
And I can't figure it out.
But when I'm with you
I don't worry about
How things will end up,
Or how things will be.
In the end, all I know is
I want you and me.

There were tears in his eyes as he reached
the bridge, and he was grateful for the voices

of Jamal, Kenesha, Zara and the other kids
backing him up.

Sometimes love gets buried
Beneath a pile of hurt and fear.
But time marches on
And makes everything clear.
Fear is a power
That love can defeat.
No matter what happens—
Fear can't compete.

He returned to the chorus, still not ready to
look at Rory again. What if his words came
too late? What if he'd wounded her too irrepa-
rably by pushing her away? But he had to trust
that she knew his heart, that she could forgive
him for letting the fear infect him as it had.
He wrapped up the song by repeating the last
lines of the chorus.

Times will get tough
Without a doubt, I know.
But you're the only one
Who will never let go.

He strummed the last few chords, and the
echo of the music faded. He stood there, his
face lowered for several breaths. The world

had fallen silent. He could almost believe everyone had already departed. But when he finally lifted his head, they were all still there. His gaze swept the crowd and then, at last, came to rest on Rory.

She was standing while the rest of the crowd remained seated. His heart stopped.

"Rory," he said. It didn't matter if the microphone picked him up or not. Things were so quiet that he knew she'd hear him from her position in the front row. "I love you. Don't give up on me."

And then she was moving. He tracked her with his eyes as she came around the front of the stage. She was barefoot, but her steps were fast and determined. The security personnel stepped back to let her through as she ran up the steps. Sawyer shifted his guitar behind him, and the kids parted as she passed.

And then, she was in his arms, her lips finding his. In some distant part of his brain, he was aware of cheers from the crowd and shouts from the kids. But all he cared about was Rory, and the feel of her, and her forgiveness. They kissed long and hard, finding each other all over again in their embrace.

When they finally pulled apart, he traced his knuckles down her cheek and then reached in the pocket of his jeans, pulling out the ring he'd chosen years ago and had held on to for so long.

"Rory Callahan, will you do me the honor of standing by my side, for better or worse, in sickness and health…as my wife?"

Tears shimmered in her eyes, but her smile was bright.

"I thought you'd never ask."

Then she pulled his lips down to hers as the crowd erupted into thunderous applause, and Sawyer knew that despite what the future held, everything that mattered was right there in his arms.

EPILOGUE

One year later

SAWYER HELD ONTO Rory's hand, only vaguely aware of the cameras aimed on his face. He was far too busy enjoying how beautiful his wife was in her designer gown of deep red satin with lace overlay. His simple black suit and tie with a red vest that matched her dress was sure to put them on a few fashion blogs' best-dressed lists tomorrow. When designers had learned how he was being honored at tonight's awards show, they had clamored for the opportunity to dress Nashville's latest A-list couple. But fashion had become the least of his and Rory's concerns in the last year.

Following their autumn wedding, they'd thrown themselves into the dual work of promoting his new album and funding the nonprofit they'd established for patients and families dealing with Alzheimer's. Rory had found new purpose as his partner in philanthropy, and most days, she worked harder than he did as she lobbied for funding, not only for their own charity, but also others, including the Harbor House Youth Center back in Maryland.

They made the visit back home as often as they could, usually at least once every four weeks, to check in on their family and friends. But Rory also worked to make their Nashville house a home so that in the midst of their breakneck schedules, they still had a haven to return to where they could shut out the rest of the world and be together for a couple of days at a time.

"You'll know him not only for his gold-certified single, 'Rory's Song,' but his extensive work with charities and families dealing with Alzheimer's across the nation."

Rory slid a glance his way at these words, and he squeezed her hand. He accepted the awards and accolades because they served to bring more awareness to the disease. But in truth, he had found he was happiest just making music and focusing on his wife.

"Are you paying attention?" she whispered to him, her voice low.

"Only to you," he replied and managed to drop a kiss onto her jaw as their heads bent together.

She gasped and pulled back slightly. "Sawyer, remember that we're on camera."

"We're nearly always on camera," he replied. "If I waited for them to pan away from us, I'd never get to kiss you."

She grinned, not bothering to challenge him.

"Well, you're about to be called up onstage so pull yourself together, mate. The sooner we finish here, the sooner we can board the plane for our long-overdue honeymoon," she reminded him.

He released a happy sigh at the thought, and it was those words that propelled him from his seat as his name was called to come to the stage and accept his award for Humanitarian of the Year. As he walked the aisle to the steps leading to the platform, he tried to reassemble his thoughts, preparing for his speech.

He accepted the plaque honoring his efforts and then stepped to the microphone, focusing his attention on the audience.

"Thank you so much for this honor you've all bestowed on me tonight. I am humbled by the recognition and appreciation." He drew a breath. "But I should remind you that I'm just one person in a world of families struggling with Alzheimer's. And I'm one of the lucky ones. While my dad is afflicted with this disease, he still has far more good days than bad ones. My brother, after having tested for the mutant genes that cause early onset Alzheimer's, learned that he does not have the DNA that causes EOA. His diagnosis gives me hope, even as I've chosen not to be tested myself. Not all families are this fortunate."

The lights were practically blinding, but he still searched the crowd to find Rory. And there she was. He glimpsed her in the first few rows, beaming with pride.

"You all know my wife, Rory. My single 'Rory's Song' was written for her at a time when I feared Alzheimer's might take everything from me. I never feel quite right standing up here, accepting an award, when I know the truth—Rory is the one who deserves the accolades. She's a talented musician in her own right, and she still performs occasionally. Yet she spends most of her time helping others... and supporting me."

Rory had shifted in her seat, and he couldn't quite make out her expression now with so many lights in his face.

"Rory is at the heart of everything I do because without her unwavering faith and steadfast love, I wouldn't be able to keep making music. Rory, sweetheart, would you join me up here?"

There was a hush in the audience, and he sensed that Rory had hesitated. But then, the applause started, and he knew she was making her way to the front. He caught sight of her as she walked the aisle, finding her way to the steps that led to the platform. He stepped back from the podium and added his own applause to the rest of the auditorium's.

As she reached the stage, he moved forward to take her hand and draw her back toward the mic with him.

"Ladies and gentlemen, my wife, Rory Landry."

The applause became deafening as the audience swept to their feet. Rory was blushing and shooting daggers in his direction. She never liked being the center of attention in situations like this, but for once, he couldn't resist. He owed her too much and loved her too well to let her escape recognition yet again.

He drew her into his arms, with the entire audience watching, as she whispered in his ear, "You're going to pay for this, cowboy."

He felt her shiver in his arms and whispered back, "Well, here's to having a lifetime together for you to take your revenge."

And though neither of them could guarantee the future, he knew that however much or little time he had, they were going to spend every minute of it together.

* * * * *

Get 2 Free Books,
Plus 2 Free Gifts—
just for trying the Reader Service!

Love Inspired®

Get 2 Free Books,
Plus 2 Free Gifts—
just for trying the
Reader Service!

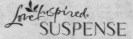

LIS17R

HOMETOWN HEARTS ♥

HHBPA17

Get 2 Free Books,
Plus 2 Free Gifts—
just for trying the Reader Service!

Love Inspired HISTORICAL